Out of Eden

A spectacular new novel of passion and adventure

KATHLEEN SAGE

Claire swam in the placid river, her golden hair swirling behind her. He could tell she was naked. He couldn't quite see her body, but her pale skin reflected beneath the water . . . The whole scene conspired against his good intentions. The hot sun poured over his back. A light breeze puckered his nipples. The scent of pine tickled his nose. He found it easy to abandon scruples . . .

She turned in the water. Her eyes widened and her lips parted . . . Now he stood there naked before her . . . She waited. Her pale face above the green water, her skin blurry beneath it. He dove. He reached her . . .

He kissed her. He tried to be hard and heartless about it, but he knew he had failed. Her mouth was too tender, too soft and expressive. He pressed himself to her, full of hunger and love, and every emotion but anger. He didn't want this and fought against it, but his lips lingered over her softness . . . and she pulled herself to him, twining her legs over his waist, more giving, more wanton, more open and needy than he'd ever imagined . . .

Out of Eden

Kathleen Sage

JOVE BOOKS, NEW YORK

OUT OF EDEN

A Jove Book / published by arrangement with
the author

PRINTING HISTORY
Jove edition / June 1996

The Putnam Berkley World Wide Web site address is
http://www.berkley.com

ISBN: 0-515-11875-3

A JOVE BOOK®
Jove Books are published by The Berkley Publishing Group,
200 Madison Avenue, New York, New York 10016.
JOVE and the "J" design are trademarks
belonging to Jove Publications, Inc.

PRINTED IN THE UNITED STATES OF AMERICA

10 9 8 7 6 5 4 3 2

My career as a novelist began as a series of schoolgirl notes passed between my best friend and I, recounting the further adventures of Fielding's rascal *Tom Jones*. Our miniature novel went on for some years. My friend's last name was "Francis," mine "Foley," and our alphabet-minded teachers sat her behind me in all our classes. Luckily for me, she became a teacher herself and still reads all my drafts. Even better, she's still my best friend.

Thanks, Fra. I couldn't have done it without you.

ACKNOWLEDGMENTS

Special thanks to the staff members of Bodie State Park and Yosemite National Park for their unfailing courtesy in answering my questions. And to my family (Todd, Tim and Tony, Wes and Larry and Joan), who backpacked most of the terrain described in the book with me. Finally, to John Muir, whose stories, as retold by my father, have inspired many, many a ramble.

Chapter One

"They're going to hang Johnny Christmas, and it doesn't seem fair."

Claire Butler stared at the brassy-haired woman whose low-cut red dress exposed the last of her faded charms.

"You want me to defend an accused rapist?" Claire asked.

"You got it, honey."

Claire clutched the top of the ladder and glanced at the sign whose ornate white letters proclaimed her name and new occupation. She'd hoped the law business would pick up in Bodie, but she hadn't expected an offer so quickly, and during a lifetime of admiring her father's profession, she'd never envisioned a proposal like this. She set the claw hammer down and wondered what a fancy lady would know about justice. "And you're offering to pay his expenses?" Claire hitched up her skirt and inched down the wood steps, mentally cursing the female apparel that made masculine chores such a burden. When she reached

1

the bottom, she brushed off her sleeve and turned to face the small crowd of women gathered on the porch of her house and office. "Do you mind if I ask you why?"

"Why what? Why do we want to hire you? Or why would we pay his expenses?"

"Both, as a matter of fact."

The scarlet-clad hussy turned without answering and opened the door to Claire's office. Her satin skirts rustled as she sashayed inside, followed by a bevy of girls whose angled cheekbones belied their plush figures and betrayed the hardships that had driven them to the oldest profession. Claire retrieved the hammer and hustled inside. The women posted themselves next to a table Claire had set up to interview clients. She walked quietly to the desk, glad she'd already furnished the study. Given her dismal experience in San Francisco, she'd never expected an offer of work when she'd barely even hung out her shingle.

Reaching the table, she turned and faced the clutch of young women ranged behind their crimson-clad leader. A soft breeze fluttered their smocks. Claire knew from her childhood that they wore them loose to give men quicker access. She shuddered inside, thanking the heavens that even in her lowest moments, when she'd had no notion where the rent money would come from, she'd never been driven to such desperation.

Still, she didn't have next month's rent yet.

She thrust her hand at the fancy lady with the overexposed bosom. "Claire Butler. Attorney-at-law."

"I'm Cleo." The middle-aged woman ignored

Claire's gesture and shifted her weight so her hip tilted forward. "I run the town's most popular whorehouse."

The scent of cheap lilac water tickled Claire's nose, but she remained standing, gaze level, hand forward. The plump woman studied Claire's ladylike suit and wool-encased figure, then brought her gaze to meet Claire's. "We've come about Johnny Christmas. I imagine you've heard what he's charged with?"

Claire nodded. Everyone in town knew what had happened, or at least what was supposed to have happened.

"He's a friend of ours, and we want to help him. We want to hire you to defend him."

Claire gestured the woman into the chair. She didn't have enough seats for the others and briefly considered finding them some, then dismissed the notion. If the madam came with an army of backers, they'd just have to find their own places. "I understand he's engaged Patrick Reddy."

"A fine lawyer, Patrick, but not the right man for this case."

Claire took her own seat. The idea shocked her, defending a rapist. She found herself wanting to crawl under the table. She braced herself with the smell of old leather, the heft and weight of her father's fine pen. "You seem pretty certain of your opinion."

"In my line of work, you learn a lot about lawyers."

"Then you must know Reddy's one of the best."

"He's too softhearted to defend Johnny Christmas."

Claire glanced at the circle of whores. The youngest looked as if she'd been crying. "And you think I'm not?"

"Only a woman can shred up a woman. A man won't go hard enough on the victim."

"You don't like Louisa Cantrall?"

At the question, the other whores fluttered. The youngest one set up a wail. All the rest bunched closer together, and the prettiest one, slightly older than the rest of the girls, slipped her arm around the crier's waist. The wailing subsided into a sniffle, which the bosomy madam outwaited with patience.

"No, as a matter of fact," Cleo said finally.

"May I ask why?"

"I've seen that little schoolteacher in action. She thinks she's better than her fallen sisters, but she's just holding out for a better bargain. I can't grieve that she got her comeuppance."

"I see."

"Maybe you do." Cleo plumped a fat reticule on the desk. The jeweled handbag winked in the sunlight. "But that's not why I'm here."

Claire's mouth went dry. She didn't truly fear that she'd fall victim to the fate of the whores. Uncle William would help her, as he always had. But lifelong dependence on a generous uncle was not what she wanted from life. "Why are you here, then?"

"For Johnny."

"Do you think he did it?"

"No."

"What makes you so certain?"

The madam leaned back in the Windsor chair, a

half-smile on her face. "Let's just say . . ." The line on the side of her world-weary mouth deepened. "I'm very familiar with the . . . character . . . of the accused."

Claire arched an eyebrow. "I suppose you'd lose a good source of income."

Cleo's smile deepened. "Johnny pays well."

The simpering youngster set up another moan. "Don't be so crass. He's a real gentleman, Johnny." All her sisters nodded, clustering in closer. The young one continued, speaking between sniffles. "He not only pays promptly, he holds his weight on his elbows. He wears clean underwear. And . . ." She pulled a hankie out of her pocket. "And . . ." She blew her nose and buried her face in the white kerchief. "And . . ." A small sob escaped her. "Look what he did for Hattie."

"Shush, now, Emmy, that's none of her business," Cleo said softly.

Claire rose from the chair and walked to the window. She'd allowed herself white cutwork curtains, the one feminine touch amidst the leather of her father's old books and yellowing papers, the Daumier satire of arguing lawyers. "You know, I've never handled a case."

"I figured," Cleo responded.

Claire fingered the lace of the curtains. Pale sunlight streamed through the design, making shimmering patterns on the wooden floor. "I should probably start on something smaller."

A sniffle wafted up from the sniffler.

Madam Cleo must have shifted her weight in the

Windsor; Claire could hear the creaky squeak of its protest. "Of course you should." The middle-aged madam had a comforting voice. Now that Claire couldn't see her flashy apparel, she could hear how soothing it was. "Nobody knows better than a whore that a woman without money has very few choices."

Claire turned to face the little grouping and found herself curiously jealous. She'd never so much as met Johnny Christmas, but she had to admire this display of devotion. He must have some goodness in him for these women to offer this kind of friendship, she figured. She reflected briefly about who would know better whether a man might be a rapist. And if he were truly innocent, who would need a good lawyer more badly? "Why can't I be choosy?"

Madam Cleo jerked her chin toward the wall. "How long have you had that law license?"

"Six months."

"How many women got a paper like that?"

"In the state?"

Cleo nodded. Garnet twinkled against pearly earlobes, splashing patches of red on the golden oak desk.

"Three." Claire cleared her throat and spoke a little more loudly. "I'm the third woman lawyer in California."

"You tried working yet at this occupation?"

"Yes."

"And?"

"There were disadvantages in San Francisco."

The madam opened her sparkling purse and pulled out a small leather bag. She loosened a thong and displayed the contents, a tiny mountain of greenish-gold flakes. "You think Bodie will be any better?"

"I grew up here."

"This is a mining camp, sweetheart." The dust looked deceptively leaden, but Claire knew from experience that the humble poke's contents would probably pay her rent for a winter. "A first-class contender for the legitimate title of the baddest town in the West."

"So there'll be lots of need for a lawyer."

"There's plenty of crime, I'll grant you that, but if the forward-thinking folks in San Francisco won't bring their cases to a woman lawyer, what makes you think the Bodieites will?"

"My father—"

"Is dead."

Claire suppressed a sob of surprise.

Madam Cleo held up her hand. "I'm sorry, honey, but this is pure business. Your father was a wonderful man. There's not an old-timer who doesn't remember how Judge Butler tried to bring law to this town. There's many here who'd give you a handout; and many more who'd be glad to come courtin'. I could hire you out ten times a night." Claire touched the top button of her heavy wool suit dress. "Don't worry, I'm not proposing nothing like that, but think hard about your situation. Your father died trying to tame Bodie. How you gonna prove to these miners you're more of a man than the judge was?"

She'd come back to haunt him. Jonathan Robert Van Kessel, otherwise known as Johnny Christmas, rolled over onto his shoulder and smiled at the woman whose slender figure barely darkened the jail cell's squat doorway. He hadn't seen her in eight years at least, but time hadn't dimmed the memory of her loveliness, or how her soul-stirring beauty had changed him.

"Come on out, Johnny," Sheriff Franklin Flowers said, nudging the little lady with him. "You've got visitors out in the front room. Patrick Reddy has come to see you, and he's brought this little woman with him."

Johnny rose from the bunk, his eyes fixed on the face of Claire Butler. Even in the shadowed light of the hallway, she had the vivid blue eyes he remembered. He nodded, wishing he had a hat to take off. "Nice to see you again, ma'am."

She frowned, rose-colored lips pressing together, and shifted her dark green carpetbag from one hand to the other. "Have we met?"

The bearded sheriff tugged at the sleeve of her suit coat. "There'll be time enough for introductions. Let's get Johnny here out of his cell."

She backed up slowly, clearly not frightened, but obviously still puzzled.

Johnny straightened the red flannel cuffs of his uniform shirt. "This is low of you, Sheriff. It was bad enough you had to arrest me, worse that you nabbed me in front of my friends, but I must have made somebody awfully angry if you've brought such beauty to see how I've fallen." He flipped an unruly lock of brown hair sideways, turned his body away, and tucked in the flannel. As he did, the stocky sheriff stepped inside with the handcuffs.

"Aw, Frank." Johnny held his hands out meekly. "You don't think I'd try to escape and cut short my time with this lovely lady?"

"Save it, Johnny. I'm not taking chances." The powerfully built lawman cinched the cuffs tight. "I don't approve of this visit. I won't give you the chance to take advantage of either the lady or me."

Ignoring the gibe, Johnny stepped over the threshold and into the short, narrow hallway. At some other time, the sheriff's insult might have rankled, but Johnny wanted to know why she'd come to see him; why, eight years after he'd watched her dice up her heart and bury her hopes along with her father, she'd shown up at the door to the jailhouse. As he strode down the hall, Claire Butler hustled before him, the wool of her skirt whispering softly.

He reached the front room and stopped. Patrick Reddy, the town's foremost lawyer, stood in the front room. He offered his hand, but Claire Butler held Johnny's attention. She shimmered, framed in the pool of clear mountain sunlight filtering through the square jailhouse window. A tiny slip of a girl with hair that glowed like the state's golden hillsides and eyes to match the sparkling blue lakes that sheltered beneath the slate-gray Sierras.

"Have we met?" She touched the white ruffled collar that softened the severely cut suit dress.

"Once." He glanced at the lawyer he'd hired to defend him, nodded, then swung his gaze back to the lady. "A long time ago."

"I see." Clearly she didn't. How could she? She'd

been only sixteen and completely carefree, until the day her father had died. The rough citizens of the old mining camp would have kept the details—both good and bad—from a gentle, civilized girl from the flat-lands.

"Sheriff." Patrick Reddy removed his bowler. "Perhaps we could see Mr. Christmas without you." The one-armed lawyer pointed at a door and partition. "I think this side room should do quite nicely."

The sheriff's mustache tugged downward as he rif-fled through the keys on his ring, "I don't mind you, Patrick, but I can't see including the lady."

"I understand your hesitance, Frank, but if Miss Butler's to serve as his lawyer—"

"Beg your pardon?" Johnny's red flannel shirt prickled his skin. The gust of wind didn't explain the goose bumps. "What the—what in Hades are you talking about?"

"Now, Johnny." Reddy stepped forward, his movements offset by his low husky voice. "Just settle down. Cleo and the girls have offered to hire her to defend you. They're having a bake sale."

"They're baking?" Johnny couldn't have been more surprised if the fireman's ball had gone stag.

"Well," Reddy said as he shrugged his broad shoulders, "They can cook, you know. And, Johnny"—he glanced at the woman—"don't worry. She's not that expensive. Besides the Chinese from King Street have also kicked in."

"What the—" With a curse to himself, Johnny bolted. He brushed past the blue-eyed beauty. The sheriff pulled out his British bulldog, aiming it upward in warning. Without a backward glance at the snub-nosed revolver, Johnny lifted his boot and kicked open the door. Two shots rang out. Pat Reddy shouted. Claire Butler made no sound at all. Johnny turned, bracing his manacled hands on the top of the doorframe and resting his forehead just beneath it. "Put that gun away, Frank." He cast a sarcastic glance at the heavens. "I'm not escaping. This jail is built for midgets like you. It makes me crazy ducking through doorways, and I spent the night folded up like a jackknife. Just give me a minute to loosen up."

He dropped his hands and hunched up his shoulders, working the kinks out of his back. He had to think fast. The doxies had hatched up a plan. Right away, he could see the logic in it, a kind of weird, perverted scheme with a twisted charm that might work, except... "Tell the ladies I'm sorry, but I've already hired my own attorney."

The handsome, muttonchopped lawyer turned a bright Irish smile on Johnny. "I know you've hired me, but the ladies have come up with an idea. And I believe it has considerable merit."

Johnny shook out the muscles of his left thigh. "I don't know what you think you're doing, but I hired you, not some funny-looking little yellow-haired female." In the periphery of his vision, Johnny could see Claire Butler stiffen. "How do I know she's even a lawyer? I've never heard of a woman in court—except, of course, being fined for streetwalking."

Reddy smoothed the lapels on his jacket. "Put that gun away, Frank." The frowning Frank Flowers paid no attention. With a shrug, Reddy returned his gaze to Johnny. "She's a perfect greenling, but she's a real lawyer. She's got a fine pedigree. She's Judge Butler's daughter. She read law in San Francisco and the legislature passed the women lawyer's bill last year."

A fine tension worked through Johnny's chest, an edgy heat behind his rib cage, like a cinder smoldering in a bale of raw cotton. The sheriff still clenched the squat snub-nosed bulldog, but the blunt businesslike weapon didn't make Johnny so nervous as the proposition that Claire Butler defend him. "Goddamn it, Pat. I know you're all for social progress, but this is my freedom we're talking about. I'm not volunteering my ass to a novice just to prove some new theory, especially one I don't agree with."

"Mr. Christmas." Miss Butler had a resonant voice, surprising in someone so tiny. "I take exception to those remarks."

"Yeah, so—"

"Your ass is quite safe with me." She threw a withering glance at the part she referred to. Johnny grinned. She colored, wet her lips lightly, then raised her gaze to his eyes. "I'd never risk any man's freedom just to prove my mettle in court."

"Then just what do you think you're doing?"

"I'm trying to save your life."

She'd saved him that summer and did not even know it. "I'm not charged with a hanging offense."

"Under the laws of 'Judge Lynch' you are."

A chill ran down Johnny's spine. He stepped back inside the jailhouse, then turned and stared down Bonanza Street. In the morning, the scent of sagebrush drenched the whole mountainside and even the red-light district smelled sweet. The neat row of cribs was completely deserted. As always Johnny was struck by their order, the subservient way the small numbered houses waited patiently to receive their patrons. But the peaceful arrangement did not fool the street-hardened firefighter. He often prowled Bonanza at night. Men lined up outside those houses. And not just any men either, but that prideful and swaggering type whose drive for adventure outweighed the need for love, home, or feminine softness, except of course what they got on Bonanza. "There's never been a lynching in Bodie."

"Then perhaps it's time there be one." This time Pat Reddy spoke.

Johnny turned slowly, his gaze fixed on the sheriff's bulldog, its barrel still trained on his heart. "That's a fine way for a lawyer to talk."

"Listen, there were ten men gunned down in Bodie this year. I defended every one of the killers and got every one of them off."

"So, that's my point." Johnny strolled to the window. The sheriff tensed. Claire Butler's eyes narrowed. Johnny hesitated a moment, then rested his hand on the sill. "Why would I want anyone else? Especially a woman, not to mention a novice who's probably never been before a jury before."

"Because if I defend you, the closest you'll come to a jury is the posse that is going to hang you."

Johnny's hand trembled a little. The iron bar brushed against his cheek. He grinned and wiped the sweat from his brow. "You think this thing's got some people upset?"

"Some people, yes." Reddy seemed to be watching the sheriff, who still had his gun leveled at Johnny. "There's some folks think this town is long overdue for a hanging, that the rowdy element needs putting down."

"Now wait just a minute." Johnny winked at the sheriff. "Whoever said I was rowdy?"

"That the rowdy element needs putting down." Reddy kept his voice even. "What's worse, you're accused of hurting a woman."

"I didn't do it, you know."

"I hear what you're saying," Reddy replied as he closed the front door of the jailhouse, then drew a chubby cigar out of his pocket, "but there are rumors of a vigilance committee. If I defend you, there's apt to be trouble. Some of the miners won't wait for justice—they'll take the job on themselves." He tossed the cheroot to the sheriff, who fumbled, then caught it without letting go of his weapon. Reddy frowned. "If Miss Butler defends you, the committee won't be so eager. I can help on the sly. I've checked her out, and she ought to do well in the courtroom. And of course, there's the obvious fact—"

"There's nothing wrong with my eyesight." Johnny rapped the metal bar with a knuckle, then held up his manacled hands with a sigh. "Do you think I could speak to Miss Butler alone?"

Chapter
Two

After a few minutes of wrangling, the sheriff allowed Claire to interview Johnny Christmas in the cell to the side of the front room. Annoyance shimmered through Judge Butler's daughter. She'd expected problems as a lady lawyer, but she'd never considered her very first client might be an accused rapist whom she'd have to interview in a jail cell.

Still, she didn't feel very frightened, even though Johnny Christmas looked villain enough, tall and solidly built, with a broad, square-jawed face that should have been brutal except for the way his smile redeemed it. Nonetheless, she left the door ajar. She fancied herself a competent woman, but right at this moment she felt like a mouse set to pull the thorn from the lion's paw.

With a last glance at the crack in the doorway, Claire seated herself at the pine table in the room's center.

Johnny Christmas chose to look out the front window. "The mountains are pretty this time of day."

This seemed an odd subject to discuss with a lawyer, but Claire let the remark lie. Bending down, she riffled through her carpetbag for a pad. As she did, Johnny Christmas pulled up a chair and rested one booted foot on it. His manacled hands hung loosely before him, as if he'd forgotten their presence. "I love life," he said softly.

"Most of us do, Mr. Christmas."

He smiled. "I'm God's gift to women, you know."

He had even, white teeth and an olive complexion, and the mountain air seemed suddenly thinner. "Don't try that line in the courtroom."

He straddled the chair and lifted his hands, casually inspecting the steel that bound them. "Why would a woman consent to defend me, especially given the crime I'm charged with?"

"For pretty much the reasons you speculated."

"You want to prove that females are equal?"

"Close, though I wouldn't describe my motives quite that way."

He jiggled the chain, watching it closely. "How would you describe them?"

"I've got bills to pay." Ignoring the faint chink of the metal, she drew out her paper and a black fountain pen handed down from her father. "I came here from San Francisco. But I grew up in these mountains. I know a lot about towns like Bodie. I know it won't be easy getting the men to accept me."

"Maybe not the women either."

"No, maybe not."

Removing the pen's cap, she tested the nib on a corner. A blot of dark ink splotched the paper. "I have to show people that a woman can be a competent lawyer.''

He stood and returned to the window. Bending at the waist, he peered out. ''You don't believe you're betraying your sex by defending a man who could be a rapist?''

''It would be a far deeper betrayal to turn down a case because I'm a female.''

''Does Louisa's honor mean so little to you that you'd defend a rapist just to prove you could do it?''

''Honor's important, but so is due process.'' She laid down her pen and arched her eyebrows, an expression she'd acquired from her father. Johnny Christmas still watched the mountains, but the assertive look made her feel better. ''No one needs a lawyer unless he has trouble. If I want to live up to my late father's example, I'll need to put finer feelings aside.''

''I'd be your first client?''

''Yes.''

''Do you believe I did it?''

''I haven't made up my mind.'' She snatched up the pen and scribbled the date, with his name and hers in the corner. ''I'm impressed the ladies want to defend you, though I doubt their opinion would count much in court. As for the rest, I'll just have to listen. You've yet to tell me what happened.''

''And what if my tale is pretty salacious?''

''I told you before.'' Pen poised at the top of the paper, she reasserted herself with her best lawyer look. ''This isn't a job for a blushing female.''

He met her gaze and held it. To her immense chagrin, those long-lashed green eyes roved lazily over her figure. Heat rose in her cheeks, and she knew she had pinkened.

"I'll practice," she said quickly. She dropped her gaze, relieved to be out of that contest. "There'll be no blush in my cheeks in the courtroom."

"And if you came to believe I was guilty?"

She stood and tossed her pen down. "I'd still defend you, of course."

"Seems pretty cold, if you ask me."

"I'm a lawyer." Rounding the table, she shut the door. She didn't know what made her do it, except perhaps she wanted to show him she wasn't frightened. "In some ways it's much like gunfighting. I'm paid to be ruthless."

He smiled slightly. "So you'll defend me, no matter what actually happened?"

Fine hairs prickled on the back of her neck. She'd trapped herself in a room with a possible rapist. It occurred to her she should run. Now. Before she came to regret this foolishness. "My father taught me always to be honest and counseled his clients with the same advice, but he defended many a fable, and I'd do the same for you if need be."

He peered back out at the mountain. The breeze toyed with a shock of brown hair. Claire could see why the prostitutes loved him. For all his size and pugnacious manner, there was something ineffably boyish in him.

He jiggled the manacle chain steadily. "I read about your divorce in the newspapers. You beat some pretty fine lawyers in that case."

She leaned back against the door. She hadn't known anyone in Bodie had heard of the scandal. "I had truth on my side."

"Let's hope you come to believe that of me." He perused the bracelets with studied indifference. "What have you been doing for money since the divorce?"

"I get by."

"I see."

"Then you're going to let me defend you?"

"Maybe." Pushing away from the window, he strode to the table and picked up the pen, holding it awkwardly in one hand. "I have three conditions."

"Which are?"

"One." He scrawled a vertical line on her pad. "I pay your fee. I don't want the doxies—"

"They offered."

"They're lovely ladies, but I'm not pressed for money."

"And two?"

"And two." He held the pen stiffly and scratched the number two on the paper. "If the lynch mob comes in spite of this tactic, you stay as far away as you can." With thick, slashing strokes, he underlined the second figure. "You're only to help out in the courtroom. It's the sheriff's job to handle the rough stuff."

"That's fine." The door handle poked into her back. She was beginning to wonder about the wisdom of this whole ridiculous plan. "And three?"

"And three." He smiled wryly and traced out a

number. "There are some animals out at my place. . . ."

"Some animals" had been an understatement. Johnny Christmas collected cats, four-legged as well as human.

"The man's got more women hanging around him than the Pasha of Egypt has in his harem," Claire said to a black-and-white tabby, one of a dozen sleek feline creatures who primped and purred beneath Johnny's porch. The pretty kitty didn't respond, except to roll in the dust and lick one of her paws. Claire had never owned a cat. She had never owned a dog for that matter, but she liked her new client, and she couldn't expect Johnny Christmas to trust her if she couldn't even take care of his pets.

Sighing, Claire reached beneath the wood slats and pulled out a tin miner's pan. As she did, a growl, fierce and distinct, rolled from behind the red clapboard shack. For the second time that day, fine hairs stirred on the nape of Claire's neck. She ran for her pinto and pulled a shotgun out of her saddle scabbard. Hand on the stock, she crept warily toward the back.

Johnny Christmas had warned her about his dog, a half-wild scoundrel who protected his master but had little use for anyone else. "He'll probably head for the hills when he hears you," Christmas had told her. "He'll defend the house when I'm in it, but he's not especially brave in my absence. Still, it never hurts to be careful."

Claire tightened her grip on the gun. There was a short burst of yelping, followed by the sounds of a scuffle. Breaking into a trot, Claire rounded the corner, then stopped. Behind the house, a pair of dogs dueled. They roiled in the dust. She fitted the butt of the gun to her shoulder and shouted, ''Hey!''

Neither creature paid any attention. Breaking away from each other, the two dogs squared off. At least, Claire thought they were dogs, though on closer inspection one appeared to be a coyote and the other seemed wild, though he probably wasn't. The second canine met the description Christmas had given—a small, white, wolf-shaped dog. Claire thought him a suitable pet for her client, for the chalk-colored dog bristled and snapped without the slightest regard for the fact that the coyote was taller, leaner, and probably meaner, and certainly used to squabbling for dinner. She lowered her rifle and looked around for a stone.

''Scat.'' She lobbed a rock at the coyote. He yelped, then twisted. The white blur attacked. With a fierce snarl, the small dog flipped his opponent, who tucked his tail under and ran. The white mutt streaked after him, faster even than the dun-colored figure, and made a wide harrying circle. The coyote snapped at his pursuer, then doubled the pace of his flight.

Fang—for by now Claire remembered the little dog's name—gave a lighthearted chase. As the coyote streaked over a bluff, Fang slowed to a trot, growled for a minute, then dropped down on his haunches. He curled his lips and pricked his ears forward. Claire relaxed the grip on the gun barrel. She didn't know who the dog was protecting, but clearly she was low on his list of potential intruders. Keeping one eye on his watchful figure, she returned to the pinto, re-sheathed the shotgun, retrieved the scraps she'd bought at the butcher, and returned to the back of the house.

"Hello, Fang." She approached slowly, her eyes near leaving the dog. "I've brought you some treats." She held out one strip of raw meat. The dog's lip was bleeding and one ear was torn, but he otherwise appeared to be in pretty good shape, breathing lightly, proud and undaunted. She backed up two steps. "Come on, you mongrel. I'm trying to help you. Look." She jerked her chin toward the rock. "I threw the first blow. Without the distraction, you'd probably be a dead mutt by now." Fang lowered his head and lifted his bottom, curled his lip briefly, then dashed beneath the wooden porch.

"Fine." Claire lifted her chin. "Be stubborn. Just like your master. I'll get these cats breakfast." As she headed toward the front porch, Fang sped out from beneath it, furry black shape squirming in his mouth. Claire stopped. Fang did likewise. Clutching the brown paper package, she propped her fists on her hips. "Now what have you got?"

The dog plopped flat on his stomach. The shape in his mouth twisted and wiggled, a high-pitched mewl letting Claire know that this was a kitten pleading for its mother. Claire winced. The screech was worse than nails on a blackboard.

"Here, Fang." She edged toward the dog, holding the package out at arm's length. He dropped the kitten between his paws. The tiny furball scrabbled and fell, its insistent piping revealing more fright than hurt.

Fang rested a paw on its tail and licked its puckered face with his tongue. The mewling subsided. Claire Butler sank down on her haunches and inched one bloody scrap forward. The dog freed the kitten and watched. The tiny fur bundle stretched out a leg, tottered forward a step, then stumbled. The desperate wailing started again. Fang dropped his chin to his paws, regarding Claire with a weary expression.

"Oh, I see." Claire dropped down on her knees. "You think I'm a sucker." She scooted up slightly. Her eyes on the mongrel, Claire set down the package and picked up the kitten. Fang lifted his head. "It's all right." Claire cradled her hands around the tiny furball. She felt like a fool, but this little creature, with hazy blue eyes and a helpless expression, was too adorable to ignore. "Well, you're probably right." The dog whimpered slightly and dropped his chin on his paws.

Claire walked back to the porch. "Are there any more under there?" She peered into the dark recess beneath the brightly painted red house. "No?" She listened, but the only mewing came from the dainty creature she sheltered. She closed her fingers gently over the kitten. "Did the coyote get your brothers and sisters?"

The kitten didn't respond, but the furry white dog snatched one of the scraps and retreated. Claire unbuttoned the top of her jacket and tucked the kitten into the front of her bosom. Wearily she filled up the bowl. The gaggle of cats had disappeared, but Claire supposed they would return for their breakfast. She wondered about the fate of the kitten. She hadn't noticed a nursing female among the sleek felines, and she couldn't imagine how the dog had acquired the role of protector except in the absence of a mother. Since cats, whatever their faults, were highly maternal, and coyotes, whatever their virtues, were quick to prey on anything helpless, Claire surmised the kitten to be the last survivor of a cozy little family grouping.

She scraped the last of the meat out of the package, then scratched the head poking up from her bodice. The kitten had started mewling again. Claire walked to the pump and dipped her pinky into the primer bucket. She pressed her finger to the tiny mouth. To her immense satisfaction, the kitten started in suckling.

Claire stroked the top of the fuzzy black head. "What am I going to do with you, kitty?" The mouth felt funny, soft, rough, deliciously ticklish. "I wish you had a more sensible master." The kitten ignored her, intent on his chore. Fang had finished his scrap, trotted to the front, and brought back another. The noonday sun beat down on the shack, a much neater place than Claire had expected.

As she cuddled the kitten, she realized with a pang how much she wanted to believe Johnny Christmas was innocent. She found him attractive, though she couldn't quite explain why to herself. Sure he was good-looking, but Claire wasn't one to be swayed by appearances. Were she a less sensible type, she might have said he appealed to her womanly instincts. But Claire thought of herself as an incorrigible tomboy, and her disastrous marriage had proved it.

Turning, she studied her client's house, a well-kept bungalow, bright red, cheerful, and so achingly homey she wanted to weep for its imprisoned owner. She saw no sign of his supposed wealth. Rumor had it in Bodie he'd frittered a fortune away—on women and wine and fire equipment. Claire smiled in spite of herself. Maybe that was why she liked Johnny Christmas. He was so different from her former husband. More like the men she'd grown up with. Unpretentious and wild. As untamed as the mountains. A true son of the bad town of Bodie, but suited, like her, to its haunting beauty.

"He's a fool, you know." She nuzzled the kitten. She still couldn't place Johnny. She'd worked hard this morning, interviewing her client and all of the whores, as well as discussing the case with the sheriff. In spite of all she'd learned about Christmas, she still didn't know when she'd met him or whether or not he was guilty. "He's hiding something from his own attorney."

Sighing, she sat down on a step. As the kitten continued his licking, Claire stared out at the mountains. Johnny Christmas had dodged most of her questions, except to deny he'd raped Louisa. He wasn't sure why she would lie. They had—in his words—been spooning that day. He had—his words also—gotten carried away. But he'd stopped when she'd asked. He'd been angry and threatened obliquely that she ought to think twice about her behavior—and here he got a little indignant—and not let a man under her blouse unless she intended to let him complete the act. But he hadn't come back that night or ever.

Claire fiddled with one jet-black button. He didn't know why Louisa would say he attacked her. He volunteered that she wasn't a liar. If she said someone had forced her, Johnny believed that part of her story. She could have mistaken him for another—the rapist had worn a mask on his face. Still, Johnny allowed that a mistake didn't seem likely, given his size, his build, and the way her description matched his pistol.

Claire's toe tapped on the step. The pistol damned him, of course. Louisa had described a very large man, but the mining camp had its fair share of bruisers. Bodie had only one silverplate Colt, however. Johnny had never worn the handgun in public—too fancy a piece for everyday life. When Louisa had reported the crime, one of the deputies remembered a gun he'd seen at Johnny's. Sheriff Flowers put two and two together. He had gone to the commissioner, asked for a warrant, and found the pistol under Johnny's bed.

As Claire rebuttoned her jacket, the kitten climbed up her blouse. Tiny claws scratched her breasts. They'd arrested him at the fireman's ball, too frightened to come for Johnny Christmas in private. His crimes and killing might be only rumors, but he had a penchant for hardfisted brawling and eight years' experience as a crack firefighter. All of which made him a serious threat when it came to the business of taking him in.

"He came quietly, though." Claire nuzzled a velvety ear. She found the fact puzzling, if reassuring. Johnny Christmas didn't seem like a rapist, though she scarcely knew what a rapist might be like. She didn't suppose he'd do her the favor of sporting horns and a tail. As she tucked the kitten back into her jacket, the sensible lawyer reminded herself that the wickedly handsome carouser and outlaw might not have a soul to match his exterior. The lopsided smile she found so disarming meant nothing except that God had blessed him with a fine set of even, white teeth, and one dimpled cheek to offset them.

Chapter
Three

⤳⤳⟋

The next day she brought Johnny Christmas the kitten.

"Here." She practically shoved the poor creature at him. "If you won't help me help you, at least you can make yourself useful."

He took the tiny, sleeping ball in his hand. She'd used the kitten as an excuse to be allowed to visit his cell. Why the sheriff had allowed it, Johnny couldn't imagine, but he didn't like the idea. He'd only been in jail for three days, but confinement told on his nerves already. She did far more than crowd up the small space—the scent of her drenched him. He hungered for freedom. He dreamed of the mountains. He awoke in a sweat, stifled for air. And she, her gold-spun hair smelling faintly of roses, transformed all those smoldering dreams into passion.

He grinned. "Did you bring milk?"

"Yes." She pulled a glass bottle out of her carpetbag, the forest-green one she'd carried before. "He drinks pretty well. I didn't know if you'd named him . . ."

"I haven't."

". . . so I took the liberty of calling him Flowers."

"Good choice." With a free hand he plumped up his pillow. "Did the sheriff like it?"

"No, but I thought the name would amuse you."

Suppressing a smile, he nestled the kitten into the cushion.

Claire pulled two more objects from her valise. "I brought a bowl and a dropper. He'd mostly been licking milk from my finger. I don't think he's ready for solids. . . ."

"Whoa, there." He settled the milk bottle under his cot. "Where did you find the little bugger?"

She snapped her bag shut. "Under your porch."

"Were there any more with him?"

"No." She fingered the lace of her collar. She wore a gray cotton dress that made her look softer than the dark suit she'd worn yesterday had, though still too somber for his taste. "I think a coyote got them."

"That's a pity." He picked up the dropper. "You're probably right. One of the cats gave birth last week. What a shame." He tucked a blanket around the kitten. "He lost his whole family to Louisa's mistake."

"Is that what it was? A mistake?"

He squared his shoulders and looked straight at her. "I told you before. Louisa's a dear, but she's made an error. I'd never hurt a woman that way."

"I've been thinking about what you told me." She hugged the bowl to her bosom and paced the brief length of the cell. "You said the gun was part of a set; that you'd lost the mate a long time ago." Stopping, she held out the metal bowl. "You don't suppose the real"—she glanced at the kitten, the tiny dropper—"rapist . . . could have used the gun you misplaced?"

"No."

"What makes you so sure?"

"Like I said." He kept talking quickly, determined to make this part of the story convincing. "That pistol's been missing for eight or ten years. It's highly unlikely someone could have found it."

"But maybe—"

"No." He took hold of the other side of the dish. "Don't waste your time." He wanted to touch her. He'd never been this close to her before, and her closeness, her tangible presence, tangled his insides and tightened his muscles, not to mention more intimate parts. "There's got to be some way to help me that doesn't involve chasing down phantoms."

"Then give me a better idea."

"Help me escape."

"Be serious."

"I am."

She let go of the bowl. He rolled the dropper into the basin. The slight chink of glass against metal was the only sound in the jail cell.

"I'm a lawyer."

"So?" He arched a questioning eyebrow.

"An officer of the court. They'd disbar me first thing if they found out."

He tucked the feeding utensils next to the milk, then sat down and stroked his new kitten's back. The baby purred slightly. He felt glad for its presence and softness. "And that's your only scruple against it? That you'd lose your precious job if you did it?"

"No!" Swift as a spring storm in the mountains, those pretty blue eyes iced over. "Of course not." A shaft of sunlight fell through the small window. The bright sunbeam caught her hair and glimmered and flickered in the cell's darkness. He smiled. A ghost of a grin tugged at her mouth. She pressed her fingers over her lips. "What am I saying?" She glared. "You've got a lot of guts, Johnny Christmas."

"Courage—" he flashed his brightest smile at her—"is my middle name."

"I thought it was Kid."

He glanced at the tiny, sleeping newborn. Not for the first or last time in his life, Johnny Christmas wondered why God made some creatures so strong and others so weak. "It was—a long time ago."

Johnny stood up, gesturing for her to sit on the cot. She colored, hesitated a moment, then picked up her bag and sat down. Ruffling through the green valise, she pulled out the pad of long yellow paper she'd used yesterday. She retrieved a black fountain pen and unscrewed it.

Without looking at him, she flipped the first page over and wrote a neat date in the corner. "I remember when you were called by that nickname." She spoke so softly he almost didn't hear her.

"Yeah?"

"Yes. It took me a while." She doodled a small cloud in one corner. "That was a tough time in my life, but it came to me as I was feeding the kitten. In the old mining camp, you were the gunman known as Kid Christmas.''

"Sure was.''

She drew a profile of Mount Whitney, its uplifted peaks recognizably jagged. "That is a pretty interesting fact.''

"Seems pretty boring to me.''

Whitney Portal bloomed on the paper, its gray arms embracing a stream. "Do you remember my father?''

"Sure do.''

"He was killed by a Colt.''

Johnny fought to control the rush of his blood. He'd dreaded this moment the first time she'd shown up at the jail. "How do you know something like that?''

"Because I still have the bullet.'' She set the pen down and pulled a silver chain from beneath her collar. An ugly squat plug of lead dangled from the end of the necklace.

"You kept it?'' he asked tightly.

"Yes.'' She lifted her braid and slipped the grim souvenir over her head. "And I was thinking . . .''

"There's a lot of Colts in this country.''

"True. But some Colts are special.''

"It's a beautiful gun. I'll grant you that.''

"That's not what I mean.''

"Then what?''

"Look.'' She held out her palm. The silver chain fell over her fingers like water. The blunt instrument of her father's death lay sullen and brutal, telling no tales and asking no quarter. "There's a scratch on the ball.''

"Yeah?" Johnny squinted. He could see little here in the darkness.

"That means there's a defect inside the barrel. If I found the weapon, I'd know if it shot him."

"How the he—heck could you know something like that?"

"Because." She slipped the gruesome pendant over her head. "If you shot another bullet through it, the gun would make the same mark."

"Is that why you came back? You want to convict your father's killer?"

"No. Not exactly." She touched Flowers' tail lightly. "I doubt my theory would hold up in court, but I'd still like to find out for myself."

He wanted to pace. He didn't trust her. She knew about law, and he didn't. Her assertion that she could not convict him did not assuage his feelings one bit. "You can't fire all the old Colts in Bodie."

"No . . ." She toyed with the kitten, but very sweetly, so her gentle touch did not even wake him. "But I can fire the ones I can get hold of. There were far fewer men here eight years ago."

"Are you going to try mine?"

"I already did."

"How?"

"I asked the sheriff."

Now he did pace, back and forth the length of the cell, a movement that took him less than two strides each way. "Damn it all, Claire. Why'd you go and do that?"

"If you'd killed my father, that would have posed a bit of a conflict." She drew back her hand and picked up her pad, holding it stiffly in her lap. "I didn't truly believe you had done it. I had to try it, that's all. Besides, it was useful. Handling that Colt got me to thinking. Why would you use that particular weapon? You own other guns. The sheriff told me. Why would you use a gun so distinctive to commit a crime that might fetch you a lynching?"

He stopped. He wanted to tear the pad from her hands, push her down on the bed, and yank off the necklace. "I could be pretty stupid."

"Come off it, Johnny." She had such a beautiful face. "You've survived ten years as a bad man in Bodie." He scarcely heard what she said. "Even your friends believe you're an outlaw." Her braid nestled against her neck, and beneath that thick plait, the clasp to the necklace. "No one knows how you make your money, but you've never been charged with a single crime, much less set yourself up for a lynching."

He shoved his hands in his pants pockets. "So?"

She has eyes like cornflowers and skin like an angel, he thought.

"I don't know if you're a good man or bad, but I do know you're not stupid."

"Maybe passion muddled my brain."

"I don't buy it, Johnny. You're not an idiot and you're not a rapist."

It would have been better never to have seen her again. Better only to remember the innocent beauty he'd admired from afar. "What makes you so sure?"

"Logic." She divided the paper in half with a line. "Louisa's assailant disguised his face, but used the most easily identified gun in this town."

He shut his eyes and waited. He expected more explanation from her, but she didn't speak to his self-imposed darkness. He kept silent through the rush of his blood, through the long, perilous seconds when he thought he might explode in frustration.

"What are you saying?" he asked finally.

"Somebody framed you. Someone, furthermore, whom you're protecting."

"Now there's a wonderful notion."

"You know I'm right, Jonathan Robert Van Kessel."

He opened his eyes. She hadn't changed one single bit. "Nobody calls me that name anymore."

"No, they don't." She'd scribbled a small list on the paper. "But the fact is, you're a man full of secrets. Nobody knows how you earn your living. You fight fires, but you're not paid much for that." She ticked off the first item. "Your gold mine doesn't produce a plug nickel." She put a check by the second. "You disappear every few months and come back into Bodie with a big wad of money. You spend it all like there's no tomorrow. On women, on wine, and on fire equipment." She drew a line through the third item. "So the question is, why?" She placed a neat dot by the word. "Why does a good man live like an outlaw? Who has your gun, and why did he take it? And why won't you tell even your lawyer the name of the man who wants to destroy you?"

After she'd gone, Johnny dropped to the floor, cursing all women, especially Claire Butler. She was right on all counts but one. Someone had framed him. He didn't know who, but he, Johnny, was protecting someone. He was protecting his very own lawyer, Claire Butler.

Pressing his palms to the floor, he braced his arms and lifted his torso. He'd killed her father eight years ago. He'd just never known it for sure. He'd been one of three. Three boys. He, at twenty, the oldest. Shooting up the small mining camp. Their wild gunplay had started a fire. They'd battled the blaze with winter snowballs, then pulled the judge out of a burning cabin. No one knew whose bullet had shot him. He'd bled to death in the moonlight. They'd buried the guns and taken an oath never to reveal what had happened.

As he continued his exercise, Johnny's arm muscles bulged. At the time of Judge Butler's death, Johnny had thought silence the correct course of action. He'd never known until this morning exactly who'd killed the judge. But he'd never been free of the regret of it either. He'd been half in love with Claire Butler that summer. He'd never approached her, of course, being far too full of himself. He'd noticed her, though. And he'd thought if ever he did settle down, she'd be the girl he'd settle down with, though those were the days when he still believed he'd never live past his twenty-first birthday.

Johnny laughed as he lowered his nose to the floor. Funny, how life played tricks on weaklings. He'd come alive with the death of Judge Butler. Watching Claire bury her father had ended his brief career as a gunman. He'd been in many a brawl since, and he'd had guns drawn on him, but he'd never drawn his own. He fought fires instead, subduing the monsters that boiled inside. It had turned out to be simple really. Each time he entered a burning building, he had to face down the same hazard. Death by suffocation. The monster he'd feared all his childhood.

He jumped to his feet. He'd have to escape. He did not want to hate her. For eight years, he'd followed her life in the Frisco papers. With each new scandal or triumph, he felt always the twinge of regret. He'd never gotten to tell her he loved her. In those days close to boyhood, he had not realized life might stretch on toward thirty.

He leaned his shoulder against the door. The wood felt solid against his muscles, but Johnny had battered down his share while firefighting. He felt fairly certain he could dislodge this one, but he'd have to fight his way past the sheriff, a prospect he didn't relish at all.

Cursing, he flung himself at the cot and just missed crushing the kitten. With another foul curse, he picked up Flowers. The tiny kitten started purring. Johnny sat down and, his head bent and his shoulders slumped over, cradled the furball. This called for thinking, never his strong point. He just hated thinking, having spent every childhood winter in bed, engaged in a fierce interior battle with a strangling disease that never quite killed him.

He lay down, the kitten on his chest, and crossed his arms over his eyes. For Claire, he'd try to think. She'd been the first hope he'd known; a debt so precious he could never repay it. His childhood asthma had disappeared slowly, but his joy in living had never abated. He owed her the best eight years of his

life, and it made him ache just to think how he'd hurt
her. He'd find a way to help her law practice, but she
could never defend him—and never find out who'd
killed her father. For her, he'd keep plotting. He'd
find a way out of this jail. He'd hurt her once, but
never would again. He'd not disappoint Judge Butler's daughter.

Claire awoke to the rustle of feet in the darkness.
Her clock chimed twice in the blackness. She bolted
straight up in bed and listened. Whispers ruffled the
night. She could not make out words, but she didn't
need to. She lived on the good side of Bodie, the
respectable part, where men had wives, businesses,
and ambitions, and not very much went on at night.
But something stirred here this evening. Voices and
footsteps swirled in the darkness, mingling with the
honky-tonk airs that carried from the town's red-light
district.

Quickly, she flung back the covers, bounding out
of bed and to her armoire. She'd worried about this
from the beginning. She knew in her heart what odd
night sounds meant. The good men of Bodie were
going to take over justice on the bad side of town.

Claire pulled on her boots, slipped on her coat, and
tucked a double-shot Remington into her pocket. She
considered the promise she'd made to Johnny Christmas and right away decided to break it. Though she
knew they might seem ruthless to some, her father
had taught her a lawyer's scruples.

"An attorney does not owe only his client," he'd

said. "A lawyer stands for civilization, for logic and reason over emotion."

Crossing her bedroom, she patted the small bulge made by the weapon. She wouldn't be her father's true daughter if she lost her first client to a vigilante hanging. She slipped into the alley and hustled through the back streets of Bodie. Her mind worked surprisingly coolly. By the time she'd reached Bonanza, she'd come up with a workable plan.

She knocked on the back door of the jail. "Sheriff."

No crowd gathered here, but Claire's run through the town had further convinced her: Judge Lynch's minions were working. There'd been a small crowd at the stables. Shadowy figures were rolling a buckboard beneath the tall frame used to fix wagons. Claire had shuddered as she'd snuck past. They'd have to find a large structure for Johnny, but the thick wooden beams would certainly take the weight of the fireman.

"Sheriff." She banged again. As a true jurist's daughter, she had learned all about hanging. When it was done correctly, the neck would break, but an amateur could botch the procedure. These fools would feel pretty stupid, she thought, if the rope beheaded their former companion. Or worse. She pounded harder. Christmas could die by strangulation, the slowest, most painful hangman's mistake.

"Hold your horses." The sheriff's voice sounded sleepy. His face appeared at the window. "Miss Butler?" Surprise replaced his drowsy expression. "What are you doing here this time of night?"

"Let me in." Claire rattled the handle. "They're coming for Johnny."

Metal scraped, then the door swung open. "Give me the key." Claire gestured at the door of the cell, where Christmas's face appeared in the window. "I'm going to hide him. I'll bring him back to you in the morning."

"Like hell you will," the sheriff said thickly.

"Fine." Claire pulled the derringer from her pocket. "Then let me help you defend him."

"Like double-damned hell!" A thump jarred the cell. The wooden door shuddered. "You gave me your word!" Johnny yelled out.

Claire ignored the commotion. "It's your choice, Sheriff. You can face down a mob with me beside you, or you can let me slip out of here with him."

"No!" A deeper thump shook the door, raising a squeak from the hinges.

"Quiet." Claire stood on her tiptoes and peeked in the tiny window that allowed the prisoner to look out of the cell. "It's the only chance for freedom you've got. Lucky for you there are no trees in Bodie. They need a few minutes to rig up the scaffold."

"Damn." The sheriff fumbled through the keys on his belt. He unlocked his handcuffs and tossed them through the bars. "Put those on Johnny." He glanced at Claire. "If you can hide tonight, maybe I can scrape up reinforcements. And you better be telling the truth."

"You know I am."

"I'm afraid I do. Everyone knows what Judge Butler stood for."

"I'm ready when you are." Johnny's voice sounded tense.

The sheriff thrust a key in the lock. "You'd better not hurt this little lady. I ought to leave your sorry butt in there, but I don't like losing prisoners to lynch mobs, and I really hate having a woman protect me." He jerked Johnny out of the cell, pulled out his bulldog, and pressed the muzzle to Johnny's forehead. "You touch a hair on her head, and I won't wait for the rabble to hang you."

"Don't worry. I won't." Johnny grinned sweetly at Claire. "I only hurt women who cross me." He held the kitten out to the sheriff. "But what about you?"

"I'll be all right." Frank Flowers frowned. He shoved the pistol back in his pocket. "Here, take this." He handed a key over to Claire, then accepted the sleeping fuzzball from Johnny. "You ought to die, but you ought to die legal. I'll do my best to convince them of that."

"Come on, Johnny." Swiftly she plucked off her necklace and strung the key next to the bullet. "They won't hang the sheriff."

Johnny buttoned his red flannel shirt. "What makes you so sure?"

"There are men from my side of town in the crowd." She opened the door and peered out. No dark figures haunted the back of the jail. The stars and the mountains looked down on the town, cold and indifferent to human affairs. "The rowdies would hang a lawman for sport, but the good citizens won't go so far.''

''I hope you're right.'' Johnny said softly.

''I'm always right.'' She shoved the derringer in her pocket. At Johnny's quizzical look, she responded: ''All right. Strike that comment. I'm always right on certain subjects. Come on. Can't you hear them out there?''

The mountain air carried the sound of a somber tread and murmuring voices. Johnny Christmas didn't change his expression. He turned and spoke to the sheriff. ''I'd be deeply grateful if you'd be careful.''

The sheriff's dark eyebrows drew down in confusion.

Johnny pointed a manacled hand at the kitten. ''He's had a tough life already, and I think he's going to need a new owner.''

Chapter Four

Claire grabbed Johnny's hand and hustled him into the narrow back alley. The night air nipped his skin, but Johnny's heart boomed in his chest, chasing the chill out of his bones. Eight years of firefighting had steeled him to danger, but his dangerous sideline had not taught him how to accept a woman's protection, especially one as stubborn as this one. Checking his stride, he glanced around. The jail stood at the far edge of town, as suited its function, a remote location for bandits and outcasts.

"Come on." Claire tightened her grip on his fingers, dragging him toward the blackness marking the start of sagebrush and mountains. "Hurry up."

He held his pace. "Where's the fire?"

She whirled, ready to pounce. He shielded his face with his manacled hands. "Hang on there." Clasping her elbow, he guided her to the jail's corner and pulled back close to the wall. She struggled, but he held her lightly, in easy control of such a small woman. "Just calm down a minute." He gave a sharp tug on the cape of her coat. "Listen to me." She stilled. He could feel her warmth and excitement, but she seemed to get control of herself. "That's better." He loosened his grip. "How far away are these vigilantes?"

"Can't you hear?"

He listened. Sound carried here on the mountain, borne on the wind with little to stop it. The rinky-tink of saloon pianos mingled with the noise of drunken amusement. Beneath both, from farther away, came the sobering tones of low, angry voices. "It sounds like they're gathering on Main Street."

"For heaven's sake, what do you care?"

"It's the first rule of firefighting—make an assessment before you run into a burning building." He pushed her behind him and peered around the corner. Bonanza Street seemed its usual self—dark and frowsy, patient and humble—but much more deserted than normal. The cribs, washed in gaslight from the saloons, waited silently to receive their patrons. A few customers lurked in their shadows, but no one seemed edgy or rowdy or troubled. Johnny flattened himself against the wood siding. "Where were you thinking of running with me?"

"Up one of these canyons." She moved around him and peered out herself. "Why does it matter?"

Awkwardly, he turned up his collar. "We'll have to spend the whole night up there."

"Are you afraid of the dark?"

"No, but it's cold." Dangling loosely next to the bullet, the key shimmered between her breasts. "Unless you're up for a snuggle, we have to keep warm, and I think a campfire is out of the question."

Moonlight turned her bright blue eyes midnight. She poked her chin in the air. "Got a better suggestion?"

"Yeah, as a matter of fact."

"So tell me."

"I've got friends who'll help me."

She fiddled with the silvery chain. "We don't want to endanger anyone else."

"I don't think that will happen." He brushed a wisp of blond hair from her forehead. The chains on his cuffs jingled lightly. "The mob will search the whole town for me and then scour every bit of the surrounding country, but these fools won't even consider the notion that a woman might hide me."

She blushed. "I can't take you home."

"I didn't mean that." He glanced out at the cribs lining Bonanza.

Comprehension dawned in her eyes. "That's a brilliant idea."

"Yeah, well. Sometimes I have a good thought."

"Do you think one of your . . . lady friends would help us?"

He grinned. "For a sweetheart like me? Yeah, I think so."

Frowning, she peered out again and studied the dark row of low shacks. "How do we get past those men?"

"First you unbutton your coat." She threw him a furious look. He held up his manacled hands in response. "We need to get to crib number seven. Those fellows seem to be minding their business. No one knows I've escaped yet. If you'd do me the favor of helping to hide these, it ought to be easy for us to slip by them.''

She clutched at the key to the handcuffs and measured the breadth of his chest with her eyes. The night could have erupted in gunfire, and it would not have disturbed Johnny Christmas as much as that gaze.

Blinking, she dropped her hand to her side. ''All right. Shut your eyes.''

Though puzzled, he did as she asked. She must have moved swiftly, as he'd scarcely had time to decipher the distant sound of the gathering crowd before he felt her press lightly against him.

''Put your arms around me,'' she whispered.

He complied, cursing the day he'd first seen her and every haunted daydream since then. The soft brush of flannel assailed him. He didn't remember what she'd worn in his dreams, but it could not have been more erotic than this flower-sprigged flannel concoction. Not that the gown wasn't modest enough. It covered her skin from neck to ankle, but her body, free of all stays and female restrictions, had a supple, unrestrained quality that threatened to rob him of breath.

Cursing tightly, he hunkered down and circled his bound wrists around her. She tucked one arm around his waist and draped her wool coat over her shoulder, loosely enough so it covered his handcuffs. The derringer in her pocket bumped the back of his knuckles. She stiffened. He tried to move, but she didn't move with him. He could have lifted her easily enough, but he had no desire to hold her too tightly.

He stopped. "You got a problem?"

"Maybe. A little."

"So spill it."

With her free hand, she clutched her collar. "You really think one of the . . . ladies will help you?"

"Yeah." He had to get going. He thought himself crazy, but one more second next to this nightgown, and his sensation-starved body would surely embarrass them both. "You object to that?"

"No, but I don't understand their motives. I mean, I'm sure they're nice women, but why would—you know, why would those women do all this for you?"

He lifted her feet off the ground. "I told you." Ignoring her struggles, he carried her forward. He pitched into the street, pretending to be drunk and raising his voice so every bystander could hear him. "I told you before: I'm God's gift to women. I'm handsome. I'm rich. And I'm great in the sack."

He lurched crazily forward. She wiggled against him, but she might as well have been Flowers the kitten for all she hampered his stride. He burst into song, levering her against one thigh.

"Johnny, quiet!" she whispered fiercely. She couldn't imagine what he was doing. His deep baritone was so filled with joy it rolled off the mountain and drowned out the tinny pianos. "Someone will hear you."

He hefted her higher and blew a kiss into the curve of her neck. "I certainly hope so."

A crib door flew open. A female figure appeared in the doorway, followed by a half-naked miner.

"Hey there, sister," the woman called out. Claire

did not know the voluptuous whore, but the prostitute appeared to know Claire. "You need some help with that fella?"

Before Claire could answer, the kimono-clad harlot turned the miner around, booted him into her boxlike bedchamber, and shut the door quickly behind him. Then hustling into the street, she winked at Claire and slipped her arm through Johnny's elbow.

"Where are we going?" she asked casually.

"I want a twosome with this one an' Molly." Johnny's voice boomed down Bonanza.

Claire pinched his ribs. Much as she admired his acting, she could certainly have done with a slightly less graphic description.

"I like that." The new woman leaned forward. Brassy red hair tumbled around her shoulders. Her loosely tied robe revealed lush cleavage. She fell in step with Johnny Christmas and Claire. "Of course, it's even better with *three* lovely ladies."

"Can't do it three times." Johnny staggered heavily sideways. "Unless you want to wait until morning."

"Honey"—the harlot's voice dripped the word— "I'd wait all night for you."

At the far end of the street, a yellow light pierced the darkness, and behind it, a shadow.

"Molly!" Johnny bellowed loudly.

The door to another crib opened. Thinking to quiet him, Claire brought Johnny's mouth to hers and planted a firm kiss on his lips. She hadn't meant to, but fear—it must have been fear—had set her heart pumping. Her blood rushed with two kinds of terror.

One was that she might be caught on Bonanza kissing a man who might be a rapist, a client she'd helped to escape.

But the second misgiving pressed more deeply. Johnny Christmas might be an outlaw, but that was an unproven assumption. She did not know if he was guilty. What she did know was that he was living—living, breathing, and right at this moment responding. The crowd at the end of the street—the men massing behind that dim beacon—intended to snuff out that sweetness, to take from Johnny Christmas this very joy and all of life's lesser but still lovely moments. The lawyer in her, the stern judge's daughter, believed that shouldn't be done without proper due process. If she had to hide Johnny Christmas with kisses, she would.

She kissed him again, watching the crowd from the corner of one eye. The dim light grew closer. No longer the size of a pinprick, it had grown to the size of a candle. For a moment Claire thought Johnny Christmas was oblivious to it. His arms tightened around her; his body was surprisingly warm and his masculine interest amazingly obvious. Then he broke off the kiss without prompting and nestled his face in the curve of Claire's neck.

"My little sweetheart," he whispered softly. "I'll kill you after we get out of this pickle."

He clasped her closer and began to sing, this time in a thick Irish brogue. Claire couldn't believe it. Surely the mob could hear him. So, evidently could several more doves, as four more crib doors flew open.

"Hey, ladies," the brassy woman cried out, "we're

going to have an early Christmas.''

Claire tried to get a glimpse of the cribs, but their doors slammed shut, and with them the light. Before Claire could quite grasp what had happened, a small circle of harlots had surrounded Johnny. He sagged into Claire's arms as if he had passed out. She nearly fell backward, but a glimpse at his face made her indignant. He was grinning with joy and boyish pleasure.

"Delectable fool.'' She lowered him into the dirt, the fine dust that covered Bonanza. "You almost make me wish they'd catch you.''

The muffled thump of male boots grew louder. Claire glanced up quickly. The shadow had massed into movement, a dark wave made more fearsome by the fact that only one lamp lit its way. Cold night air seeped under Claire's nightgown. From this distance, she couldn't make out individual faces, but she could tell some had been covered. She panicked. Glancing at the circle of whores, she barely kept her voice from trembling. "What do we do?''

"Tug,'' said the brassy, kimono-clad harlot.

A visible wave of despair fell over the circle of loosely dressed women, but the redhead stood up, grabbing Johnny's collar. "Come on.'' She jerked Johnny up by the shoulders. "For Hattie.'' Claire did not follow the comment, but the sinking row of fallen women seemed galvanized by the remark. Claire couldn't see their expressions, but a sense of purpose came into their posture. The smallest of them, a girl so tiny Claire could only imagine how she practiced the oldest profession, stood up and took hold of Johnny's feet.

"Hey." She spoke in a quavering voice. "He's a rock, but I'm sure we can move him if we work together."

Claire grabbed his wrist. Her heart skittered, fast as water striders darting across the deep pools beneath Whitney. The blue light approached. Its low light painted shadows on the crowd's leader, a broad-shouldered man, his face masked by a wool scarf and darkness, his black duster flapping behind him.

"We're coming through, ladies."

Claire ducked, sweeping her coat over Johnny's face. The voice tugged at her awareness. She could not place its owner, but felt certain she knew him.

He hoisted his lamp, revealing his pistols, two Peacemakers tied to his thighs. "I suggest you get off the street for a while."

Ignoring the grim figure's order, the whores crouched in a circle. They ruffled Johnny's clothes and patted his pockets. The vigilantes swept by them, more than two dozen brisk, silent men glumly ignoring the sight of a drunk being rolled by Bonanza Street's finest.

"Come on," Miss Brass whispered fiercely. "Let's get him to Molly's." The whores stood up in a chorus, rolling Johnny over, each taking a part of his body. On a whispered order, they pulled and proved rather quickly that a half dozen cooperative women could easily move one recalcitrant man.

Johnny remained limp, except for his dimple, which reappeared at odd moments. Claire wanted to kick him, so smug did he look, and she instantly wondered what kind of man would inspire such loyalty from this kind of woman, and what he had done to earn this devotion, and who in the world Hattie was.

They reached crib number seven in less than a minute.

From the end of Bonanza, a distinctive voice sliced the air. "Open up, Sheriff. We've come for the rapist."

A low rumble joined the sharp order. Claire didn't dare glance at the jail.

Miss Brass tapped on the door of the small wooden shack. "Molly, come out," she whispered.

A click, then yellow candlelight glowed in the darkness. Working together, the tattered group of determined women whisked Johnny's hulking male form into the tiny, freestanding, square building.

"Thank you, kind ladies." Johnny tried to stand up, but the minuscule wood structure barely contained room for two people, and his massive bulk had no room to move. Three women backed out the door. Molly flattened herself in the corner. On the single bed lay an inert figure. His naked flesh gleamed like a fish belly, the pale complexion of a deep-rock miner.

"You didn't kill him?" Johnny rose to his feet, then bent down and examined the sleeper.

"No." Molly had crow's-feet and a sallow complexion, but enough springy curves to keep a man's interest. "I just knocked him out. It took a few minutes, but I keep drops around for contingencies."

"Are they going to hang you?" asked one of the youngest women, the pretty one from the jail.

"Not if Molly can find me a horse." Johnny smiled at the wide-eyed young whore. "Why don't you la- dies go back to your places. The morning should find me a long ways from the sweet town of Bodie."

One by one, the women slipped out. The last of them, the well-built Miss Brass, blew him a kiss and left on a husky "Keep your chin up, Johnny."

As the last of the ladies disappeared out the door, Claire freed her derringer from her pocket. She turned it on Johnny. "You're not leaving Bodie."

"Why not, may I ask?"

"I didn't spring you to help you escape."

Johnny glanced at Molly, then leaned against the iron bedstead. "I know that, Claire. But think about this from my point of view. I'm sure you're a really fine lawyer, but do you believe for a minute a jury won't hang me? You can see for yourself." He jerked his chin toward the street. "I can't get a fair trial in Bodie."

"I'll make a motion for a change of venue."

"Ah, venue motions. I suppose you're an expert at those."

"I'll figure it out."

"Claire, look—"

"Back off, Johnny." She lifted the dainty, pearl- handled gun and pointed its barrel straight at his heart. "I know how to use it."

Molly gasped, but Johnny Christmas showed no re- action. He kept his elbow flat on the bedstead and stared at Claire's bosom. "I'm sure you shoot well, but the question is will you."

She worried her lip and glanced at the pistol. She knew how to use it, but not well enough to only wound him. Besides which, she couldn't fire the weapon anyway, as even one shot would bring the mob down on them.

He grinned. "Molly, get me a horse."

The middle-aged hooker moved a couple of feet, but Claire tightened her finger over the trigger. "Molly, stay put," she said, then moved in front of the door. "I promised to bring you back in the morning."

"How are you going to stop me?"

"Molly, bring us two horses, will you?"

He straightened and nearly hit his head on the ceiling. "Goddamn it, Claire." Ducking, he shook his wrists and jiggled the steel chains that bound him. "Why don't you just shoot me?"

"I may be a lawyer, but I'm not a killer."

"So, what's the point here?"

"I can be very persuasive."

"Persuasive?" His gaze shifted toward Molly. "With what?"

"Logic and reason." Claire kept her voice cold. "I wouldn't be much of a lawyer if I couldn't persuade my own client to believe I can free him."

From the end of the street, a low sound made a rumble. Molly dropped to her knees. Johnny remained quiet. The aging whore bent creakily and pulled a shawl from her bed. "I can't wait all night. I'll bring horses for both of you."

"Traitor." Johnny frowned. Like a preening wrestler in a backcountry circus, he flexed the muscles beneath the red flannel.

Claire tightened her grip on her gun. The double-shot Remington seemed much too small to make much of a hole in such a massive bulk.

Molly stood up and shook out a burgundy, feather-trimmed wrap. "I'm not going to stand here and listen to you argue. That mob out there's got this figured out."

Claire moved away from the door. "How will you get us horses?"

"No trouble." She wrapped the feather-trimmed shawl around her. "I'll tell them I heard about Johnny's escape and decided to go visit my mother. But, listen," she said as she stepped toward Claire, her bosom puffed out, her plump hips swaying, "I think the best way to do this is for both you and I to ride in a buggy and let Johnny hide in the back."

"Goddamn both of you women!"

Christmas smashed the wall so fiercely the boxlike crib rattled and shook. Both women froze. The naked miner rolled over. Outside, footsteps swirled past them. On saloon row, the pianos fell silent, but true to Johnny's prediction, none of the mob seemed to be searching the whores. "You're not riding out there with me. There could be shooting." He drew his eyebrows together. "And worse."

"Worse?" Claire and Molly asked in a chorus.

The sputtering candlelight fell on the dark triangle surrounding the sleeping miner's limp privates. Johnny scowled at Molly, then awkwardly pulled a blanket over the man's lower body. "How do you know I'm not a rapist?"

"Oh, Johnny, don't be silly." Molly turned toward the door.

"Fine." Johnny shoved the miner's feet over and plopped himself down on the bed. "I won't go. I'll just wait here until morning. By then, I'm sure they'll all be in a better mood."

"Now, wait a minute." Claire Butler felt a little unsteady. She listened. Slamming doors and shouted curses echoed through the squat row of cribs. Though she couldn't figure out what possessed him, her worry for Johnny grew with each oath.

"Take me back." Johnny laced his fingers and rested his manacled hands on his unruly curls. "See if I care."

Molly looked stricken. Claire took the threat a little more calmly, but she stuffed the derringer into her pocket and moved away from the door. "What if you can't get a fair trial in Bodie?"

The drunk twitched in his sleep. He rolled to one side, twisted in a spasm, and kicked Johnny in the buttocks. Johnny winced, rubbing one cheek, then re-adjusted the blanket. "How could my trial be *un*fair? I'm being defended by the first female lawyer who ever hung out a shingle in the whole mining district."

Claire looked from Molly to Johnny, then pushed her arms into her coat sleeves. "I've never even handled a case."

"I believe we've discussed that." Rising, Johnny settled one shoulder on the unpainted wall. "But all my friends will sit in the gallery. I'm sure they'll make a fine impression.''

Claire shut her eyes and pressed her fingers over the bridge of her nose. "What if I lose? They'll hang you for sure.''

"What do you care? As long as it's legal.''

"You ought to be guilty.''

"Does the law concern itself with such details?''

Claire opened her eyes and toyed with the key that hung on her bosom. "There's a federal marshal in San Francisco.''

Johnny's green eyes reflected the light of the candle. He stared at her bosom, then tucked the thumbs of his manacled hands in one pocket. "We'd still have the problem of how to get there.''

A bay-scented candle covered the smell of the miner, but the sharp incense couldn't disguise the sickly-sweet smell of a joss stick wafting over from King Street. Claire chewed on her lip, dangling the key between her fingers. "I could take the buggy and sneak out to meet you.''

"You trust me that far?''

"No, I don't trust you, but I don't seem to have that many choices.''

He brushed past her and peered out the door. Claire peeked around him as best she could. Bonanza Street seemed completely deserted, the whores pretending to feel terror; the good men of Bodie intent on the lynching; the bad men electing either to hide or to spend the night indulging the fiction that they possessed a sense of justice.

"No good.'' He shut the door with a quiet click.

She thought she should choke him, but buttoned her coat up instead. "Then you think up something better."

"I'm going to kidnap you."

"Now wait—"

He looped his handcuffed hands over her head and grabbed her, pressed his calf under hers, and threw her off-balance. She didn't scream, but she kicked him. Hard. He grunted and lifted her onto his thigh. "Look. You broke your promise."

"But—" He felt solid, warm, and extremely determined.

"You're right about me." He took one step toward the center of the room. "I'm low and conniving and not to be trusted, but I do try to be manly about it. I fight my own battles and I don't like depending on women."

She could have screamed, but she didn't. "I'm your lawyer, you scoundrel. I won't get in trouble."

"Like hell you won't. If it comes out you helped me leave Bodie, you'll never practice law in this town."

"A good lawyer—" She struggled, but he held her immobile. She could feel his hard muscles. His strength surprised her, though she didn't know why. For three days she'd looked at those shoulders. Logically she ought to have deduced how easily he could manhandle her. But she hadn't. As she reached for her gun, her mind groped for a reason. Had the smile disarmed her? How had he seemed so harmless? "A good lawyer—"

"A good lawyer be damned." He tightened his

grip and squeezed her. "This town's had its fill of good lawyers. Look where it got them. The streets are so bloody a man can't walk to an outhouse." She tried to retrieve the gun from her pocket, but his grip was so strong she nearly fainted. "And now somebody's assaulted a woman. Believe me, lady. I know these miners. They've got a lot of respect for women, but none whatsoever for your lawyers." She looked wildly for Molly. The plump tart had dodged around them and waited, wide-eyed, by the wooden door. With one hand he motioned toward the chill outdoor darkness. "Get Tiny, will you?"

"Sure, Johnny, but don't you think that might lead the lynch mob to you?" Molly's loose shift fell short of her ankles, revealing partially fastened high-button boots.

Claire dug her fingers into Johnny Christmas's forearms. Though her nails made no dent in his muscles, he shifted her weight on his thigh. "Tell them the girls have decided to hide him. That there are rumors out I'll come for my horse."

Molly nodded, then disappeared into the darkness.

Claire stilled. "Will you let me go now?"

"Not yet. You have to listen to reason."

She kicked him again.

He winced but didn't drop her. "If that mob finds out you helped me escape, who knows what effect that would have on their scruples. If that rabble finds us somewhere out in these mountains, and thinks we're in cahoots, our friends will never know where we're buried. On the other hand, if the vigilantes think you've been kidnapped, they'll think twice before starting to shoot. Then if I get caught, no one's the wiser. As far as they'll know, you'll have been one of my victims.''

"Put me down.''

"I'd rather you didn't come with me, but if you come, you come on those terms.''

"Put me down first, then I'll answer.''

He set her on her feet. She took one last look at those shoulders. She'd be helpless, she knew. But she just had to trust him. He'd never get a fair trial in Bodie. Sooner or later that lynch mob would get him. Why the idea pained her she didn't know, but the grim image niggled: the face of a dead man, neck broken, tongue swollen and purple; the handsome face of Johnny Christmas forever robbed of light, joy, and sweetness.

He grinned. Something swirled deep in her stomach. Like a brown trout in a warm pool in summer, some latent emotion flickered to life, and she swallowed. His strength didn't lie in those broad shoulders. She'd been helpless, she realized, from the first time he'd smiled. She had no choice but to help him. Johnny Christmas might not think much of lawyers, but she wouldn't be her father's true daughter if she gave up an innocent man to a lynch mob. With trembling fingers, she pulled the silver chain from her neck, slipped the key from it, and handed Johnny Christmas his freedom.

Chapter Five

Molly brought them two horses, a small brown-and-white pinto and Tiny, the Clydesdale Johnny Christmas loved above all the animals he'd ever owned.

He noticed Claire peek out of the door, then step back. "You expect to sneak away from Bodie on that?"

Tiny lowered his head and nickered. Johnny smiled as the middle-aged whore tied the gentle giant out front. The Clydesdale's mane now reminded Johnny of Claire's tresses, cascading in waves touched by lamplight and starlight, shimmering, the way Claire Butler's hair would if she ever decided to loosen her braid.

Stepping around the fragile lawyer, Johnny rubbed the horse's velvety nose. "He's perfect. Now give me your pistol."

Claire hesitated. Johnny didn't. He grabbed one of her wrists and pulled it behind her.

"What are you doing?" Her voice had risen, but not to a shout.

"Now hold on there, sweetheart." He kept his voice steady, his body a distance from hers. "You have to look properly kidnapped." He snapped a manacle over one hand. For some reason he found this erotic and stifled the thought that he'd soon have the object of eight years' worth of daydreams tightly bound and helpless before him. He turned her around, closed the second handcuff, lifted her chin, and checked her expression. Her eyes had widened. The flower-sprigged flannel rose and fell with her breathing.

"You okay?" he asked.

She nodded tersely. He wanted to kiss her. He didn't know if that kind of attention would help her, but he wanted to put to rest all the questions that danced behind those dark pupils. Instantly he discarded the notion. Eighteen years of squabbling with sisters had taught him to be gentle with smaller opponents, especially once you've got her pinned down.

He buttoned the top of her coat, then slipped the gun out of her pocket. "Here." He opened the barrel and slid out the bullets, tucking them in his jeans pocket. "Does this make you feel better?"

"Not really."

Molly entered the crib and strolled to the unconscious miner, who'd rolled toward the wall during this conversation.

Frowning, Claire examined the steel that now circled her wrists. "How did I get talked into these?"

He grinned. "Perhaps you succumbed to my charms?"

Her hands dropped like a plumb bob. "Professional

pride. I refuse to let rabble hang my first client.'' She tugged at the ruffle on the sleeve of her nightgown. ''What will you do if the crowd starts shooting?''

''Push you behind me and take a few bullets.'' At the arch of her eyebrow, he shrugged. ''Fine. Don't believe me.'' He shoved the dainty derringer in his belt. ''This peashooter won't help, though. You'll just have to trust me. I've survived eight years in Bodie, and I haven't shot a man since . . .'' He checked her wrists and ran a finger under the handcuffs. ''Well, since the last one I shot.''

''How reassuring.''

''Look.'' He squelched an urge to smack her bottom and instead smoothed down a fine spray of her silky tendrils. She seemed pale, maybe frightened, and he really did want to kiss her. ''Don't get smart with me. I could leave you trussed up here with Molly, and in many ways I'd rather do that.''

''You'd never survive.''

''Don't you ever keep your thoughts to yourself?''

Outside, Tiny nickered and bumped his haunches against the much smaller pinto. The drunken miner turned onto his stomach, and Molly straightened the blanket over his shoulders. Quickly Johnny stepped out of the door. He ignored the slap of cool air and peered into the crystalline darkness. The saloons had calmed down. The sound of the crowd had traveled to Main Street.

''Can you ride astride?'' he asked Claire tersely.

Behind him, the steel bracelets chinked, and wool rustled. ''You'll find me well suited for this . . . adventure. I think like a man, but that's not my only

masculine virtue.'' She moved beside him, a tangible
warmth in the cool mountain darkness. ''I can ride
astride. I'm a fine fisherwoman. I shoot well, too, if
you must know.''

''Yeah . . . good. Molly.'' He signaled the pale,
middle-aged strumpet whom he'd visited lately only
for comfort. Since Hattie had died, he'd started to
miss his three sisters, and the soft, fallen woman who
was becoming almost mouselike, had been just what
he'd wanted in terms of a woman. ''Thanks.''

She hugged his waist briefly. ''Here.'' She rolled
up her shawl. Fat, quiet tears plopped off her eyelashes. ''You got no coat.''

He grinned, tucking her offering under his elbow.
''I'll remember you always, sweet lady. Take care.''
He blew her a kiss, then commandeered Claire by the
small of her back. ''Let's get going, counselor. I hope
you are a really good lawyer, 'cause you may have
to do some pretty fast talking.''

Once they were outside, he tossed Claire on the
back of the pinto. He didn't hurt her, but neither did
he handle her gently. Rather, he jolted her into the
saddle, as if his mind were running toward some other
business and transporting a trussed-up attorney was
only a small part of his task. He pulled the reins over
the pinto's head, then vaulted onto the Clydesdale.
Claire couldn't imagine how he planned to sneak out
of town on the largest, most striking and muscular
horse she had ever seen in her life.

''Hey,'' he said as he tugged on the reins and

started to pull the much smaller pinto toward Main Street.

"Hey, yourself," Claire called, eyes forward. "Where are we going?"

"I told you when we broke out of jail, never run into a burning building unless you can hear someone screaming."

"Could you just spare me your strained aphorisms and tell me why we're riding straight toward the gallows?"

"I'm going to make sure we're not followed."

"You realize by now they've constructed a scaffold right next to the stable and are likely to hang you the minute they see you?"

Turning, he grinned.

"And don't think I won't enjoy watching," she said.

He flashed her a dimple, but didn't respond.

They rode down Bonanza in silence. The night chill had deepened, and so had the stillness. The normally boisterous din of the red-light district had settled down to the hush of a graveyard. Claire could still hear the lynch mob, its raucous shouts and noisy door-banging reduced to the murmur and tread of frustration. Fear salted her mouth. She had to admire Johnny's bravado. It took a certain lunatic courage to face down a crowd of vengeance-bent miners, most of whom believed you'd dishonored their town by raping a woman.

Surreptitiously, she studied his back. He had a broad, wedge-shaped torso and powerful shoulders, as well as the thick neck of a practicing boxer. He didn't have a pugilist's bearing, however. He carried himself with a good-humored grace, as if he'd long ago made peace with the demons that sometimes lead men to build up their muscles. His posture conveyed he accepted his size as a gift with no meaning beyond its obvious practical uses.

"Now, come on up forward." He tugged the brown-and-white splotched horse toward him. Claire felt the heat of both man and Clydesdale, their solid mass of bulky muscle producing enough pure energy that they warmed the chill air for at least a few inches. "Try not to be frightened."

He drew the derringer from his gun belt. The tiny gun looked almost silly, and Claire didn't know whether to admire him or laugh.

"Do you think I look brazen?" She glanced at her boots—halfway buttoned—and her pale calves poking out from her nightgown.

"Fetching." He wound the reins around one bare hand and palmed the gun in the other. "Now, follow my lead."

They rode down Bonanza, their saddles creaking. She felt as if she could have counted the stars, the infinite extravagant millions that spangled the black above the Sierra and lent a single softening touch to the dark profiles of the town's looming ridges. The piano music having shut down, the distant sound of the mills seemed much louder. The tremor and low metal groan was a hellish staple of mining camp life she only noticed on rare occasions. They turned off Bonanza, plodded down Main Street, and approached the stable from the direction of the Green Street fire station.

Claire squinted. She made out the outlines of the darkened buildings, but couldn't pick out very much more. The moon had not risen, and the stars were not helpful. Their cool brilliance lent Claire no guidance. She had to stay focused to pick out the skeletal shape of the scaffold.

Once she found it, though, she could see shadows moving. Some of them moved with evident purpose, going to and from the scaffold, while others milled around the black framework, quietly listening to the broad-shouldered leader, the man whose voice Claire couldn't quite place.

Johnny halted, bringing her close. The pinto shied. Johnny calmed him, then waited. Claire shut her eyes, frightened and sick at the sight of the blunt, resourceful, mechanical construction the crowd had adapted to the purpose of justice. She wasn't sure what Johnny Christmas was doing, but she gathered he didn't mean to sneak by. She longed to ask him about his plan, but decided she shouldn't. She listened. The men's voices floated over, some high-pitched with whiskey, some low and more sober.

Gradually, though, the voices subsided. She felt glad enough for it. Her hands had grown cold along with the steel bracelets, and she wanted this charade to be over. She could sense the crowd stirring, the mutter and shift as the leader stopped speaking.

She opened her eyes. The dark blotch had in fact moved closer, discernible now as individual bodies. Masks covered each of their faces, as if the rapist had sprouted a few imitators. She drew herself up, perhaps not wise for one who'd been kidnapped, but she couldn't cower in front of a lynch mob, even if she was supposed to be frightened of Johnny Christmas.

The leader stepped forward, the husky man in the black duster. "What you got there, Johnny?"

Johnny tipped his head in Claire's direction. "You can see for yourself."

"Let her go, friend. We're going to hang you. Hiding behind a woman won't change your fate."

Johnny grinned. "I'm going to do my damndest to try."

"For chrissake, Johnny." A small, bandy-legged miner stepped forward. "Ain't you had enough? That's Judge Butler's daughter. You'll have the whole state looking for you if you hurt her."

"From the looks of that scaffold, I've got grief already. Now, listen. I'll make you a bargain. I didn't do what you accused me of—yet." The comment was met with a deep silence and a hushed rustle of disapproval. "You don't have to believe me. Just listen. I'm leaving Bodie. Tonight. And forever. And I'm taking this pretty young woman with me." A low murmur ran through the crowd. No moonlight glinted off the dark rifles, but Claire had a sense of movement and stirring. Johnny held the pearl-handled gun to her head. "Settle down, fellas."

The shadowy mass shifted, bunching together, then thinning out, the noise of the men's protest ebbing away as they touched their triggers one after another, then visibly measured the distance between the derringer's barrel and the pulse that throbbed in Claire's temple.

"That's better," Johnny said to the palpable silence. "Think hard, fellas. She's a pretty thing. I don't want to hurt her. Keep your distance, and I promise I'll free her—"

An angry voice interrupted, "Why should we trust you? You messed with one woman already."

"You don't know that, do you? But that's not the point. Rush us, and I'll kill her. If you let us leave Bodie, we can all take our chances. I promise you this, though: You get anywhere close to us as we're running, and you'll have more than her blood on your conscience. You understand, fellas?" He scanned the crowd, who met his speech in absolute silence. "Now I'll seal this deal." He pulled her over and kissed her. To her surprise, he shut his eyes, though the barrel remained pressed to her temple. She kept her eyes open. To her deeper surprise, her body responded. In spite of the death threat, or maybe because of it, her nipples tightened, her knees turned to jelly, and her thighs hugged tight to the pinto. He deepened the kiss, as if here at this moment, in the teeth of the lynch mob, he wanted to drag her off her horse, lay her down on the ground, and take her. She found his bravado appalling and outlandish, primitive, barbaric, and somehow appealing. She could not see the crowd, but she could sense their tension, perhaps even their heat, two dozen furious men torn between shame for their manhood and a blessed thread of sensible thought.

She trembled. Johnny pressed his horse closer, his thigh brushed hers, the cool metal barrel a steady pressure. She found herself wondering about the nature of passion. Would most women find this display thrilling? Certainly Claire did. Why this was so she couldn't fathom, but her blood rushed, while other parts softened. He crushed her into his chest, his hard muscles straining against her soft bosom. She tried to look frozen, but some wicked, willful, passionate impulse wanted to respond, and for some reason she couldn't plumb, his hot mouth drove her to a frenzy.

A low moan broke in her throat. He broke off the kiss. For a suspended instant his gaze locked with hers, then he cursed softly and glared at the crowd. Pulling back, he waved the gun. The derringer wasn't loaded, and that fact made her nervous. Men took virtue seriously in Bodie. Some misguided miner might really plug her ravaging brigand. The vigilantes could pick Johnny off in a second, though they'd run the risk of shooting her, too.

Johnny raised himself in his stirrups. "Do we have a bargain?"

The crowd wavered, then murmured. A few of the men touched their guns, but none of them drew a bead on the broad-shouldered man dressed in red flannel.

The leader, a big man, nearly as well built as Johnny, stepped forward. "Let her go, Christmas."

"No dice."

"We'll hunt you down like a scat-sniffing coyote."

"Every dog has his day."

The leader tightened his grip on his rifle. The small man from the crowd grabbed the barrel. "Let it up, pal. He's got guts, and we oughtn't cross him."

"We gonna let him sully another woman?"

"Gentlemen, please." Claire lifted her hands in supplication. "Don't do anything rash." She tried to think of them as a jury and wondered what logic might sway them. In the end, she settled on flagrant emotion. "I know you think he's threatening a fate worse than death, but whatever he does out there in the mountains"—here she choked and let tears into her voice—"I'll still wake up to see the sunrise. I like the sunrise . . . It's not that I don't trust your shooting—"

"That's enough, Claire." Johnny swung her off the pinto and into his saddle, then pressed the derringer close to her temple. "So, gentlemen, do we have a bargain?"

He rode out of Bodie with the pinto behind them, Claire firmly ensconced in the front of his saddle. She didn't argue, but when they reached the Toll Road, she wiggled half sideways and clutched his red sleeve. "Whatever possessed you?"

"What do you care?" He liked the solid feel of her fingers. "I needed a hostage." He held her slim waist, his arm tucked beneath her rib cage. "I didn't want to miss my last chance to kiss you."

She turned and rested her manacled hands on the pommel. The silver chain gleamed on her neck. "If I'm expendable, why aren't I riding behind you?"

"I told you before: As best as I can, I'll take the bullets."

"I suppose you walk on the outside of board-walks?"

"Of course."

She settled in slightly, and he eased himself back as far as he was able. The freezing air rushed in between them. She trembled. He sighed and moved in closer. "I'm sorry I got you into this fix."

Ignoring his comment, she stared stolidly at the horizon. "Oh well. I never thought practicing law would be easy."

"I bet you never thought you'd get kidnapped, though."

She didn't answer. Tiny clopped lazily over the dirt road, the rock-strewn path that led toward Lee Vining, the last camp before the Tioga Pass. Claire's wool coat prickled, but Johnny was glad she wore it. He wouldn't have liked her to be cold. In general, he liked thrilling adventures, but Claire's presence made his predicament sobering. He still found it hard to believe she had risked her life to defend him. "Do you miss your father?"

"Of course."

The moon had set behind the horizon. The silver-tipped night gloomed into dark shadows. "I liked him."

"Did you know him?"

"Not really. But everyone knew what he stood for."

They'd reached the deepest part of the night. No birds. No crickets. No sounds at all. The earth had lost all the warmth of the daylight. Johnny couldn't quite see what Claire was doing, but she seemed to be fiddling with the ruffles of one of her nightgown sleeves. "Could you take these manacles off?" she asked.

He listened. The wind blew in layers, a feathered and eloquent chorus, echoing down from the mountains, caressing the hills. The breeze might drown the approach of hoofbeats, and he wasn't a man to take foolish chances. If the vigilantes caught up, he wanted her to look like a captive. "Do you still think I'm a rapist?"

She tightened her grip on the pommel. He covered her hands with his own. His fingers were cold, but hers were much colder. She smelled like lye soap and lightly scorched flannel, and he wondered if she did her own laundry. "Well?"

"I don't know. . . ."

Fine, he thought, let her stew for a while in her suspicions. He didn't know why she should believe him, but it still annoyed him that she didn't. They rode for a while longer in silence. Her hands warmed up—and so did his body. He cursed silently. He'd be better off without a conscience, he told himself. He didn't like to imagine what went through her mind when she felt the hard prod of his masculine interest. "I wish I could let you free safely."

"You do?" she asked hopefully.

He listened again for hoofbeats and spurs. He heard the clump of Tiny's vast hooves, the higher notes of the pinto, the creak of the saddle, the Sierras' soft sighs, but he didn't catch any sharp chinks of metal or distant clinks of horseshoes on rock. He didn't fool himself, however. Two men besides him had known where the Colt was. Johnny didn't know who dug the gun up, or how it had come to be used on Louisa, but it didn't take a Philadelphia lawyer to realize someone had framed him, and the really dangerous part of his plight was that one of his friends must have revealed his secret, and someone who knew about Judge Butler's killing might be among the vigilantes who followed. "I wish I could take those manacles off you, but I'm thinking I'd better not."

Chapter
Six

She didn't like that decision. In fact, she sincerely regretted the misguided impulse that had gotten her into this predicament. From the hard outline pressed to her bottom, she gathered the nature of Johnny's interest. She found this disturbing. In the cold, clear chill of the night, she tried to assess how much danger she might be in. As she ticked off the list, a lumpy weight settled deep in her stomach. She'd made herself helpless before a total stranger, a possible rapist and a notorious bad man. She could have escaped, but she hadn't.

What had possessed her? Her notions of justice? She thought herself a logical woman, but now that the chain of events had slowed down, she could not re-create the sequence of thoughts that had gotten her into this situation. Attraction? She rejected that notion. She'd never been ruled by hot-blooded passion. Her marriage had been proof of that. A sense of adventure? Maybe. If she were honest. She found Johnny Christmas exciting. The tomboy in her, the girl who'd grown up in these mountains, liked his good-humored sense of bravado, the wild escape, the make-believe abduction. It felt good to be riding beneath the night sky, especially after life at her uncle's and her dismal failure as a wealthy man's wife.

She consoled herself by reading small signals. Christmas had tried to move back on the saddle; he wasn't taking undue advantage. The attraction, what's more, ran in both directions. She liked the brawny feel of his arms, the vast expanse of muscular chest, not to mention the memory of the kiss and the warm rush of pure titillation his masculine hunger evoked.

Some lawyer, she scolded herself. Her first chance to uphold the law's honor and she'd taken off with an outlaw.

"What are you thinking?" he asked.

She jangled the chain on the handcuffs. "When do I get these manacles off?"

"When I think we're safe."

The steel bracelets chafed, but not as much as his answer. "When will that be?"

"Don't know."

"How do you plan to get to San Francisco?"

"Don't know that either."

"I see." The wind had come up. Moonlight outlined the high cumulus clouds that pushed against the towering mountains. She liked Johnny's touch, if not his attitude. His hands sheltered hers, keeping her surprisingly warm. "Do you mind if I make a suggestion?"

"No."

"We've got to outwit them."

"Fine." His thigh muscles tightened. "I declare you the brains of this outfit."

She ignored his sarcasm. Her intellect was both her downfall and freedom. Planning came naturally to her; dissembling didn't. She'd never been able to simper and swoon, or to hide the fact that she was smart. That fault had cost her a husband. She supposed it wouldn't sit well with Christmas either.

"Do you think they can track us?" she asked finally.

"Of course."

"How?"

"For one thing," he said as he leaned forward, let go of her briefly, and patted the Clydesdale's blond mane, "there aren't that many horses like Tiny."

"True." She glanced at the ground. The gargantuan creature had hooves twice the size of a normal breed's, and very likely a gait like no other. "Maybe we could replace him."

"Not a chance, counselor."

"I was not suggesting we break the law."

He fitted his warm hands back over hers. Why did he have to feel so delicious? She figured he probably ravaged more women in a night's carousing than she would bed men in her lifetime.

"I was thinking of something more like a trade."

"That's out," he said tersely.

"Why?"

He tugged on the reins of the pinto. Tiny clopped along slowly, but the smaller horse had nearly to trot in order to keep up the pace. "I don't think we should show ourselves much. The vigilantes won't only track us—they'll ask questions at all the ranches.''

"I wasn't thinking of asking. . . .''

"How, then, if not horse theft?''

"Just a fair trade. If we took a horse in exchange for Tiny—''

"Not a chance, lady.''

"Why not?'' Briefly she stroked the golden neck. "He's a wonderful horse.'' The massive animal had developed a lather, and his body heat made the night warmer. "There's not a rancher around who'd press charges if you left this giant in some nag's place.''

"This giant's mine. I'm not leaving him with a stranger.''

"For heaven's sake, Mr. Christmas.''

"No dice. Come up with a better suggestion.''

She moved forward slightly. So far Johnny'd shown no temper, but she didn't want to test him, especially while she was still helpless. She studied the mountains. She knew these hills well, having rambled in them as a child with her father. "Could we hide?''

"Don't think so.''

"Why not?''

"Ambush.''

The moon had passed behind the clouds, illuminating the massive gray shapes that swelled and surged behind the real mountains. She liked traveling at night, seeing these vast natural displays that generally happened while she was sleeping. "Well, what's your recommendation?''

"Ride day and night for San Francisco.''

"No, I don't think so.''

"Why not?''

"I'm apt to develop a very sore bottom."

He chuckled at that. "Got a better idea?"

"One, actually." She declined to blush. She hadn't meant the remark the way it had been taken.

"Yeah?"

The night air caressed her. A thunderstorm rumbled behind the dark cathedral-like peaks. The storm sang to her blood, arousing a long-dormant sense of adventure. "We'll have to work as a team." He wouldn't hurt her. He couldn't. She was his lawyer. He needed her help. "I sleep while you watch, and vice versa."

"How do I know you won't desert me?"

"How do I know you won't take advantage?"

That question silenced him for a moment. She could hear his irregular breathing, feel the press of his masculine interest. A thrill of terror ran through her. She'd made herself helpless before him, though why she'd done it she could not have explained. It reassured her a little that he seemed to be thinking. Surely a rapist could not have a conscience.

"Deal?" she asked finally.

He settled himself far back in the saddle, though his hands remained fixed over hers. "You drive a hard bargain."

Claire didn't dare ask what he meant by that comment. She felt it was wiser to let matters rest. The mountains rolled with an irregular thunder, layer upon layer of sound. Tiny's pace quickened a little. Johnny seemed to be searching for something; though Claire could not see him, she had a sense of him moving forward, as if he were scanning the distant storm.

"Are you getting hungry?" he asked.

"No." She glanced back at the pinto. "But I have been thinking about how to get food. I camped these mountains a lot as a girl. This time of year there are buffalo berries, fish, rabbits, and maybe some piñon nuts. I won't eat larvae, of course, but I think I could stomach ants in a pinch."

"Ants?" His voice pitched above the distant thunder.

"I hear they're nutritious."

"Are you trying to kill me?" He sounded angry. And hungry. A bad combination.

"Have you got a better idea?"

"I think so. . . ."

His better idea involved a woman, of course.

An old woman, to be fair to Johnny, and a Digger Indian to boot. She was sleeping soundly beneath a twig shelter. A faint white glow had turned the horizon silver. As they approached, a black-and-white magpie burst into song. From the back of the Clydesdale, Claire didn't know whether the sleeper was male or female, but a certain frailty about the body told her it was a woman.

"Mary?" Johnny called out. Startled, Claire turned. She studied the long, thin trail behind them. She had a vague idea Christmas should whisper, though they'd not seen the vigilantes since they'd left Bodie.

"Chreesh-meesh?" The old woman had an indescribable accent and evidently very few teeth. The skin blanket stirred. Dark eyes squinted from beneath brown furs. "Chreesh-meesh?"

Johnny grunted, then slid off the horse, taking Claire with him. As her feet hit the ground, her knees nearly buckled. Only the care with which he clutched then released her kept her from stumbling.

"Thanks." She pulled away, glad to be free of his closeness, though she missed his warmth immediately. Her back ached. Her bones creaked. And she didn't want to think about her bottom. The toasty mass of solid male body had been more of a comfort than she'd been aware of. She shifted forward, stretching the kinks out of her muscles. Johnny steadied her by taking her elbow.

"You got food to trade?" he asked the Indian woman.

The old crone sat up. Long gray hair fell over the ragged remains of a calico dress, but neither quite covered her bronze, flattened breasts. She didn't seem self-conscious, however. She clutched the brown furs loosely around her and studied Claire's manacled hands. "Trouble, Chreesh-meesh?"

Johnny nodded. The old woman scrambled up quickly, leaving the rabbit furs in a heap. Behind her hovel lay three gourd-shaped baskets, their intricate and beautiful patterns a startling contrast to the shambling disarray of her rude shelter. She lifted the smallest and shook it. It rattled.

"Piñon nuts?" Johnny asked.

She smiled, nodded, then pointed to a stick scaffold where short strips of flesh were drying.

"Rabbit jerky?" he asked.

She nodded again, then patted the largest gourd

with a mournful expression.

Johnny peered in. "You don't have much bread. Maybe you ought to keep it." After a short pause, he said, "I've got some tobacco to trade."

The old woman's grin widened. Frowning, Johnny dropped Claire's arm and turned to his saddlebags. He hesitated, however, evidently torn between morals and hunger. Claire understood. Among the Indians tobacco had value. The old woman could trade it for food. But if she smoked it, rather than traded, she might be hungry in a couple of weeks. Considering her rather wizened condition, that seemed a lot to have on one's conscience.

Turning, Johnny walked back to the woman. "Let me see your teeth, Mary."

She offered her mouth without protest. Taking her chin, he glared into that inhospitable cavern, whose few remaining yellowing teeth showed clearly enough the effect of her vice. "You're an old sinner, you know."

She shook her head vigorously and grappled for a small wooden cross nearly lost among her tatters. "No." She held the crucifix up to Johnny's face. "Mary good Chreesh-tian." Shaking her head again, she lifted her piñon nut gourd and pressed it on Johnny. "Take." She waved one hand in the air, shaking the pretty basket for emphasis. "Tobacco. Bah." She spit on the ground. "Take. Chreesh-meesh. Friend. Chreesh-meesh. For Hattie. Take."

"Naw." He opened the saddlebag and pulled out a plug of tobacco. "We're not really hungry. But if you can manage, go down to my place and see what you can do for my pets. It might be a while before I can tend them.''

Johnny grabbed Claire and lifted her onto the Clydesdale. The Indian woman pursued them, rattling her small gourd of nuts. ''Take. Chreesh-meesh. Take.''

He fished through his saddlebags, tossed down the plug of tobacco, and grinned. ''Thanks, sweetheart. I'd love to, but I think we're in the mood to go fishing.''

''That was the stupidest thing I've ever seen anyone do in my life!''

''Just stuff it, Claire.''

Though Johnny doubted Mary could hear them, he could not resist looking over his shoulder at the squat figure watching them leave and the low hovel fading into the distance. At least, he thought, Claire had waited until they got out of earshot before she launched into her tirade.

''Well, I'm hungry.''

''I'm hungry, too.''

That admission cost Johnny, for he hated hunger more than any other discomfort, except the painful press in his chest he'd experienced during his childhood bouts of asthma. Or maybe his chagrin at riding with Claire. He'd been pressed against her for half of the night, and the steady rhythm of the broad-backed Clydesdale had only increased his sexual frustration. Still, he didn't regret his predicament. He'd be dead, after all, were he still back in Bodie. Nor did he quite regret having Claire with him, even if she seemed a bit crabby. He regretted his empty stomach, however. For the second-largest firefighter in a town of gold miners, breakfast was a serious matter.

"Some outlaw," she said.

"Can't you be quiet? I'm thinking."

He could feel the sulk in her posture. A light breeze fluttered her nightgown and drew attention to her bared calves. Johnny stifled a groan. His thighs ached. His groin was sore. He had been looking forward to more than just breakfast, though cold logic told him Claire wasn't that kind of woman, and he knew his chances of sating either stomach or other were growing dimmer with each passing minute. He tried to move backward, but couldn't. He should have mounted her on the pinto, but he'd been so distressed by his encounter with Mary that he hadn't been thinking especially clearly. She couldn't move much wedged into the saddle. He could feel her distress, though she didn't slump forward. Anxiety stiffened her spine.

She curled her fingers over the saddle horn. "How did someone so softhearted survive eight years in Bodie?"

"Not by cheating old ladies."

"And who's Hattie? All these ladies love her."

The sun had come up behind them. Johnny could not see the bright circle, but the day had gone from golden to glaring. The meadowlarks settled into cheerful song, but Claire's wool coat scratched against him. "She was a whore."

His answer did not change Claire's posture, but a new tension came into her shoulders. " 'Was'?"

"She passed away last year."

"Did she . . . support . . . you?" she asked quietly.

A pimp. She pegged him for that? In spite of his outrage, he didn't answer. Claire could think what she wanted. What he'd done for Hattie was private. The whole mining camp knew about it, of course, but public opinion had never been the point for a minute. Whatever he'd done, he'd done for personal reasons, and no prying lawyer was going to judge him.

"I'm hungry," she repeated.

Her complaining annoyed him. He did not have an alternate plan, nor would he likely make one. He worked best in tight situations. The lack of a system didn't bother him much, except for the state of his stomach. "You said you liked fishing?"

"I'm too tired to fish, and we don't have tackle." The burgundy shawl had slipped off her head, and her golden hair shimmered. "Though . . ." He could just see the curve of her cheek, the delicate strands of toast-colored eyelashes. She should have looked gray, or tired, or disheveled. Instead, she looked pink, cream-colored, and fetching. She frowned and looked at her manacled hands.

His stomach growled. He jerked on the reins of the little pinto and immediately regretted his roughness. "Look. Goddamn it. If you've got a suggestion, spit it out."

"It's just an idea." She clung grimly to the saddle horn.

"So spill it."

"There are fish in some of these streams. When I was a girl, I used to catch them."

He cleared his throat discreetly. "You said yourself we don't have tackle."

"Bare-handed."

He chuckled out loud.

She shrugged. "It's not so hard if you know what you're doing. You've got to find just the right place, but if we rode for a while in a streambed, I think I could find a good fishing spot."

His muscles relaxed. He didn't know he'd stored up such tension, but the night ride had affected his nerves. And hunger always sharpened his temper. "I think I like that."

"Good." She glanced over her shoulder. "It might throw the trackers off, too."

"Not likely."

"No?"

He gazed at the barren ridge rising before them. He knew these mountains by heart, though not from hunting or even from fishing. "An experienced tracker can follow signs in a stream."

She readjusted the manacles clamped over her wrists. Faint red marks welled beneath the steel circles. "How?"

"Mostly from rocks. Horseshoes leave scars; hooves turn them over. You watch the bank and see where your man exits." He twitched the pinto closer. "Yeah. I think fishing's a fine idea. And I'll take the manacles off when we get there."

"Do you know a lot about tracking outlaws?"

"I've been on a couple of posses."

She dropped the burgundy shawl and looped it awkwardly around her waist. She also seemed to be watching the mountains. The sky had turned pure blue and relentlessly clear. The day wouldn't get hot enough for discomfort, seldom did at these altitudes, but Johnny's growling stomach and his frustrated nerves couldn't take much more aggravation. The stream sounded good, and so did the fishing. The vigilantes were out there, probably supplemented by a posse. He wasn't so foolish as to think either would give up the search. But the mountains were grand and largely abandoned. Though he and Claire might not be able to stop for a while, if they rode straight into the wilds, they'd likely find some secluded place.

"They used to like you in Bodie," she said abruptly.

"Yeah. They used to like me in Bodie."

"I'm sorry for all the trouble you've had, but I think I can help you in San Francisco."

"I'm touched." He spoke more sullenly than he intended, and his stomach added a growl to his protest. He'd been thinking cheerily about a fish picnic when he realized with a bright burst of frustrated insight the point of her elliptical comment: She didn't trust him, and he couldn't blame her. He'd never prove his innocence either. He wouldn't admit it, of course, but he intended to bolt when they reached San Francisco. He could leave her there safely and escape to the Islands. He'd always wanted to visit Tahiti.

"Honest," she said.

"You'll excuse me, counselor, if I don't jump for joy, but all I care about right now is where you think we might find these trout."

*   *   *

Fortunately for both their frayed tempers, Claire's skill at finding a trout pool had not abated.

"I'm good at this," she whispered to Johnny as he stood next to the deep pool she'd chosen and unlocked the steel bracelets that bound her, "but I do have a couple of quirks."

He didn't answer, but she knew he was listening. He kept his gaze lowered, his shoulders hunched over. She spoke softly, both out of fear of the posse and from long experience with fishing. "The main one is, I don't like to touch fish. I mean," she hastened to add, hoping he wouldn't think her a coward, "I don't mind worms. I don't mind worms at all. It's fish, mainly dead ones, I can't abide. Even alive, they're . . . I don't know . . . slimy and cold."

"And rough?" He ran his thumb over the marks on her wrists.

She shuddered. "Well . . . yes. Frankly. And smelly."

He greeted that declaration with a slight lift of his eyebrows. He held her hands lightly. For a moment she thought he wanted to kiss her, but he dropped his gaze, bounded over the stream, and threw himself on the opposite bank, up a little, where he could watch for the posse.

She removed her coat and both her boots, which left her only in her flannel nightgown. She briefly considered seminude fishing, but immediately discarded the notion. She'd done it, of course, when she'd been much younger. Well, not fishing exactly, but swimming and catching lizards. Her father had left her alone on an island—just for the day to teach her survival—and she'd spent the day like an Indian woman, bare-bosomed and pagan. There'd been no one there to see her, however.

She glanced up at Johnny. He grinned. She lowered her lashes and hiked up the nightgown, twisting the material into a loose knot at her waist. The movement revealed her feet and calves, but her thighs were covered by white pantalets, and the flannel gown covered her top. Still, she burned at the thought of uncovering herself. He looked more like an outlaw than ever. He'd grown a good stubble in only one day, a gold-burnished start of a beard that made his face look rugged and hungry with an elegant slash of bronze shadow, transforming the broad, straightforward expression into something more raffish, less boyish.

As she fought down the thump of her heartbeat, she searched the ground for a club of bleached piñon. She pulled a gnarled branch from the ground and lowered her feet into the water.

"Are you keeping a lookout?" she asked.

"Sure." She didn't trust the tone of his voice, and she glanced briefly upward. True to his word, he was gazing at the distant horizon. She sincerely regretted the bizarre circumstances that led her back to these childhood pursuits. She wanted to enjoy these sensual pleasures—the pure hot blue of the sky, the cool music of swiftly running water, the pungent scent of sagebrush and piñon, the sand and stone under her toes and the deep-down primitive thrill that all these sensations engendered.

She entered the water and paused. She'd picked a small pool at the foot of a fall. She knew from experience that trout lurked in such places, hiding from the bright heat of midday. Slowly she walked toward the center. Three of her quarry lazed in the shadows, plump brown and tempting, so still and at home in the vast mountain fastness that she delayed for a moment in order to savor their peace.

Johnny's stomach growled. She glanced up, surprised, and he grimaced. He didn't look as though he'd gone hungry often. In fact, out here, away from the jail, she could see he'd led a prosperous life. He exuded good health. Strength and muscles, even white teeth, and a tan complexion. Good bones, high coloring, and confident posture. All that vigor spoke privilege, though not necessarily leisure. She wondered if he'd grown up on a farm or somewhere in these mountains, or even if he'd had a childhood so pampered he'd devoted time to physical education, a degree of refinement she'd not been exposed to until she spent time as a wealthy man's wife.

"Do you see anyone?" she asked quietly.

"No." He spoke softly also. "Though they'll follow, I'm sure."

She nodded agreement, holding the branch out to the side.

"Not the whole crowd—" he continued.

Eyes on the fish, Claire couldn't see him, but she thought he shifted position a bit.

"—but a few fanatics. Most want to restore the town's honor. Clearing me out will be fine for that purpose, but . . ."

"But . . . ?"

"But . . . there are bound to be a few zealots."

"Do you think Sheriff Flowers will come?"

"Flowers will follow for sure. He's suffered the double dishonor of losing both a prisoner and a judge's daughter."

"He knows I'm your lawyer."

"True. But by now he'll think you're the lawyer I've kidnapped."

She peered into the clear, placid water, hoping to catch a glimpse of her quarry. "I'm sorry if I've made your plight worse. That wasn't my intention at all."

"Naw. You did fine. And I never expected help with the fishing."

Claire edged toward the trout, her feet almost drifting. The stream's undercurrent slipped past her ankles, but the surface was placid, the fish in plain sight. Johnny shifted, the derringer in one hand. Though he'd taken her manacles off, he kept the gun brandished, explaining that she should look threatened if they were ambushed. In retrospect, she regretted they hadn't thought to secure a better weapon. The lady's pistol might help her look kidnapped, but Johnny would never outgun a rifle, the sheriff's bulldog, or even the Colts of some vigilante.

Earlier, Johnny had made light of that observation, though. "Guns! Who needs them?" he'd said.

"Not even for hunting?"

"Yeah, that would have been useful, but I imagine we'll get by without one."

She thought his attitude odd, for the bad men in Bodie lived by their guns, and Johnny owned more than the silverplate Colt. She ascribed his disdain to swagger and bluster, the masculine habit of denying errors, and a hearty dislike of feminine nagging.

Fortunately for the fate of their stomachs, she liked fishing and did it quite well. She'd rather have used tackle, of course, for clubbing a trout was a brutal business, but that had been one of her father's best lessons. She thought killing moral when followed by eating, and frivolous waste a far greater sin.

She'd reached the pool's center and stood very still, not even watching, just waiting. Water striders skimmed over the surface. Bees and butterflies brimmed in the meadow, and an ouzel flitted through the small waterfall. She waited some more, not thinking of much, just quietly renewing her love for the Sierras, the hot sun, the gentle embrace of the cool mountain water, and the infinite, peaceful, sensual pleasure she generally felt in these mountains.

A trout nuzzled her toes. The nip felt like the gentlest of kisses. There was something about a fishy cuddle that always both thrilled and revolted her. She shivered in spite of herself.

"What's the matter?" Johnny Christmas asked, unbuttoning the top of his shirt.

She silenced him with a gesture, but the tiny kisses beneath the surface were too much for her strained composure. She giggled.

"Are you all right?" he asked.

She answered in her tiniest whisper. "They're down there. I feel them."

He stood, all six-foot-whatever, and the trout disappeared in a flash.

"You oaf." She dropped her arms to the pool's

surface. "That was our dinner you scared with your shadow."

"What the hell are you doing?"

"I'm letting them nibble my toes."

He cast her a skeptical glance.

"It's hard to explain, but that's how I catch them. I used to fish all the time with my father. He rode circuit, you know. Winters I'd live in Bridgeport, but we'd come up here in the summer. He loved the mountains. Me, too. I remember the first time a trout tried to eat me. Scared me to death. I screamed my fool head off. Daddy laughed and laughed. He called me a girl. But I got the last laugh when I started catching them that way. He loved it."

"You're lucky he didn't hide you."

"He never hit me. Sometimes he should have. And sometimes I wished he would have. A judge's tongue-lashing is a fearsome weapon."

"And you miss him?"

"Of course."

"I suppose your life's been pretty lonely without him."

"A little."

"Is that why you married that banker?"

"Let's just say I made a mistake. Now shush if you want some dinner."

He gave her another skeptical look. "Have you really caught trout by this method?"

"Certainly. I came up here with Indian children. Fishing's easier when you've got no scruples. The young braves spear their quarry. Girls just drive the trout onto the shore."

"And which method are you using today?"

"Well, kind of a combination. I thought I'd lure them up to my toes, then thunk them over the head with a club."

"Doesn't seem very sporting."

"It isn't. But I'm hungry. So if you'll sit down, I'll catch us some dinner."

He trudged to the top of the rise, took a long steady look at the horizon, then sat down on a small dome of granite.

She spread her arms to her side and tried to let her mind float, but the thought of his watching was somewhat unnerving. The day had grown hot, and the water felt lovely. She would have liked to truly go swimming, but that couldn't happen with Johnny Christmas staring at her. Still, it was good to be home. As she tried to lure the lazy brown trout, she felt the delicate silver chain weigh heavily on her neck. She'd not only been lonely, she'd also made such mistakes without her father. Her disastrous marriage. Now this adventure. An innocent man should never hang—but what if John Christmas was guilty?

She sighed, but kept her thoughts to herself. She waited patiently for the slow-floating creatures, and it didn't surprise her when she felt a trout nibble her toes.

She drove the stick downward, hard and without hesitation, then freed the knot at her waist. Splashing down on her knees, she scooped blindly and caught him. She gathered the nightgown around him and shivered, nearly dropping the fish as she felt his thrashing. He twisted inside the flannel, probably in-

jured, but fighting for life. She scrambled to gather
the material more closely, the keen edge of her hunger
pressing her on. The fight made her stubborn and
zealous, determined to win. She propped herself on
one knee and rolled the gown around the struggling
shape. The fish shuddered, then flapped in a frenzy,
almost causing her to drop him. Climbing to her feet,
she looked for Christmas, who stood smiling on the
far bank.

"That's a girl. Slowly." He held out his hand, still
darting looks at the distant vistas. "Didn't think you
could do it."

"Yes. Well." The fish had stopped thrashing. She
could still feel him panting, suffocating in air as
surely as she would have drowned in his watery
world. She charged the bank, her face scrunched up
in a grimace. "Take him." She shuddered. "Hurry.
You promised. Oh. Heavens." She puckered her
mouth and abandoned all pretense of tomboyish bravado. "I hate this part."

He steadied her with a hand to her elbow, the derringer stuck in his pant waistband. Carefully he un-
rolled her nightgown and took the still-gasping fish in
his hands. The silvery trout trembled, curling his tail
in impotent protest against the change in his condition.

She shuddered again. "How in the world can you
stand to touch him?"

"Why not? He won't hurt you."

"No. But I don't like this part." Her whole body
trembled. "I like to catch them, but I don't like to
kill them."

He swung the fish toward the stream in mock protest. "I could throw him back."

"Don't you dare even think it. I caught him; you clean him. It's a family rule."

He shot her a look, crossed the stream in two strides, and picked up her shawl. The movement revived their potential dinner and he convulsed several times in death spasms. Johnny held the trout's head and dragged the shawl in the water.

"There." He wrapped the shuddering body in the burgundy cloth. "Is that better?"

"Yes." She hopped gingerly over the water. "How are you going to clean him?"

"I think I can manage, but after I'm done, we'll need to find a safe place to cook him."

"Are you going to say thank you?" Claire tossed a delicate fish bone into the charred embers.

"Thank you," Johnny said.

"That's all?"

"What would you like me to say?"

"Oh, not much really. Maybe something flowery— like 'Good fishing, Claire.' "

"Good fishing, I think. Or at least interesting."

She tucked her feet under her freshly dried nightgown. "Now what's that wisecrack supposed to mean?"

Johnny grabbed a branch and stirred the ashes of the small cooking fire they'd risked. He regretted the loss of the wet nightgown. She had a small-boned, dainty body, slender, not lanky, and he'd liked the look of the wet flannel against her curves. "You're a fine fisherwoman, but you don't have the courage of your convictions.''

''Sure.'' She stretched out on the ground. She looked exhausted, her hair escaping in pale, dispirited tendrils. Her eyelids drooped shut, then bounced open. ''You just didn't like cleaning him up.''

''It's women's work, I'll grant you that, but fair's fair. You did your part. I've got no complaints about splitting the chores.''

She rested her head on her bundled-up coat. He could tell she was weary from the tone of her voice, the sag of her shoulders. He could also tell she still feared him. She watched him intently, trying to keep her eyelids from drooping.

''You're still hungry, aren't you?'' she asked.

He wanted to kiss her. ''Rest.''

She gave him a dubious look.

He couldn't touch her, he knew. He'd probably never be able to touch her. ''Lie down.''

''What about you?''

She thought him a bad man, a pimp, and an outlaw, he told himself. She'd go to her grave with that impression. ''I'll take my turn later. You've had a good lunch. The world will look better when you've had some sleep.''

''I don't know . . .'' Her voice trailed off, and her expression softened. She adjusted the coat. Her fingers relaxed, and her eyelids dropped shut. Johnny poked the stick into the campfire. He wanted to tuck her into a bed, lay her head on a pillow, unpin her hair and spread it over white cotton, watch yellow sunlight play on her face, and see what she looked like sleeping.

He swirled the stick through the embers. She looked wonderful, even if the world didn't. The vigilantes were out there. He sensed them. And also the posse. And Sheriff Frank Flowers. Johnny had gotten Claire in a desperate fix, and the gnawing pang in his stomach reminded him with some forcefulness of how dire their plight was likely to get before it might possibly get any better.

But her company meant he needed a plan. Risking his own life had never seemed foolish, but risking hers seemed somehow different. First problem was, they needed provisions. He did not like to leave her, but he'd have to steal food to get through the mountains. He didn't want her with him for that. He wished he had Fang—the dog would have protected her in his absence. But he'd just have to trust that she'd be all right.

He pulled her derringer out of his waistband and sat it next to her hand. She looked so peaceful, her pale face relaxed in the deep golden sunlight. He wanted to kiss her, but knew that would wake her. He moved quietly back to the horses, gathered Tiny's reins, and vaulted onto the great draft horse's back. He headed out sideways, neither farther into the mountains nor back toward Bodie, with the vague idea of finding a farmhouse to rob. As he rode away from the sleeping figure, he missed her already and wanted to hold her. The ache in his heart was almost enough to quell the sickness souring his stomach. For the first time in his life, Jonathan Robert Van Kessel, firefighter, carouser, brawler, and bad man, also known as the gunman Kid Christmas, set out to prey on an innocent victim.

Chapter
Seven

❧❧❧

Fate saved Johnny in the form of a miner: a stubble-faced freewheeling type, in a droopy hat with droopier drawers, panning for gold in a shallow stream and humming quietly to an indifferent donkey. Johnny didn't know quite how the prospector might help him, but he knew opportunity when he saw it, so he slapped Tiny's bottom and rode toward the lightly bearded young man.

"Afternoon," Johnny called out.

The prospector looked up, readjusted a pair of small gold-rimmed glasses, but didn't waste his breath on replying.

Johnny reined in the draft horse and waited a few feet back from the miner. "Nice day for panning," he said.

The prospector nodded, but still didn't answer.

"I'm tired of mining myself."

The slender young man did not acknowledge the comment. He sluiced the water through his broad metal pan, peering carefully through his bifocals.

Johnny had spent enough time in the mountains to know the best way to rouse a gold miner's anger was to appear overly curious about his work. Although the ghost of a plan formed in his mind, he dismissed it and followed instinct instead. "Got a hand-dug shaft up Bodie way. Got no faith in it, though. I thought I'd try my luck in Tahiti."

At the comment, the young man stood up. He had a rawboned, gangly body that poked out from beneath his frayed clothes. "I heard there's still some good holes in Bodie."

"A few, but not the one I'm working." Johnny slid off Tiny's overgrown haunches, but waited a few feet back from the stream. There was only fool's gold on this side of the mountain. The young man looked well provisioned, but he didn't look as if he'd gotten rich. "Put eight years sweat into a hellhole. I got nothing to show but this overgrown pony."

The young prospector glanced dubiously at Tiny. Without acknowledging Johnny, he tilted his pan and dribbled the sand into the stream. The water's reflection played on his face as he rinsed out the bottom, then gathered the reins of his donkey. "I heard they found a geode in the Standard."

"Just one eight-foot crystal. Was nothing compared to some in the Comstock."

"What's in Tahiti?"

"Peace and quiet. I'm taking a girl."

The young man stuffed his equipment into a leather pannier. He readjusted his gold rims for a moment, then studied Johnny at length. His gaze lingered on Tiny, then skittered off Johnny's unadorned hipbones and took in the red flannel shirt. At the end of a long, frank appraisal, the owlish miner reached into his bag and pulled a loaf of bread out of a bundle. He broke off a massive chunk and offered the spongy white mass to Johnny. As the young miner chewed, Johnny tried to eat like a man trying not to look hungry. A sprinkling of crumbs clung to the miner's mustache, and he whisked them off as he nibbled. "You just leavin' your hole unattended?"

"I've got some friends watching out for my interests."

The young man scratched his beard. He readjusted his wire-rimmed glasses, then pulled some jerked meat out of his bundle. He offered Johnny a strip of dried beef, then watched quietly as Johnny devoured it. "Would you like some more for later?" he asked.

Johnny nodded.

"Why didn't you sell before you set off?"

Johnny accepted a second helping of the tough substance and stuffed it into his saddlebag. "You might call this trip a hasty decision."

The miner tightened the knot on his neckerchief, then checked the straps on his bundles. "A wise man carries provisions."

"Sure. But I'm not that wise."

"Too bad." The miner pulled a lump of sugar out of his pocket, then fed it to his brown-and-gray donkey. "Especially since you ain't even heeled."

"I wouldn't want folks to think I'm an outlaw." Johnny pulled Tiny off to the side. The Sierras had enough grass for the horse, but the bronze giant really loved sugar. It didn't pay to let him get too close to temptation.

"That's smart." The miner rubbed the donkey's soft nose. "I don't suppose you're packin' the title?"

"I don't suppose you'd take a quit claim?"

"I've got no poke."

"That's not what I wanted."

"I figured." The lanky young man pulled out a wad of chewing tobacco and plumped up his fat bundle of lumpy supplies. "Too bad, then, about the title."

"Maybe not."

"How so?" He tucked his chaw to the side and spit out a wide stream of tobacco juice.

"Would you take a quit claim if I found you a lawyer?"

"Wake up, counselor." Someone brushed Claire's shoulder gently. The touch felt familiar, and she wondered who'd interrupted her sleep. "You've got your first client."

Claire opened her eyes. The late-afternoon sun filled her vision, but Johnny stood outlined above her, larger even than she remembered. "Client? I thought you were my client."

"All right, your second. Or maybe I'm still the client, and I'm just bringing you my second problem."

Claire sat up, rubbing her neck. Her shoulder ached, her back felt crooked, and her spine had developed a crick. She wondered what had possessed her to think she'd enjoy an outdoor adventure.

Johnny pushed a spike of hair off her temple. A frisson of delight sparkled through Claire. Why did his littlest gesture affect her?

"Can you write a quit claim?" he asked.

"Now? Here?"

"Yes. I mean, if we gave you a pencil and paper. Would you know how to write a real legal quit claim?"

"Of course." She rubbed the sand out of her eyes. A dissonant movement caught her attention, and she realized Johnny had a companion, a lanky young man who stood next to a donkey heavily laden with mining equipment. She snatched up her coat and clutched the black wool to her bosom. "I could have written one when I was seven."

Johnny gave her a skeptical look.

She wanted to shake a finger at him, but it was hard to be arch in a grubby nightgown. She brushed the dirt off her sleeve instead. "Why don't you ever believe me? Until I was nine, mining deeds kept food on the table."

Johnny took her coat and held it before her, cutting off her view of the stranger. "You got a pencil?" he asked.

"A pen would be better."

"Don't get all fussy on us."

"I'm just pointing out." Turning her back, Claire shoved her arms into the sleeves. "Never write a land contract in pencil. It's far too easily altered."

The young miner's boots scraped in the gravel. "How do you know something like that?"

"I'm—"

"Her father was a judge in this district."

Claire stifled an impulse to slap Johnny Christmas. She buttoned her coat up to her neck, slipped the necklace under her shirt, then turned to face her masculine skeptics. "Randolph Butler. Perhaps you know of his reputation."

"You're Judge Butler's daughter?"

Claire nodded.

"I read about you in the Frisco papers. You're the one Chauncey Lyman charged with adultery."

She nodded again. She hated that about her divorce. Everyone remembered the scandal. No one remembered her vindication.

The sad-faced stripling glanced quickly at Johnny. "You two running off?"

"Something like that." Johnny bent over and picked up the gun and shoved it into his waistband.

The young miner frowned, and Claire wondered what he was thinking. She doubted she made a plausible captive. The pinto was tethered a few feet away. She'd clearly been free to run if she wanted. Still, Johnny had a confident air. The young man looked puzzled, but turned to his donkey and undid the straps on a leather bag. "If I sign this quit claim, will it hurt Chauncey Lyman?"

She shoved her hands into her coat pockets. "In a roundabout way."

"Good. I don't know your father, but I sure know your son-of-a-bitch of a husband." He pulled out a pencil and paper and handed the writing utensils to Claire. "I can see why you'd cheat on a bastard like that."

She accepted the pencil and paper from him. "Chauncey could be pretty ruthless."

"Yeah." The boy pulled off his glasses and pretended to shine them, but Claire could see he bordered on tears. She stared at the writing utensils, her eyes averted from Johnny's. She didn't know what he thought of the miner's comments, and supposed in a way she shouldn't care, but she felt a flame creep into her cheeks. She fixed her gaze on the wooden pencil. "Have you got a book I can use as a backing?"

"I don't carry a Bible." The miner jammed the gold rims back on his face. He pulled a battered metal pan from his pack. "Maybe you can use this."

"Thanks." Quietly she accepted his offering. She tried her best to ignore Johnny Christmas, but she couldn't help noticing he'd turned his back and made a great show of attending to Tiny. She told herself he didn't matter, but she couldn't quell her sense of injustice at being judged on her failed marriage. She curled her fingers over the pencil, sat down on a boulder, and propped the shallow dish on her knees. "What am I quit-claiming?"

"A gold mine," Johnny's voice was deceptively casual, considering the nature of the conversation.

Claire stifled the urge to ask questions. She'd just have to trust him. After all, she'd promised to do that. She adjusted the pad at an angle and printed a title in capital letters. "Do you have some kind of legal description?"

Johnny continued to groom Tiny's mane. Claire couldn't see what he was doing exactly, but he appeared to be working a burr from its strands. "I don't know the plat lines, but the mine's named Daniel Webster. I'm quite sure our friend will be able to find it. It's on the bluff up from the Standard. There's a name on the head frame."

"A name won't suffice for a quit claim—"

"Claire." Johnny spoke quietly, but Claire could tell she'd tested his patience. "Don't be didactic. The recorder can take care of those details."

She started to speak, but Johnny's expression held her attention. He hadn't stopped working on Tiny, but he'd set his jawbone at a stubborn angle, and a fine tension showed in his neck muscles.

"Owner?" she asked quietly.

"Jonathan Robert Van Kessel."

Claire glanced up, surprised. "You—?"

He nodded briefly. She glanced at the miner, then stared at the pad, wondering desperately what she'd gotten into. She'd heard about Johnny's gold mine, of course, when she'd interviewed the townspeople about him. It had been one of the less credible rumors—that Kid Christmas's wealth came from his hand diggings. The whores believed he financed his sprees from a hoard of gold he dug out in secret. The miners had been dubious, however. A hand-dug mine rarely produced enough to live on, much less to finance serious carousing. Then there was the fire equipment. Johnny had supplied the town with its fire engines, one by one over the years. Since firefighting paid a working man's wages, and fire equipment cost a small fortune, Johnny's largesse had caused much speculation. A tight knot formed behind Claire's rib cage. If the mine didn't finance Johnny Christmas's binges, that left only one source for his money.

She toyed with the edge of the paper. "How much are you selling the mine for?"

"We're trading it for his provisions, but I don't suppose you put that fact in a quit claim."

"You're trading a gold mine for dinner?"

"It's never produced much—"

"Still . . ."

"Come off it, Claire."

She thought he was crazy. Maybe not a rapist, maybe not even an outlaw, but demented for sure. "You don't trust my fishing?"

"There are no fish at the high elevations."

"Surely we can manage somehow."

He leaned over the Clydesdale's broad back, his neck muscles rigid, his shoulders taut. "Don't you ever let a man take the lead?"

"Certainly." She turned the paper over. "Sometimes." Her mouth always got her in trouble.

"Then let me trade away my own gold mine."

The sad-faced young miner broke in. "Look." He'd been unloading his donkey, a gentle beast, though far less soulful than his loose-jointed master. "If you want a rich husband, go back to that son-of-a-bitch of a banker. Any man who'll evict a widow with children will always have plenty of money."

Claire resisted the urge to argue. There were many comments she wanted to make, about love and money and other subjects, but Johnny stared hard in her direction, and the gangly miner seemed so intent she dropped her gaze back to the page. "Fine. I'll finish the deed."

"Why don't you add the house to the quit claim," Johnny said softly, his voice carrying over the afternoon breeze. She shot him a questioning glance. He shrugged.

She chewed her lip and studied Johnny. She really had a lot to say now. About hope and justice. About how he ought to have faith in his lawyer. But her heart went out to the young miner also, and she found herself admiring Johnny's quick thinking. "Tell you what," she said to the boy. "I'll fill out the papers like this. As to the mine, I'll grant you clear title. As to the house, you'll be tenants-in-common. I'm granting you a conditional interest."

"Huh?" The miner looked puzzled as he pulled a loaf of bread out of his package.

Water pooled inside Claire's mouth. "You can live free in the house, but you have to take care of Jonathan's pets."

"Can I send for my mother?"

"Of course," she answered without even looking at Johnny.

"Sounds good to me." The boy broke open a loaf.

Claire's stomach growled, but she ignored it. "And Jonathan gets the house back if he returns to Bodie."

"You two coming back?"

Johnny lifted the Clydesdale's back hoof. "I doubt it."

"I like it," the boy said.

"But I want to add two more conditions." Johnny rested Tiny's hoof on his knee.

Claire had been writing, but she interrupted her work. "Which are?"

"He'll wait three days to record it." He ran his thumb over the shoe. "And we trade for enough provisions to get us to San Francisco."

"Is that legal?" the boy asked Claire. "I mean, the part about the waiting?"

"It's legal, but not very wise." She nodded at Johnny. "He could sell the mine to someone else. If the other party records first, there would certainly be a cloud on the title."

The boy blinked behind his gold-rimmed glasses. "The judge must have been a hell of a lawyer for you to know so much about quit claims."

To Claire's infinite horror, tears sprang to her eyes, and she swallowed. She hadn't cried over her father in more than five years. She would not break down in front of a stranger. She squared her shoulders and stared at the paper. "He was the best father a girl ever had."

The boy gazed steadily at her, chewing thoughtfully on the sourdough. "You give me your word you won't let him sell it to somebody else?"

"On the grave of my father."

"That's good enough, even in pencil."

" 'Jonathan.' " Johnny stared at the crystal-flecked boulder he was sitting on. The fading sunlight had turned the rock's surface silver and made the drab granite sparkle. He bit off a piece of sourdough bread and rolled it around on his tongue. With a sigh of contentment, he savored the flavor, the distinctive tang that always recalled San Francisco. "Nobody's called me that name in years."

"Do you mind if I use it?" Claire asked from behind him, using the steep slab of rock to hide from his sight.

Johnny kept his gaze averted, though he didn't regard it as cheating to imagine what she looked like undressing. "I like 'Johnny' better."

She sighed. " 'Johnny' sounds so . . ." From behind the gray rock, flower-sprigged flannel whispered to him. "I don't know . . . youthful."

Her skin would be creamy. "That's the best thing about it."

"Don't you think 'Jonathan' sounds more distinguished?' "

"No." She'd have slender ankles. He felt certain of that.

"What's wrong with 'John'?"

"One: It's too common." He broke off another piece of the crust. "Two: It's what everyone called my father."

"Ah. Well. There's always 'Kid Christmas.' "

"Now there's a name to remember."

A slight breeze had come up. He could no longer hear the whisper of cloth. She'd be putting on the young miner's jeans. The pants wouldn't be female, but they'd surely be better than the damned flannel nightgown.

"You like that nickname?" she asked.

"Sure." He was glad of the clothes, for the gown drove him crazy. He wasn't used to innocent women, having spent all his adult life in Bodie. "I picked it."

"You chose the nickname 'Kid Christmas'?"

"Does that surprise you?"

"A little."

He gnawed on a crust, wondering if she thought the stuffy covering attractive, and what she'd look like in black lace.

"No, maybe not," she added to her last observation.

He conjured up garters; black boas, and scarlet panties. Too bad he'd never get to seduce her. "You think 'Kid Christmas' suits me?"

"Yes," she said, "as a matter of fact."

"God's gift to women?"

"No."

She sounded too certain. "Then how?"

"You're very kindhearted."

Damn. He was caught in a trap of his own making. He didn't want her to think him a rapist, but he did want her impressed by his physique and charisma. "I don't make you nervous?"

A chipmunk popped out from under a rock and peered at the scattered provisions. Johnny smiled and pulled a chunk off the bread.

"Nervous. No. Well. Maybe. Sometimes you can be pretty unnerving. But mostly you seem really kind."

" 'Mostly'?" he asked.

The little brown-and-white rodent sat up. He had a bold look to him, alert and perky, the kind of charming and confident bandit who gave more in entertainment than he ever took in provisions.

"Maybe 'kind' is not the right word." Her expressive voice quavered. He liked that about her. She tried so hard to appear self-assured, but a little girl lingered beneath the surface. "But you seem to treat people fairly."

Johnny tossed a few crumbs on the ground, then leaned back and winked at the little striped squirrel. The little thief saw his chance and took it. With a delicate scrape of small feet on pebbles, he dashed for the scraps, grabbed a white fragment, and scrambled over the boulder.

A brief squeak escaped Claire. "What are you doing?" She charged round the rock, completely dressed except for her shirt. She'd donned an oversized white cotton top, and she'd fastened all but three buttons. Her fingers hung above one, and that was enough to intrigue him. He cleared his throat and stared at her bosom, intrigued by the pert outline of her nipples, the dusky shadow her soft cleavage made. He really would love to seduce her, he acknowledged to himself once again, but how the hell did you attract a woman who thought you were a rapist? "I'm sharing our dinner."

Her cheeks pinked, and she closed up the button. "You know, you really are crazy. That bread cost you a gold mine."

"Are you hungry?" He held out the loaf, immediately remorseful. He hadn't given the chipmunk much, but he'd given Claire less. She'd been so anxious to get out of her nightgown, she'd taken only a crust behind the rock with her.

"Yes." She took the piece and tore off a chunk, then handed him the larger portion. "But that's not the point. It's a long way to San Francisco, and only Christ fed crowds with three fishes."

He accepted the fragrant offering. He loved the sweet scent of this bread. "We've more than enough for the immediate future."

"That's not the point either."

"I think it is." With a shrug of his shoulders, he tossed more crumbs to the chipmunk. "I might not be as hardhearted as your distinguished husband, but I got you food and a lovely outfit."

"Touché." She bit off a small piece. "And I'm sorry. My father taught me it isn't a kindness to tame wild creatures. They shouldn't learn to depend on man's handouts. And also . . ." She sat on the slab and grimly surveyed the scattered provisions. "I'm frightened. And that makes me silly."

Johnny sat down beside her. He felt a surge of tenderness for her. The miner's provisions littered the mountain. To him, all this seemed like a treasure, and he felt confident they would reach San Francisco. They'd have to outrun the posse. And a few vigilantes. But he'd dodged death most of his life, and he'd come to enjoy the sensation. He rested his hand on her shoulder. A lewd image returned: Claire in red garters. "I'm sorry also. That last remark was uncalled-for."

She moved slightly sideways, as if reading his thoughts. "It's all right. It's not the first time my tongue has caused trouble."

Johnny let her go. He missed her warmth, but respected her fears. He'd never courted a respectable woman, excepting, of course, his brief fling with Louisa. That adventure hadn't turned out so well, and it made him a bit gun-shy with Claire.

"In Bodie, they say you're an outlaw." She gnawed thoughtfully on the golden crust. During her nap she'd developed several tendrils, a fine spray that haloed her face and made her features softer, more youthful, also wilder, more fetching.

"That's not true at all."

"No?"

"No." He stifled the urge to tame down the wildness. She looked both pretty and boyish, the tucked-in blouse accenting her waist, her hips flaring inside the soft denims. "You know how rumors get started."

She turned her gaze toward him, unplaiting her braid as she held the bread in her teeth. Her fine hair had little kinks in it and fell in waves as she undid it. She removed the sourdough, then asked. "So how did you get the nickname 'Kid Christmas'?"

"I told you. I picked it."

"That seems so odd."

The little chipmunk reappeared. Johnny looked askance at Claire, and she nodded. He dropped a few crumbs between his round-toed work boots, trying to decide whether to answer. It wasn't so much that the truth pained him, for he'd accepted his past and all that came with it. Rather, it seemed part of a foolish youth, and she already seemed to think him too boyish. Still, he wanted her to know something about him. He wasn't sure why. Maybe his attraction to her. Maybe because she'd cared enough to defend him. Maybe because he'd killed her father, and if, God forbid, she ever found out, there might be a chance she'd forgive him if she understood that troubled youngster he'd been.

"I was very sick as a child. My mother loved me. Maybe too much. I don't know. I can't really judge her. She'd lost one son before me."

Claire fanned her hair out. It made a soft, yellowish fall, not as gold as aspen in the autumn, but more like the pale light that filtered through them. Framed by that curtain, her skin took on a transforming translucence. She seemed like a sprite, not at all like a lawyer, a notion he knew would appall her.

"I had three sisters. They doted on me." The chipmunk switched his scrawny tail. Johnny tossed a bread crumb out farther. "Now, there's a recipe for disaster: a sickly boy, four anxious women, and a distant father with no patience for weakness. I left home at Christmas, eighteen and hell-bent on adventure. The name was a gift to myself."

"Doesn't such a strange name cause trouble?"

"A little." A brown-and-white blur dashed for the crumbs, then scampered back to the fallen log. "I killed a man once because he took issue with it."

"That seems like trouble enough."

"Never had to kill another."

"I can imagine." She glanced sharply at him, then smoothed out her hair. They'd acquired a small comb from the miner. It wasn't a proper brush for a woman, but Claire seemed to know how to handle that problem. She lifted small strands and combed through them, working patiently on recalcitrant tangles.

"Aren't you still hungry?" he asked.

"Yes." She picked out a wisp of blond hair. "But

this mess bothers me more than my stomach. I've got more hair than you, but not so much muscle." She looked pointedly at his shoulders. "I don't need to eat quite so often."

"I see." He tore off a chunk and offered it to her, holding the spongy white mass in front of her mouth. She frowned at him, then opened. He dropped the small piece on her tongue.

She nodded her thanks, then went back to her hair. She seemed to be thinking; though her eyes didn't cloud, and her brow didn't furrow, she got an expression he'd seen on his sister, intently focused and drawn quietly inward. He wondered if good women all had this habit of sorting their thoughts along with their hair. "Was he the only man you've killed?"

"No." Johnny let the answer hang in the air. "And I think we should hurry. The trek down the streambed will have slowed down the posse, but they've likely regained momentum by now." He hated to push her when she felt so disheveled, but he'd decided they ought to get going. Leaning forward, he shook out the bedroll.

She didn't move from her rock. "If you aren't an outlaw, how do you get money?"

Ignoring her question, he spread out the stack of three blankets, folded them over, then began to roll one end tightly. He preferred not to discuss this subject with her. He'd spent many years as a false desperado, a state of affairs he found useful.

She stopped combing her hair and began to braid it. "I don't believe you hurt Louisa, but I can't prove you're innocent if you won't trust me completely."

He went down on one knee, picked up the neat, fat roll he'd made of the blankets, and strapped it on Tiny. "Go ahead. Say the word, counselor. I dare you to say it out loud."

She stared dumbfounded without asking a question.

"Come on. You know what I'm talking about."

" 'Rape,' " she said without blinking. "I don't believe you raped Louisa."

"Sure you don't, honey—that's why you can't even say it. 'Rape,' " he said to the chipmunk, who watched from a log. "The whole town thinks I raped Louisa. Hell, even Louisa thinks I raped Louisa, and my lawyer believes her."

"I don't—"

"Then you're a fool. How do you know what went on between us?"

"You told me."

"And you believe me?"

"Yes. As a matter of fact."

"Why?" He gathered up the other provisions— five loaves of bread, one coffeepot, a little dried meat, and some piñon nuts. "And even if you believe me, how do I prove my innocence to a jury? Strip naked in court and show them my pecker doesn't look wicked? Let them hang me so that they can watch my soul go toward heaven? No one saw what went on on that porch, much less what went on in the bedroom."

"Louisa did."

"No, she didn't, which is one of my problems. The man who raped her was smart."

"Maybe he was, but I'm pretty smart also." She

flipped her braid over her shoulder and stuffed the last of the bread in her mouth. She pulled a pannier off the pinto and held it open for him. "But if you won't trust me, how can I help you?"

"No offense, Claire," he said as he dumped the groceries into the bag, "but I've got no reason to trust you."

"Of course not." The pinto shied as she slapped the leather bag onto his back. "Why should you?" She ignored the horse and tightened down the provisions. "I just risked my neck to save you."

He picked up the gun, not the derringer tucked in his waistband, but a Colt Claire had insisted on making part of the trade. "I don't mean to sound like an ungrateful bastard, but what does my past have to do with Louisa?"

"I can't say exactly, but your reputation makes you suspicious. If you could explain how you got your money, that you haven't killed that many men—"

He strapped on the gun belt. He hadn't worn one in almost eight years, and the weight and heft felt unfamiliar. "I like my reputation."

"Are you going to die over some boyhood notion?"

"No." He checked the barrel of the Colt. Only five chambers were loaded just as they should be, so the gun wouldn't go off accidentally. "Look. That lurid reputation protects me. I let the stories grow over the years, remaining vague about my income, as well as the number of men I've killed. Even in the bad town of Bodie, no one tangled with the outlaw Kid Christmas."

She tucked her nightgown into the bag. "Well, you can't keep up that façade forever."

He slid the gun into the holster, a motion that came back without thinking. He turned and faced Claire, a gunfighter's gesture and one that also returned on instinct. "I can be Kid Christmas for as long as I want to."

"You know," she said as she picked up her coat and packed it, "I see why you never married."

"What's that crack supposed to mean?"

"Maybe I am a bit aggressive." She picked up the red shawl and folded it into the shape of a sash. "But sometimes the man gives way to the woman, especially in areas where she's an expert."

He was going to ask her what she was doing, but a puff of white drew his attention. He vaulted onto the tall Clydesdale's back. "Look, Claire. I'm just saying don't judge me by my reputation. You know nothing whatsoever about me."

"I'm trying to remedy that situation."

"Save your questions for later." He watched the horizon, his senses alert. He had a fine education in smoke, an even better instinct for danger, and some firsthand experience with posses. Claire must have had some sense of her own, for she cinched the sash quickly, mounted the pinto, and pulled him up beside the Clydesdale. She followed his gaze to the small puff of dust.

"Johnny," she whispered, "what are we gonna do?"

He turned the big Clydesdale around, bumping him up close to Claire. "Ride like hell for Bloody

Canyon.'' He pressed his knees to his horse's side, whacked the rump of the pinto, and shouted, ''And if, *if,* we get through this alive, maybe we'll finish our little discussion.''

Chapter
Eight

Bloody Canyon lived up to its nickname, in the massive red walls that defined it; in the steep, rock-strewn route that beat all other passes hands down as a hair-raising way to cross the Sierras; and in its personal meaning to Claire. As she and Johnny drew up before it, she straightened her spine trying, without much success, to catch her breath and suppress her terror. A crimson sunset turned the black slate scarlet. Fine hairs lifted on the back of her neck.

She turned around briefly. The sunlight shimmered off Mono Lake, radiating over the crater-packed plain that rimmed this side of the Sierra Nevada. She could see a great distance, though not very clearly. Nothing seemed to be moving on the barren expanse. "Do you think they'll follow?" she asked.

Johnny patted one of the Clydesdale's broad shoulders. "Maybe," he said as he urged the massive brown horse forward. Rocks crunched beneath giant hooves. Claire squelched a shudder. She remembered Bloody Canyon too well: the slate-strewn slopes, the desperate scrabble, the blood-spattered rocks, and the stench of dead horses.

She tightened her grip on the reins. "Have you been over this trail before?"

"Yeah." Johnny stopped, his fingers toying with one of the reins. An icy breeze swept down the canyon, foreshadowing snow in the passes. "And you don't have to say it: Only a fool would try this at night."

She glanced at the forbidding chasm, an angry wound in the Sierras, dropping thousands of feet in just a few miles. "Do you think we can get over by sunset?"

"Naw."

A hollow feeling formed in her stomach. "If you've got a plan, now's the time to share it."

"I told you before: ride like hell for San Francisco."

"We've been riding like hell for two hours already, and frankly I'm tired." Turning, she scanned the desolate vista again. A flock of seagulls rose off the lake, and a few of their brethren peeled off toward the canyon. "Maybe we've lost them."

"We've lost them for sure, but not forever. They're bound to figure out where we're going." Leather creaked as Johnny turned in his saddle. The alpenglow obscured his expression, but his voice was soft and attentive. "You scared?"

"Yes." There was no point in trying to lie on this subject.

Claire pressed with her knees. The little pinto scrabbled over the rocks, clambering up the small moraine that marked the start of the steep, fearsome grade. Claire thought they should hurry, and tried to ride by Johnny, but he reached out one hand and stopped her. "You want to turn back?"

She glanced at the towering walls. Hulking boulders concealed the path, but she could still remember it well: the cold, wet, dizzying terror, the treacherous footing, the constant exposure to wind and height and violent death. Another shudder racked through her. The gulls cried in the distance. The sound made her lonely for San Francisco, and she envied the birds who flew over the mountains to make their homes in Mono Lake. "No."

Johnny laid a warm hand over hers. "I don't want to leave you, but I will if you ask me. The posse's probably only a half hour away. You can take the bread. I don't really need it—"

"Stop." She untied her shawl, tossed it over her shoulders, and knotted the fringed ends around her neck. "I know I can make it. I've been through here before."

"Yeah?"

"Yes." She made a brief visual check of her bags. "I've never been up, but I've come down."

"I'm impressed." He nudged his horse closer and tightened a buckle on her saddle roll. "It's been the terror of many a drover. I don't think many women have done it."

"Thanks." She blushed. She hated to remember this part. "But I wasn't a woman when I came over."

"You came over this grade as a kid?"

"Kind of." What could she tell him? She'd gotten

her first monthly in Bloody Canyon, an event that gave the place its personal meaning to Claire and marked one of her few fights with her father, a sulky, tearstained temper tantrum that he laughed off when he realized the cause, and that she still remembered with shame. "We came through with a surveying party. My father called it our boldest adventure."

Johnny chuckled. "It's bold all right. And hard on the horses. I wouldn't do it if I had a choice."

"I know."

He squeezed her hand briefly, brushed a lock off her forehead, then kneed Tiny forward, turned him around, and leaned on his saddle horn. "What I'm trying to say is you still have choices. The posse still thinks you've been kidnapped—"

"Don't tempt me—"

"I'm offering—"

"Well, don't." She nudged the pinto forward, thinking to pass.

He stopped her with a hand on her reins. "I'm offering you a graceful way out."

"Well, I'm not that graceful."

He glanced at her jeans-clad figure and shrugged. To Claire's chagrin, his expression made her more shivery than even the fears evoked by Bloody Canyon.

"Let me see your boots," he said quietly.

Puzzled, she held out her foot, encased in black leather. She wore sturdy shoes, though palpably female with embroidered scallops and onyx buttons.

He frowned. "Ride behind me. Stay on the pinto, no matter what happens; the slate will chew up your shoes if you lead him. We should have a good moon. That won't make this easy, but if we keep moving, the time will pass quickly." He reached out and lifted her chin. Again she thought he wanted to kiss her. To her surprise, she wished he would, for she needed comfort and reassurance. "You got it?"

"I've got it."

He held her steady, but didn't move closer. "You ready?"

"Yes." Panic surged through her. The bread soured her stomach. "No." She pulled away from his quiet touch. "I'll never be ready, but that doesn't matter. I've got it."

They cleared Bloody Canyon long after midnight. Johnny had ridden reasonably slowly, but the ride had been hard on the horses. The pinto had lost three of his shoes, which Johnny'd retrieved at some cost to himself. Tiny had done a little bit better, but both horses were limping by the time Johnny and Claire reached the high meadow marking the pass.

As they moved into the parklike enclave, Claire slid off her saddle and threw herself down on the soft grass. "Oh, God." Her hands were still shaking. "I hope I never have to go through that again."

Johnny dismounted and sat down beside her. "Pretty hair-raising."

She turned onto her stomach and cradled her forehead in her hands.

Johnny rested his hand on the small of her back. "Are you going to be sick?"

She waved him away, shaking her head. His hand

spanned half her waist and had weight without pressing, but she found his touch soothing and gentle. His steadiness calmed her just as she had begun to fear she might lose her dinner. She wanted to hug him, but squelched that notion, as she didn't know how he would react.

He leaned over and looked at her face. "I didn't know you were frightened of heights."

"I'm not." She sat up abruptly. The world whooshed around her, a silver-tipped basin whose granite-ridged heights glinted with moonlight. "At least—" She unknotted the scarf and unbuttoned her coat. Sweat drenched her body, from both fear and exertion. Her heart pumped so strongly, she felt its tic in her neck. She gulped in a deep breath and blew out, a cleansing reaction that settled her stomach and lightened her soul. "I'm not easy to frighten, but even you have to admit—"

"True." Laughing, he flung himself down in the grass. She immediately missed his warm touch. "Too true." Hand on his forehead, he studied her from beneath lowered lashes. "You're a hell of a woman, Claire Butler."

Her stomach reknotted. He did want to kiss her; she could tell. Maybe he wanted to do more than that. The old wariness rose up inside her. How did she know he wasn't a rapist? Okay, so he hadn't hurt her. He hadn't hurt anyone to her knowledge, but what if his kindness was all an act? He wanted her. She'd sensed that quite plainly, in his husky voice and sultry expression. She picked a blue daisy, annoyed with herself. She wasn't sure why he intrigued her. Even if he wasn't a rapist, she was his lawyer. He shouldn't kiss her. And, more important, she shouldn't encourage his interest.

She hugged her knees and gazed up at the stars. "Got any ideas for what to do next?"

He stood, walked to the pinto, and picked up a hoof. "Maybe." Quietly he examined the horse. "I'm thinking we can't outrun them, and I should leave you behind."

"After I followed you up this canyon?" She sprang to her feet. "Don't even think it."

"Claire—"

"If they're going to catch you, all the more reason, that I should stay and protect you."

"Claire—"

"They'll shoot you down like a dog without me."

"Claire—" He grabbed her by the shoulders, and pressed his lips over hers. Her next objection fled. His caress felt like nothing she'd ever experienced, a shivery warmth deep inside her. He kissed her lightly, his mouth brushing hers. "Don't you ever shut up?"

"Sure." His arms dropped to her waist. Surprisingly she didn't feel frightened, though she did feel a sense of shame over the fact that she wanted this outlaw to kiss her. She pressed her forehead into his chest. "Sure."

He held her loosely, his hands resting at the small of her back. He was a rock-solid hunk of masculine muscle, warm to the touch, heat beneath flannel. His heart pounded loudly; hers matched it. The icy wind swirled over the pass, and patches of snow lay on the ridges, but she scarcely noticed the cold. She felt more alive than she had in eight years; female, pretty, and wanted. She touched his arm shyly.

He thrust her away. A little stream bubbled through the green meadow. He strode through the spongy grass, bent down, and splashed himself on the face.

"What are you doing?" she asked.

He used his sleeve to mop off his forehead. "I might ask you the same question."

The moonlight accented the drops on his cheekbones. He looked impossibly handsome, with a wide-open, frank expression and thoroughly masculine features. She wondered what had possessed her, until she considered how gorgeous he looked. She picked up the reins of the pinto and led him to the murmuring stream. "Surprising myself."

He rubbed his hands dry on his wool-clad thighs. "Surprised me also."

She felt her cheeks burn with shame. "I did?"

"Yeah." He chuckled. He had a resonant laugh, with a peculiar joy in it, as if life and its foibles amazed him. "I'd pegged you as Miss Prim and Proper."

"You're laughing."

"Sure."

"You think I'm funny?"

"No."

"You're pretty much right." She knelt down and made a cup of her hands. "I don't know what's the matter with me. I never get carried away with romantic nonsense."

"I wouldn't say that." He ambled over to Tiny,

who was munching the grass. "You married that banker."

"God, don't remind me."

"Did he make you unhappy?"

"Worse." She took a swift sip of the icy water. "He was boring."

"Is that why—?"

"I'm not an adulteress."

"I know that." He picked up the reins and patted the horse, then led him downstream from her. "But I never could figure out from the newspapers: What happened after you beat him in court?"

"We got a quiet divorce." The wind froze her fingers. She stuffed them into her pockets and watched as the pinto slurped the cold mountain water. "I allowed a default on grounds of desertion. In return, he financed my legal studies."

"I never heard how it all ended."

"That was part of the bargain."

He stayed behind Tiny, and she couldn't see him, but his low voice seemed a caress against this high, wild backdrop. "You didn't want him?"

"He didn't want me." The cold seeped through her coat. Her moist hands made the air doubly freezing, and she began to shiver. "It took me a while to figure him out. He wanted out of the marriage—and cheaply. The irony was he could have just asked me. I'd never cared all that much about money." She stood close to the pinto, hoping to pick up some of his body heat. "I just wanted to know why he never loved me. As our marriage unraveled, he became more confusing, filled with anger and unfounded suspicions, finally charging me with adultery. That was when I began to catch on.'' The wind picked up and assaulted the pass, plastering her wool coat to her calves. She pulled the shawl over her head and hunkered up close to the pinto. ''It was an insight I learned from my father. When someone makes a false accusation, he's revealing his own character.''

She stared at the stream, wondering what Johnny thought of her story, but he didn't comment, and she didn't ask. She might have been faithful to Chauncey, but she still felt the sting of her failure. If she'd been more of a woman, more romantic and female, perhaps he'd not have sought pleasure with others. The pinto shied slightly. Tiny's hooves made sucking sounds in the grass.

Claire felt Johnny's hand on her shoulder. ''Is that why you took my case? You knew what it felt like to be falsely accused?''

She wanted to hold him. She could hear the pain in his voice, and she suddenly realized why she liked him: She knew what he felt. She didn't think she should admit it, however. In fact, she had no idea what she should confess to a man whose mere look made her feel more wanted than she ever had during her ex-husband's lovemaking. ''I'm not sure. My motives might be baser than that.''

''Yeah?''

She sucked in a deep breath. ''Yes.''

''Were you in love when you married the banker?''

''No.''

''Then why?''

She noticed a cabin in the far distance, a tiny black patch in the darkness, illuminated by one winking light. She touched the chain on her neck. "I was very lonely without my father."

His grip tightened, and he drew her closer. "So, let's try not to get too attached."

"No?"

"No."

She could feel him stirring. She couldn't see him, and their bodies didn't quite touch, but his sheer size gave her a sense of his presence.

"You didn't have such good luck before," he said.

"True. But I'm smarter than I used to be."

"You're very smart, Claire." His thumb grazed her neck. "But smart and sensible aren't the same thing. You don't even know me. I could be more vile than Chauncey Lyman."

Her confidence fled, replaced by heat and confusion. "Are you confessing?"

"No." He moved slightly forward and planted a kiss on the top of her head. "But I've got enough troubles. I don't want problems with my own lawyer."

He couldn't believe he'd kissed her. He glanced at Claire walking beside him. Her braid made a silver cord down her back, and her jeans showed beneath the wool coat. She didn't seem at all like a lawyer. Rather, she seemed a shrouded, ethereal figure, like the girl he'd admired in his young manhood. The roar of Bloody Canyon, the wind and tumble of its waterfalls, receded. They'd skirted the small miner's cabin and were hiking downhill toward the broad plain of

Tuolumne Meadows. Granite peaks jutted above them, haunting and solemn, washed by the moonlight.

He led Tiny a little bit closer. "I think we should find a place to hole up."

She nodded.

"In the morning, I'll reshoe the horses. They'll be all right tonight, as long as we stick to the meadows."

She nodded again.

He wanted to touch her. He'd dreamt about her for years. He'd enjoyed the kiss in Bodie, of course, but that had been a show for the lynch mob, not an expression of true emotion. Silently he cursed his long tenure in Bodie. He had no idea how to treat this kind of woman. Then he cursed himself, for he had no right to wonder about how he should act. He was an outcast, condemned as a rapist. He had no right to experience hope, desire, or attraction. "But, Claire, I have to be honest." How soft she had felt. "I don't know what will happen tomorrow."

"How so?"

He gestured behind them. The horses walked patiently in the moonlight, the cold air making frost of their breaths. "They're both pretty lame."

"The posse's horses will be in the same condition."

"Yeah." Soft, fine, and creamy, with delicate bones. So fragile he thought a rough kiss might break her. "But they'll trade them at one of the mines."

"We could trade ours."

"I told you before, I don't like that idea. I don't know what would happen to Tiny."

She shivered. The moon was upon them, a harvest

moon you'd see on the prairie, a silvery disk so omnipresent you'd almost believe it was daylight.

"You know, I believe you're not guilty." She spaced out her words, as if she wished to convey some special meaning.

He tried to read the line of her spine, her proud, graceful posture. But it gave little clue to what she was thinking. "What's that got to do with the horses?"

"You don't have to put on a show of kindness for me."

"It's not a show."

"Well, I don't believe it. Even if you're not a real outlaw, no one could live all those years in Bodie and be as softhearted as you're pretending to be."

"Well, believe it." What could he tell her? "I'm tough as nails on some levels, but I can't watch small creatures suffer."

She cleared her throat.

"Okay. He's large, but he's dependent on me."

She glanced at the sky, then pulled her coat more tightly around her. Her stride lengthened. He couldn't imagine what she was thinking, but he didn't try very hard, either, as he was having some thoughts of his own. He had to escape her. The horses were lame. He could reshoe the pinto, but it still wouldn't be easy to ride him. His iron-toed boots had allowed him to lead Tiny, but Claire had stayed on the brown-and-white horse for the whole treacherous ride up Bloody Canyon, and her horse was certainly crippled. And even if they did not have that problem, he thought, he should put some distance between them. But where

could he leave her? Sure, she was an excellent woods-
man, and the pass contained miners who might give
her shelter. It also contained a few rogue Indians,
however, and some of those miners could be just as
savage.

"Johnny, I like you," she said abruptly.

He wanted to answer. He wanted to tell her how
he may have once loved her, how he'd admired her
from afar, how he cherished the memory of the slip
of a girl who'd brightened his youth in the bad town
of Bodie. And how he liked the woman she had become; an intelligent, high-spirited lawyer with a fine
sense of justice and a passion for honor. He could not
bring himself to make these confessions, however.
Down that road lay nothing but heartbreak.

"I would not like to see you gunned down," she
added in a low voice.

"There are cabins back there."

"Don't even think it. I'm too stubborn to give up
so quickly." She slowed her pace until she fell in
beside him. "But we can't just careen from one point
to another. We have to come up with some kind of
plan."

"I told you before. You're a very smart lady. I put
you in charge of the plans."

She glanced at the gnarled-looking piñon trees.
They looked windswept and barren, but their nuts
were a staple of the Mono Indians. "How well do
you know this country?" she asked.

"I've ridden through here four or five times."

"I know it well also. I rambled these mountains

many a summer. Plus, I have friends in Yosemite
Valley.''

"Yeah?"

"Yes." The moonlight caught the spray of her tendrils. The shawl had come down, and her walk must
have warmed her, for she unbuttoned the top of the
coat. "I know the Hutchins family and Mr. Muir."

She would know them, of course, he said to himself. Her father had been highly respected, and she
must have grown up among all the best people. The
wind whipped the hem of her coat. She didn't seem
daunted. There was spring in her step. Every once in
a while she looked around, but mostly she kept her
eyes on the meadow.

"I don't imagine such social pillars would be much
help to a couple of outcasts."

"Probably not Mr. Muir. Though he might surprise
you—he's tenderhearted when it comes to the helpless. I'd be more certain of Flo Hutchins, though."

"You think the hotel keeper would help you?"

"Not him. His daughter. We've been friends since
girlhood. She's very wild. More of a tomboy even
than I. And, of course, her father has had his own
legal troubles."

"Good point." Johnny knew about Hutchins, of
course. Part literate huckster, part robber baron, he'd
lived in the valley since the days of the gold rush.
He'd built part of the road and the area's first hotel.
He'd made the magnificent valley world-famous,
churning out pulp voraciously read by the traveling
public, and had fought all the way to the Supreme

Court for the right to own the enchanted domain. He'd lost, however. The Yosemite Valley had been made into a park, and Hutchins had been appointed its caretaker. While Johnny liked the fact that Yosemite was a park, he felt more than a little sorry for the hotel keeper. It seemed sad that the man had been reduced to a tenant on land he had settled and opened.

"We could get to the valley in two days' hard hiking," he said.

"I agree. And I really do think Flo would help us."

So, he had only to get her as far as the valley. "You got an idea of the route we should take?"

"The Mono Trail, I suppose."

"Naw. Too straightforward." He thought he should have felt relieved, but he didn't. He glanced up at the sky, patterned with horsetail shaped clouds backlit by moonlight. "Let's make a zigzag. We'll go down Glen Aulin, then over Cloud's Rest."

"There'll be hard climbing that way."

"Exactly. It's the route they'll least expect."

She slowed down a bit. Their passage made scarcely a sound, so lush was the grass and the flowers. The moonlight made her skin color creamy. He wished he could just kiss her. The wind and the meadow stirred something in him, a desire for freedom. He wished his troubles would all disappear, that he could lay her down in these grasses and make passionate love the rest of the night. "We could go through Pate Valley."

A chill went down his spine. "Too many snakes." This woman really was crazy. "They love that hot granite. I've killed ten rattlers a day in that place."

"But that's just my point." She stopped and waited for him. "The vigilantes won't follow. Maybe not even the posse. We could climb out of the canyon at the head of Hetch Hetchy and come down by Yosemite Falls."

"Forget it, Claire. We've come this far together. I'm not losing you to a rattlesnake."

"All right. Glen Aulin. Then over."

Chapter
Nine

They spent the night under a log, and Claire found it wonderfully cozy. She could understand why a whore might dote on Johnny. She thought him likely a considerate lover, for he certainly was a gifted cuddler. He slept hard, of course—he hadn't rested in almost two days, but his work as a firefighter seemed to have given him talents in the sleeping arena. He dug out a space beneath a fallen tree, lined it with pine boughs, wrapped her in a quilt supplied by the miner, pulled her close to his chest, and didn't let go for the entire night.

He'd kept her surprisingly warm by this method. Cold stabbed her sometimes, if a hand or foot wandered, but Johnny seemed to have some sixth sense of her movements, for each time she'd throw off the patchwork covering of discarded suits, he'd reach out and tuck it back over.

She awoke in the morning to a sense of his presence: his massive arms circled around her, one bulky thigh locked over hers, and a distinctive thickness pressed to her bottom.

"Johnny," she whispered. He didn't answer. She thought she should slip out of his grasp, but he felt so warm, and the morning so crisp, instead she turned her head slightly and took in the sight of the dawn-misted meadow. Frost iced the grass. A mother deer picked her way through the pasture, followed by two delicate fawns. She propped her head on her hand and watched. To her surprise, she had no sense of danger. She felt more at home tucked under this log than she had in the massive four-poster looking over Nob Hill from a bay window.

She also felt better being clamped to the chest of this burly firefighter. She didn't quite know what it said about her. She supposed it was a sign of her tomboyish upbringing. She'd been curiously happy for the past two days. When she thought hard on the subject, she realized she preferred the company of this rowdy outlaw to that of all the citified suitors her uncle had championed in the lonely months after her father's death.

She thought this a sign of female perverseness. Johnny had virtues, of course. He was good in a crisis. And smart enough to let her do the thinking, a quality she could get used to. He was kind and good-hearted and heart-stoppingly handsome, but none of these virtues could outweigh the fact that he seemed an utter and total wastrel, boyish and silly and full of himself—and those were only his minor faults. The best thing she could say about him was that she found his physical presence exciting. She hated the thought, but had to admit he made her feel small, female, and helpless, and that to her chagrin she liked that feeling.

She sighed, touching the chain on her neck. She'd probably been on her own too long. She had been lonely in Bodie, and the six months' practice in San Francisco had taught her that the very notion of a female attorney was so peculiar as to dissuade most men from courting her. Johnny might not be wealthy or have high social status, but he had a kind of swaggering pride in himself. He saw her as a woman, where other men saw only an attorney. This attraction was flattering and revived a hope for remarriage she hadn't realized she'd clung to.

"Claire?" Johnny whispered. Startled, she tried to push forward, but he kept her clamped tight to his chest. She could feel his warm breath on her neck. "Lie still."

Claire did as he asked, though silently she cursed herself and the lively imagination that wandered off when it shouldn't. Because for all she liked him, she wasn't sure what he'd do at this moment. He was, after all, spooned in beside her, his baser nature clearly aroused. Heat flushed her face, and other less ladylike places. "Let me go, Johnny."

"No."

She considered screaming, but that seemed pretty pointless. There wasn't room to use her elbows, so she decided on reason. "I think I ought to remind you—"

He clamped his hand over her mouth. "Quiet, Claire, I'm trying to listen."

She froze. She assumed the posse had stayed down the mountains. Only a fool would have followed them up that deadly canyon, and Flowers had seemed smarter than that. Still, it didn't hurt to be careful. She listened also. At first, she heard only the forest, a burbling stream, the distant thrum of a woodpecker, but finally she caught the rumble, a low vibration deep in the ground, that she knew could be the pounding of hooves.

"It might be the falls," she whispered to Johnny.

"Don't think so."

He scrabbled out from under the log, rolling the blanket up as he moved. "Let's go."

She didn't argue. She'd learned to trust him this far at least. He might not be the gunfighter his nickname implied, but he had a keen instinct for survival.

He took her hand, his warm touch familiar and steady as always. "There'll be no breakfast in bed for you, lady." He plopped her on Tiny and unhobbled the pinto. "I'll make that up some other time."

He swung up behind and took the reins from her. "Let's go."

Tiny moved, the pinto following. The littler horse still didn't have shoes. That didn't matter in the grass of the meadow, but the morning was bound to get rougher, especially when they reached the expanses of granite rimming the meadow. Claire could already see them on several sides, their glittering crystal-shot rock a bright counterpoint to the silvery trunks of the lodgepole and hemlock. Sheep dotted the meadow, white fluffy creatures, drifting like clouds across the green backdrop.

"Do you really think the posse is following?" she asked.

"Don't know, but I'm not taking chances. Flowers has nerve. He might have tried a stunt that stupid."

As Tiny clopped forward, Claire listened some more. The wind died down in the morning, making the little valley much quieter. They'd ridden slightly away from the river, and she could hear neither its burble nor the roar of the falls, a sound which the night winds had brought from different directions. "Do you think it could have been the shepherd?" she asked.

"I'm betting horses. That flock doesn't look like it's moved."

She looked at the sheep. She supposed to most people they would look pretty, but she remembered long summer evenings in which Mr. Muir, who loved almost all creatures, had inveighed against the practice of shepherding. "I wish they'd ban them," she said now.

"That would be nice for the flowers."

Johnny's observation surprised her. It wasn't a popular notion, that the trees and grass should be protected. "You wouldn't feel bad for the shepherd?"

"The man can adapt. The flowers are helpless."

She smiled, glad he couldn't see her reaction. She thought this was probably his oddest characteristic, that he had such feeling for the smaller and weaker. What he said about his childhood made sense, though. She supposed a long illness might develop compassion.

As Claire mused, Johnny glanced over his shoulder. He clicked to Tiny, who obediently picked up the pace. The pinto trotted behind them, but Tiny kept to more of a slow jog, a soothing rhythm that covered the ground while still seeming to have little effort behind it. Johnny rode easily, confident in the saddle, his morning arousal still pressed to Claire's bottom. She was glad in a way he felt hurried. A morning's ride slotted together so closely, would have pushed the limits of the most conscience-ridden.

"Where are we going?" she asked.

He tugged Tiny's reins and pointed him toward the edge of the meadow. "Toward Soda Springs."

"There's a hermit who lives there."

"You know him?"

"I know all the old-timers."

"You think he'd help us?"

"I don't know." She sucked in a deep breath, inhaling the sweet scent of the grass. "He's very peculiar, and I wouldn't like to get him in trouble."

Johnny circled one arm around her waist and rearranged her position slightly. The adjustment made her more firmly seated, but didn't diminish his body's response. "Keep a watch for the old fellow, will you?"

Claire nodded. Claire had met Lembert during her childhood, a harmless old man, but even more crazy than the other eccentrics who had fallen in love with these enchanted mountains. As Johnny rode toward the lodgepole forest, Claire observed the wide, verdant basin, but mostly she kept an eye out for the cabin to see if the hermit would appear there. When they reached the rise where the spring water bubbled, the cabin seemed empty, however.

Johnny stopped. "Can you call him?"

She did as he asked, but saw no sign of the recluse. Johnny turned and took a long look over the meadow. Claire saw them then, several miles in the distance, a dozen riders who, by their speed and lack of provisions, could not have been miners or herders or drovers. Johnny swung off, then lifted her after. "We'll get a quick drink and then we'll push on real hard."

Claire bent down for a drink, unable to speak. She didn't want to lose Johnny. She didn't know why, but her heart had stopped at the sight of the riders.

She took a quick sip of the mineral-tinged water. "We'll have to get rid of the pinto, you know."

Johnny frowned. One by one, he lifted the hooves of the brown-and-white horse. He glanced at the riders, then looked back at the forest, then stared at one of the distant mountains.

Claire stood and touched his shoulder. "I know you don't like it, but you have to leave him. We don't have time to reshoe him, and he can't follow us through the canyon. Look." She locked an elbow in his. She could feel the flannel beneath her cotton sleeve, sense the steady pace of his breathing. "This meadow is lovely. Someone will find him."

"I don't like to leave him with strangers."

"You did not even know him the day before yesterday."

"I don't care whether I own him, I don't like to think he might suffer."

"Then leave him, because he'll suffer plenty if we try to take him into that canyon."

Letting go of Claire's arm, Johnny turned quickly. She wished she could see his expression, but he kept his face averted from her. Whatever the rest of his faults or virtues, he seemed too tough to cry over a horse. Sighing, she removed the canteen from the pinto's saddle, then bent down and filled it with water.

As Claire filled the canteen, Johnny moved the provisions from the pinto to Tiny. She kept one eye on the black cloud of riders. They stopped at the far side of the flock, and she thought she saw a couple of the leaders dismount.

"We ought to get going," she said nervously.

"Give me a minute." Johnny removed the small horse's saddle and tucked it behind a lodgepole. He rubbed his hands over the brown-and-white withers, patted the animal's shoulder, then swatted him on his rump. "Hie." He waved a hat he'd obtained from the miner, and the little horse galloped into the distance.

Claire screwed the top onto her canteen. "Don't you think they can see us?"

"Maybe." Johnny bent down and swigged up a handful of water. He examined the hooves of his Clydesdale, picked up a small rock, and scraped out some dirt. "We could be miners or Indians. We could be friends of old Lembert. One thing's for sure. If we charge off too quickly, we'll draw their attention."

Claire draped the canteen over her shoulders. Johnny spoke the truth, but their visibility still made her nervous. There were quite a few figures spread through the meadow—the flock of sheep; an encampment of Indians. Claire couldn't tell much from this distance, but three ominous figures seemed to be speaking to a distant sheepman. Johnny straightened himself and tossed the sharp rock away.

"Come on." He hefted Claire onto the Clydesdale,

then joined her, urged the horse into a canter, and headed up toward the forest. For as long as she could, Claire watched the distant figures. She was glad the sheep stopped them and glad for the plan, as the riders stayed to the far side of the meadow, the closer route to the Yosemite Valley. As they entered the sparse forest of hemlock, Claire ventured an opinion. "I think we've lost them."

"Maybe," Johnny said glumly.

"With any luck, they'll head for the valley and maybe give up when they find we've not reached there."

"Yeah, right. And if they find the pinto?"

Briefly Claire considered that problem. "I don't know." The horse would be fine. She felt certain of that. Some Indian or miner would find him, and the little pinto would have a new home. "The posse might never see him at all. Even if they come upon him, it will take them hours to figure this ploy out."

She didn't feel as confident as she sounded, however. Claire still feared the bad men of Bodie. She had no idea which men had followed—the sheriff, the posse, or the vigilantes. Gripping the horse tightly with her knees, she scanned the landscape, trying to remember its details. Tiny plowed imperturbably forward, taking the path with the same rhythmic gait that had gotten them all to Bloody Canyon. "What if our plan doesn't work?"

Johnny chuckled. "Don't know."

She glanced back at the meadow. Through the cover of trees, she could still see the horsemen, though now only in glimpses. The dismounted figures had regained their mounts, and the group moved like dark shadows across the carpet of grass and tiny blue daisies. They scattered the flock as they rode four abreast, the white fluff-balls parting before them, a sight that Claire normally would have found pretty or funny, but that now seemed fiendish and frightening, especially because there were so many riders. No legitimate posse, she felt certain, would contain such large numbers. "I thought we'd lost them."

"Nope." Johnny sounded almost excited. "Someone on that posse is clever. Flowers has help. He's got the guts to come up Bloody Canyon by moonlight, but I don't think he's much of a leader. There's someone who's used to command on that posse."

"Do you think it's a posse, or still vigilantes?"

"Probably a mixture of both."

"Do you think they've seen us?"

"I think so."

Perspiration dampened Claire's forehead. Unfortunately, she agreed with Johnny. Someone must have put up a reward, for a true posse would have surely been smaller. Flowers had courage and patience, but greed motivated the miners in Bodie—greed, and pure evil, in the case of the bad men. "Why don't you ride farther into the forest?"

"Because I won't be able to watch them from there."

The morning was cold, but Claire couldn't feel it, and she'd forgotten completely the day's freshness and beauty. She only knew the dark, distant figures, whose silhouettes grew with each passing moment. "We're in big trouble, aren't we?"

"Yeah."

She tightened her grip on the saddle horn. "Couldn't we gallop?"

"There's no point in it, Claire. They have traded mounts with the Mono Pass miners, and we, meanwhile, are riding one tired and ill-shod horse together."

The horsemen charged through the river, silvery droplets of water spraying behind them. "So let's change our plan. What if we go down Tuolumne Canyon? Most people believe a man can't pass through it."

"Or that maybe a man could, but not a woman." He made the comment with no hint of sarcasm.

"I know how to do it. Mr. Muir told me."

"So do I, Claire." A glint of metal flashed in the sunlight. Johnny handed the handcuffs to her. "Put these on, will you?"

Fine hairs prickled on the back of her neck. "We aren't going to surrender."

"Nope."

Reluctantly Claire did as he asked. She didn't like the cold metal bracelets. She rode better without them, and considered them signs of defeat, but if they got caught she couldn't act as Johnny's lawyer if the Bodieites knew she'd helped him escape. And she wanted to help him. The fact surprised her: Now, more than ever, she wanted to see Johnny go free.

"Are we going to go down the Tuolumne Canyon?"

"Too late for that."

He tugged Tiny's reins and shifted his body. Claire

had the strongest sense of his closeness, the warmth of his body, the soft texture of flannel, the muscular thighs and hard plane of his chest, the wide no-nonsense hands with long, blunt-tipped fingers. She wanted to weep at the thought she might lose him. She wasn't sure how it had happened, but in the last two days she'd developed a fondness for him, and she had to admit her devotion no longer came only from a sense of justice.

She leaned back slightly and gripped the saddle horn. "Johnny?" He didn't answer. They were headed straight toward the meadow, and the galloping figures now clearly saw them. Several drew pistols. Rifles appeared from saddle scabbards. "We could ride like hell for San Francisco."

She could feel his arm muscles stiffen. "Thanks, but be quiet."

He slowed Tiny down. They'd reached a slope looking over the meadow. The shadowy posse turned into horsemen, grim individual riders, their faces covered, their collars turned up. "Johnny—"

"Sorry, Claire."

He swung her off the horse and faced her outward, jerking the white cotton shirt off her shoulder.

"What the—?"

"Quiet." He dropped Tiny's reins, grabbed her by the waist, and held the Colt to her head. "Look frightened."

She didn't much need that command—he'd managed quite nicely to make her alarmed. The morning breeze ruffled her hair, and the feel of the metal raised goose bumps on her bare skin. She could hear the posse by now, the heavy thud of hooves against grass. She recognized Flowers and some of the riders, though others had pulled up their coats. Johnny held steadfast behind her, and she marveled at how he kept from trembling. His heart pumped out a steady rhythm as he wedged his thigh behind hers, his arm holding her waist. The posse slowed as they mounted the slope, the breath from their horses making brief, frosted clouds in the cool morning. They stopped maybe thirty feet back, their shotguns, pistols, and rifles making a small, glistening forest of metal.

"Morning, fellas." Johnny held the Colt firmly. He was completely outgunned and he must have known it, but Claire detected no fear in his tone. "You've broken your promise."

The sheriff pulled out his bulldog. "Give her up, Johnny. Your race is run. I promise you'll get a fair trial in Bodie."

"If you get me that far."

"I'll do my best, Kid."

"Not good enough."

Behind the sheriff, the horses were restless. Claire could tell from the cut of their clothes and their grim expressions that most of these men were vigilantes. Doubtless Flowers had good intentions, but Claire very much doubted he could keep his promise, in view of the crowd ranged behind him.

"I like running, so I'll make you a bargain." Johnny nudged Claire. "I'll give the lady up for a lead."

"No," Claire said softly, trying her best to look frightened, which wasn't hard with a gun pressed against her head. "You still need me."

"You make it tempting." Johnny's hot breath wafted over her earlobe. "I might not mind dying for a woman so pretty."

Claire wanted to kick him—this seemed like such a stupid idea. She raised her voice and spoke to the sheriff. "I'm sure you're a man of your word, but he just wants to get to San Francisco. Perhaps it would be better if we allowed it."

Several gun barrels clicked in the morning stillness.

"Enough of that." The sheriff lifted his bulldog. To Claire's relief, he aimed at the air between Johnny and the group behind him. "She's Judge Butler's daughter. Her uncle's already put up a reward. And her former husband has added some money."

Chauncey? Claire thought. Why would Lyman care about her?

"That's just dandy." Johnny could make his voice harsh when he wanted, and Claire had a fleeting moment of doubt. "You fellows ride to the far side of the meadow. I'll let her go, then skedaddle, but you tell her former husband—"

"Tell Chauncey—" Claire pressed slightly into Johnny's body, an imperceptible message, one she hoped the vigilantes would not see. "Tell Chauncey this man hasn't touched me. And please . . ." She squared her shoulders and conjured up tears. The waterworks surprised her, for she'd never cried on command in her life. Then again, she considered as the hot droplets coursed down her cheeks, she'd never run from the law before, nor had a man's life ever depended on her ability to look teary and helpless.

She tried her best to keep up the reaction. "Please . . . just go back to Bodie. I believe he'll keep his promise."

"You can't trust him, lady." A thick-chested Welshman spoke from the crowd. "You're better off dead than crossing the state with a bastard like that."

"I'm all right." She looked straight at Flowers. "I know the law wants him. I promise you when we reach San Francisco, he'll turn himself in to the federal marshal."

"You're crazy, lady. Look what he did to Louisa."

"He didn't—"

"Enough." Johnny virtually lifted her off her feet. "Louisa Cantrall's beside the point. I'll give you ten minutes to ride back through the meadow. It's a small enough lead, when you consider it."

"Why don't we just shoot you?" The voice came from the back of the crowd.

Johnny tightened his grip around Claire's waist. "Because you'd have to kill Judge Butler's daughter, the former wife of the state's richest banker, and one of our first female lawyers, and I'd be willing to bet good money on this: The reward's only paid if she's returned unharmed."

A visible wave traveled over the crowd. Several of the gun barrels lowered.

"That's better," Johnny said slowly. "Do we have a bargain?"

No one spoke. They simply stared. Claire realized, with some sense of dismay, that all but the sheriff were intent on the bounty. There wasn't an honorable man in the group. One by one they turned their horses, until only Flowers faced Johnny. "Just let her go, Johnny. I'll give you a lead."

"No!" Claire said to Flowers in spite of the vise-like hold on her ribs. "You can't let them kill him. That wouldn't be right."

"You still trying to defend him?"

"He came to me as a client."

"And you still believe him? Even after what he's done to you?"

"He's done nothing to me. And believe me, by this time he could have. So, just let us get to San Francisco. We'll straighten this out in the city."

The sheriff lowered his bulldog. "I know what you're thinking." He looked directly at Johnny. "But it won't work. I'll be waiting for you in San Francisco."

"That's my problem, Sheriff."

"Her husband's got influence in the Bay City."

"He's her *former* husband."

"That doesn't mean he'd like to see her raped."

Johnny eased the Colt from Claire's forehead. "You just tell those thugs to keep back."

Flowers muttered an indistinguishable curse. He turned his horse slowly, the bulldog still clutched in his fist. The vigilantes had melded back into shadow and were slowly approaching the Tuolumne River.

"Ten minutes, Johnny. And if you don't let her go, you're a dead man," the sheriff shouted over his shoulder.

As the sheriff plunged his horse down the slope, Claire's mind raced over her options. She couldn't leave Johnny. The vigilantes would catch him in less than ten minutes. Without her as a hostage, they'd shoot him down for sheer pleasure, and Flowers would be helpless to stop them.

As the sheriff rode down toward the river, she spoke softly to the big man behind her. "Johnny, don't leave me. I don't want to lose you." She knew she should have more pride, but fate hadn't left her with the more proper option of ladylike silence. "I know this sounds foolish, but I'd really miss you if something happened after we parted."

A perceptible tremble ran through his body. The reaction surprised her, because until this moment he'd been as cool as a Mississippi River boat pilot.

"I'll miss you, too, Claire." He eased his arm from her waist. Suddenly she could no longer feel him, and a sense of panic set in. "If I make Tahiti, I'll send you some money for your law practice. But remember this no matter what happens: I always thought you were terrific, and never more so than at this moment."

"Johnny." She turned. He'd reached the Clydesdale. She took one step in his direction. A clap, like thunder, boomed in the distance. Dirt splashed around Johnny's feet. He swung into the saddle. Another boom. Something hit Claire. She felt impact, not pain. She fell.

"Claire." Johnny must have screamed, she knew from the tone, but the sound seemed to come from rather far off. The next moments all ran together. Johnny's arms circled her waist. She knew they were Johnny's, not so much by logic as because she'd come to know them by instinct. She couldn't see much because there was liquid and dirt in her eyes, but a logical thought asserted itself and told Claire she should get going. She threw herself forward, but that must have been the wrong choice. Johnny shouted again and pulled her in close, then lifted her in his strong arms. Another explosion rained dirt around them. "Up you go, sweetheart."

Johnny pushed her into the saddle. He mounted behind her, covered her with his body, and urged the giant horse into a gallop. A wicked pain stabbed Claire's forehead. She clung to Tiny's mane, trying to control the nausea that racked her. She listened for shots and didn't hear any, then realized suddenly that Johnny had stopped.

"Are you all right, Claire?"

She was trembling and sweaty, sickish and dizzy, and she knew by now there was blood on her forehead. "I think so."

Johnny's attention seemed to be divided. She could feel his muscles, hot and rigid behind her, and she knew with an instinct she could not have expressed that he was looking steadily toward the vigilantes. She tried to look also, but couldn't. The sun stabbed her eyes and pounded her forehead.

Johnny pulled her in closer and turned her chin toward him, giving him a view of her profile. Gently he touched the blood on her face. She winced, and he trembled.

"It's nothing. Really," she said. "I think I just got hit by a pebble."

Johnny said nothing, though she could still feel his anger, a palpable tension in his muscular body. He tugged the reins and turned Tiny sideways, walking them slowly toward the Tuolumne River. It took Claire a moment to realize what he was doing. "Johnny?"

"Shush."

Claire remained down. She knew she'd been shot, but didn't want to admit it. Whoever had done it had stopped their shooting, and she had an ominous feeling about what might have happened. A dark blotch lay next to the river, the whole posse ranged out behind it. One mounted individual posed by the shape which looked like a body. Claire shivered. Evidently Flowers had gunned down one of the vigilantes, probably an overeager bounty hunter who had tried to put a bullet in Johnny and accidentally shot her instead.

Johnny reached the glittering water and stopped. "You all right, Sheriff?" he shouted.

"Sure," Flowers's deep voice reached them. "But you better skedaddle. I'll hold off these dogs if you'll leave the woman."

"No." Claire raised her voice to a shrill tone. "Somebody shot me. You're a good man, Sheriff, but the men with you aren't. I'd rather take my chances with Johnny."

"They weren't aiming for you." The sheriff's voice bounced off the rocks. "They just wanted Kid Christmas."

"Can't prove it by me." She lowered her voice so only Johnny could hear it. "I won't let you leave me. I'll track you down by myself if I have to."

"Claire—" Johnny put in.

"Don't try to argue. I'm more than your lawyer, and we both know it. You wouldn't abandon your horse to these thugs, so why would you leave a woman who loves you?"

Chapter Ten

~~~

They'd almost killed her. The thought still made Johnny tremble. And much later that night, when they'd gotten far into the forest and he knew Flowers had kept his promise to let him take her away safely, he still felt sick to his stomach that he'd almost gotten Claire Butler killed—and stunned that five minutes later she'd said she loved him.

She loved him. He thought about that as he cleaned her face, scarcely daring to touch her. Her cuts had been superficial, though she had been right—someone had shot her, leaving a shallow crease in her forehead.

She loved him. He thought about that as he collected pine boughs to fashion into a shelter. She couldn't have meant that declaration, though he couldn't imagine what else had prompted her refusal to leave him. In eight years in Bodie, he'd collected quite a few friends, including some of the town's fancy women, but no one had loved him, except for Hattie, and her grateful devotion wasn't the same feeling as Claire's seemed to be.

She loved him. He thought about that as he tucked her in, determined to watch while she was sleeping. How could she have come to that conclusion? He loved her, of course. Maybe he'd always loved her, but certainly he'd fallen hard since she'd shown up on his doorstep, determined to act as his lawyer and willing to risk life, limb, and honor just to stand up for her idea of justice.

But what would possess her to return that feeling? And why on earth would she declare it? And risk her life, not for the law's honor, but for a man condemned as a rapist? He tucked his arm over her waist. Moonlight gilded her face. He could feel the movement of her muted breathing. And what would he do when they reached San Francisco? Could he ask her to come to Tahiti? Did they have lawyers on the South Sea Islands, and would she give up her special status to follow a man considered an outlaw?

He laughed softly. He wasn't an outlaw, but he was a wastrel, and he had a feeling that might not be much better in her estimation. He could support her. He'd always had money and he always would. Alice Van Kessel might be the world's most protective mother, but solicitous mothers had certain virtues, loyalty being one of their finest. Alice had never stinted with Johnny. She sent him money whenever he asked, and many times when he didn't. She'd always indulged him and always would. She'd wonder about Tahiti, and fret over whether the weather would be good for his health, and then she'd send him a fortune if a fortune was wanted.

Johnny looked thoughtfully at Claire's peaceful expression. But would Claire accept that kind of refuge? Clearly she admired her father, a man who'd worked hard all of his life. And she hadn't liked being a wealthy man's wife. Johnny wasn't a bastard like Chauncey Lyman, but in his own way he wasn't much better. Lyman might cheat and steal for his money, but at least that showed some talent. Johnny merely sent home to Mother and never had he been ashamed of that fact.

He hadn't bragged about it, of course. He liked being one of the boys. In a town full of men scrabbling for wealth, you didn't advertise that you had more than you wanted. He let the Bodieites think him an outlaw. He worked the mine to confuse them and let the rumors fall where they might. His true love had been the fire department—the risk, the bone-deep thrill and adventure that came with having a fire to fight. If nobody paid him, that didn't matter. To him it was useful, and he'd never, until this moment, thought about doing anything else.

Now he had Claire. The state's third woman lawyer. The daughter of a prominent judge. The former wife of a wealthy banker. Even if they got out of this pickle, even if they reached San Francisco, even if she would come to Tahiti and consent to life as a bauble, how long could he keep his secret, and what would she do if she ever found out she'd left honor and country and hard-won occupation to follow the man who'd killed her father?

"You have to leave me," Johnny whispered to Claire when her eyes opened. "I know you don't want to, but this is foolish. You can't follow me to San Francisco.''

''Good morning, darling.'' She stirred and put her hand on his cheek. ''What did you say?''

''Oh, God.'' He buried his head in her shoulder. Her whole body felt warm against his. He'd fallen asleep, in spite of his promise, and awakened for the third day in a row full of desire and passion for her. He'd never awakened next to a woman, having never spent the whole night with a whore. He found this a different, more desperate craving than the simple lust he'd felt for the town's fancy ladies. ''You have to leave me.''

She propped herself on one elbow, then ran her hand over his shoulder. ''Even after what I said yesterday?''

He could still feel her. The small, soft, delicate bosom; the rounded thighs and feminine apex. ''Especially after what you said yesterday.''

She dropped back down and toyed with his collar, a turned-down flap of red flannel. ''Can I ask why?''

''You don't know me, Claire.''

''I disagree.''

''How could you love me? You don't know the first thing about me?''

''Feminine instinct.'' She smiled, soft and seductive.

He brushed back a lock of her golden hair. Her eyes looked so blue in the morning, the color of sky and the tiny blue daisies that hid in the meadow grasses. He wanted to love her. God, how he wanted to love her. It was like a starvation, a hunger and madness. And added to that he wanted to take her. But sexual possession had its own price, a cost much higher than that charged by the whores. He'd learned that in caring for Hattie. Women weren't toys for his pleasure. Nature had made them vulnerable creatures, a fact they ignored only at their own peril. "Hogwash. You told me . . . You're mainly a tomboy."

"All right. I used logic. You're brave and resourceful and . . . well . . . virile. What else do I need from a man?"

A charge passed between them. There was some truth in her comment. She was smart and determined. He was a man of action. If that wasn't exactly a match made in heaven, there was a certain odd logic to it. "But I can't protect you." He wanted to weep. The years in Bodie had finally caught up to him. He'd spent all his adult life flirting with death. His childhood asthma had slowly disappeared. The impulse for self-destruction had lingered longer, but just when that wild passion had left him, too, his hellish, alluring childhood companion had come back to haunt him in the form of this false posse. But he also knew it didn't pay to argue with her. He'd never beat her in verbal gymnastics.

He touched his lips to her earlobe. She shivered. A bolt of desire ran through him, and with it a plan. What if she thought he was a rapist? She'd surely leave then. Whatever faith she had in her judgment would surely be shattered if he attacked her.

He slid one hand up to her wrist and held her. "I don't need your love, but I surely could use something else."

She froze, her eyes wary. Uncertainty crept into her expression. "What do you want?"

"I think you know."

He kissed her. He supposed a rapist did not dispense kisses, but he wanted to feel her soft lips. To his surprise and chagrin, she responded. She parted her lips and made a small sound. Desire stormed through him. He felt charged and heavy, drugged and intense. He also felt panicked. A false rape wouldn't work, if she responded. He'd have to do something far less seductive. He heaved himself up, his chest blowing in deep, ragged breaths. "Jesus Christ, Claire. You don't make love with total strangers."

"You knew all those . . . ladies . . . before you went with them?"

The scent of the pine boughs made him dizzy, and she looked so pretty, wild, and disheveled in the miner's shirt and surrounded by greenery. "No, but that's different."

"Because you're a man?"

"Because I regret it." He had an ache in his groin, a throb in his chest, a wild thrum of blood in his veins, and a serious pain in his forehead. "You remember Hattie?"

"Yes," she said warily.

"She was a whore. She died of consumption. That's why the whores love me. She spent her last year in my cabin."

"What's that have to do with you and me?"

"Because . . . what is a rapist?" he said, groping to make sense. "He's a man who thinks there's no price for his actions. Men are all rapists on some levels, trying to get what we want from women and thinking there's a cheap way to do it.''

She sat next to him. Her feet were stockinged in lisle, the only delicate part of her outfit, but even togged out in the miner's rough clothes she managed somehow to be so pretty. ''You're frightened, aren't you?''

''Yeah. I suppose so.''

''Have you ever had a lover before?''

''Only Louisa.''

''Were you and she lovers?''

He stood and faced away from her. He wanted some breakfast. He wanted some water. He wanted to be rid of his lust for Claire's body. ''No, we weren't lovers. But she was the first woman I courted.''

''Did she have other suitors?''

''I don't know.'' He turned and looked at her. Her face had a pure, straightforward expression. ''Why do you ask?''

''No real reason. Just a stray thought.''

''Don't let your thoughts stray in too many directions.'' He approached Tiny stiffly, determined to walk off his sexual frustration. ''We're going through the Tuolumne Canyon.''

The trail was wicked. Johnny was grumpy, and there were good reasons for his foul mood. Claire didn't like the frustration herself. She didn't love him exactly; she'd lied about that. But she did know she liked him. She'd realized that truth out in the meadow. This had nothing to do with the law's honor. Somehow he'd touched her. His absurd innocence.

His boyish wonder. The sense of adventure she'd thought she'd lost. He was like these mountains. Wild and enchanting. She'd thought she'd come to Bodie to tame it. Johnny made her remember a truth she'd forgotten: Part of what she'd loved about Bodie had been its untamed beauty and wildness.

Even now, as they slogged over the boulders and descended into the forested canyon, she didn't mind the pain in her toes, the soreness of her thighs, the clenched buttocks muscles. Her heart lifted in wonder whenever she gazed at the blue skies above her, listened for the echoing falls, or caught a glimpse of the silvery water. And she responded the same way to Johnny. She cherished his straightforward nature. She'd never loved any man but her father, and had begun to believe she never would. There'd been plenty of suitors in San Francisco, good men, but boring, concerned about money and social status, with none of her father's passion and honor. It had clicked into place back there in the meadow: She'd tell a small lie, an easy one for a lawyer. She liked Johnny and wanted to save him. For all his fine speech about masculine nature, she didn't believe he was a rapist. If she told him she loved him, he wouldn't leave her. And she could defend him. That's all that mattered.

Now if she could just get him to accept her protection, which seemed a pretty tough task in itself. He was hiking ahead and leading Tiny. There had been no real path through this canyon. They'd trekked past miles and miles of falls, more varied and beautiful than she'd known existed, even though she'd visited the famous Yosemite Valley. He hadn't spoken in five miles at least, and most of the time he'd looked angry.

She sat down on a rock overlooking a little side canyon and called out. "I'm hot."

He stopped, turned around, and led Tiny close to the river, which in this spot was shallow and braided, slipping over a wide formation of granite, forming dozens of falls with pools behind them, and gathering several hundred feet down behind one deeper pool she knew foreshadowed a wild leap into a chasm, a hard hike that would be rewarded with a view of a dazzling cascade of billowing water.

"Do you think Flowers has followed?" she asked.

"No. And I don't think once we get past Waterwheel Falls the vigilantes will follow either."

"Why?"

"Too many snakes in the inner canyon. Your Mr. Muir might have done it, but very few men like picking through rattlers when they're three days' hike from the nearest doctor."

She nodded. She didn't like rattlesnakes either. She'd seen them, of course, big brutal creatures that always gave warning, which didn't make them less frightening, for they were quick, deadly, and vile-tempered and blended in well with their surroundings.

He pulled a kerchief out of his pocket, bent down, and wet it in the river. "Do you know where we are?"

"I think so." She looked at the gray walls arching above her. She'd never been down the Tuolumne River before, but she understood the geography well. The stream ran parallel to the Merced, and after a wild run down its canyon, created a second enchanted valley, very much like its more famous neighbor. "We're going down toward Hetch Hetchy. Yosemite's over this ridge of mountains, about two days' hike if you're lucky."

"How does your head feel?" He handed the kerchief to her. He didn't touch her. She noticed that.

She pressed the cool cloth to her forehead. "It's not really hurting," she lied. "Johnny, I meant what I said when I told you I loved you." The lie did not come so easy this time, but she couldn't tell what he was thinking, and his sulk made her nervous. Until yesterday, he'd been happy-go-lucky. Now he seemed peevish, defensive, and nervous. He eyed her, suspicious, then turned on his heel and stalked back to Tiny.

He spoke, but his voice came out husky. "We'll spend the night below Waterwheel Falls."

He wished he knew how he was going to do this. He ought to plan it, he told himself, but he'd never been good at the simplest planning, and how on earth would he plan to rape a woman? Not that he planned to rape her exactly—only pretend to, enough to frighten her. In theory, a sham display should be easy. He'd been a false outlaw for so many years, why couldn't he be a counterfeit rapist? As he made up their bed, though, the idea didn't seem simple. He knew he couldn't wait until morning. Half asleep, she might give him access. She'd certainly seemed willing this morning, though the kiss still seemed like a dream. And then there was her profession of love. What if she were willing? He couldn't ravage a cooperative woman. He dismissed the thought, however. She might deign to kiss him, but she wouldn't go farther. He'd already learned that with Louisa. A respectable woman might lead a man forward, but she would not let him finish, except at the price of a marriage license.

Divorced or no, Claire was clearly a respectable woman. Brainy and classy, honorable and determined. He cut down a pine bough. The false-rape idea made him sick to his stomach. Not so much that he couldn't succeed at the sham, but it made him unhappy to think of parting this way. Hell, it made him unhappy to think of leaving her at all. For all her scolding, he enjoyed her presence. He enjoyed the tomboy in her and was touched by her vulnerable, feminine side. He wished desperately he could protect her, but he simply couldn't, and the thought unmanned him.

Her only safety lay in retreat. She knew her way to the Yosemite Valley. He'd seen enough of her skills as an outdoorswoman to know she would make her way with few problems. And he might even be safer if she weren't with him. Flowers would follow him down the Tuolumne Canyon, but the real vigilantes would probably trail her for the reward.

The thought made him sick. To the end of her days, she would think him a rapist. It had been one small consolation, that he might convince her of his innocence. For a moment, he considered the notion seriously, that he should ride to the Yosemite Valley and deliver himself up to the law. But surrender meant death swift and certain, and he hadn't outwitted that monster for so long only to give himself up to it now.

He tossed the pine bough into a stack. She'd gone down to the water to bathe. The thought created a quick reaction, and he considered the ache in his groin. He should do this now before he reconsidered. He didn't intend true penetration, but he'd never make a credible rapist if he couldn't exhibit the physical symptoms. While he'd never had trouble along those lines, with Claire or with any other woman, the thought of doing her harm made him cringe and he had to conjure up her nude image in order to get the proper effect.

He picked up the knife. The pistol would have been better, but he wasn't about to take the chance of having a firearm accident with her. He stripped himself naked and ran. Some little part of him thought he should plan, but skin, bone and sinew said "No!" His life in Bodie had taught him: in a tight situation, take action. He charged into the clearing.

Claire swam in the placid river, her golden hair swirling behind her. He could tell she was naked. He couldn't quite see her body, but her pale skin reflected beneath the water. He thought himself lucky. The whole scene conspired against goodness. Hot sun poured over his back. A light breeze puckered his nipples. The scent of pine tickled his nose. He found it easy to abandon scruples in such a natural and sensual setting. He took one quick step forward.

She turned in the water. Her eyes widened, and her lips parted. His heart broke, and he threw down the knife. Not once in his life had he harmed an innocent creature. He couldn't start with Claire Butler. Now he stood there naked before her, bare-assed with a full erection. She waited, her pale face above the green water, her skin blurry beneath it. He dove. He reached her in less than two strokes.

"What are you doing?" she asked.

He kissed her. He tried to be hard and heartless about it, but he knew right away he had failed. Her mouth was too tender, too soft and expressive. He pressed himself to her, full of hunger, and love, and every emotion but anger. He didn't want this and fought against it, but his lips lingered over her softness, a fatal mistake, for she opened her mouth and pulled herself to him, twining her legs over his waist, more giving, more wanton, more open and needy than he'd ever imagined in his wildest daydream.

A small groan escaped him. He couldn't stop. He knew that he ought to. He'd not intended true penetration, but at her invitation he slipped in. He doubted he hurt her. She clung to his shoulders, a ragged breath coming from her.

"Oh, Jesus, Claire." She loved him. He hadn't believed it, but now he had to. He couldn't drive her away by this method, because she'd made up her mind to accept his lovemaking. She loved him.

He lifted her up. He was chest-deep in water. She was lapped against him by the little wavelets the falls generated, the gentle but powerful current that drove the river into its canyon. Holding her tightly, he explored her mouth. It was hot and accepting, a vivid contrast to the icy cold water. But as he kissed her, he no longer had a sense of its coolness. The Tuolumne River had faded away, along with the sky and the pines and the late summer flowers. The roar of the falls, however, had grown louder, supplemented by the thrum of his blood, the powerful pulse of his heartbeat.

Although he wanted to thrust, he held himself back. He had no trouble holding her up, but he thought he might hurt her. He'd been only with whores, making love in a horizontal postion. He'd never had to consider a woman's sexual pleasure and was certainly learning under novel conditions. Still, he felt he could satisfy Claire, if he followed his instincts. He lifted. She made a small, passionate sound, arching back to bring herself closer. He took one nipple into his mouth. Her fingers dug into his shoulder. She tightened around him, a moan in her throat. He suckled. The roar of the falls seemed to double in volume. The breeze on his back, the push of the current, gave the act an added dimension. He felt transformed in that moment. One with her. One with the river. A lover who'd found his first lover. If rational thought came only in snatches, that did not matter. She loved him.

He released the bright bud and swept her back toward the falls, keeping himself sheathed inside her. She clung to his neck, murmuring softly, her long golden hair swirling around her. They reached a sheltered spot by a sandbar, and he eased her slowly onto the wet grass. She hadn't let go and did not do so now, but lay back with the sun in her eyes, droplets of water running lazily off her.

"Johnny," she whispered.

"Ah. Claire."

He kissed her again. God, how he loved this. His fantasies had not been erotic, at least not until the last couple of days. She'd simply seemed like a soul mate, a beautiful, privileged, vulnerable girl who'd grown up to become a remarkable woman. But to have her trapped naked beneath him, that creamy skin glistening, the hungry mouth moist and compliant, her body joined fiercely to his, seemed totally natural. He explored her with kisses, her mouth, her earlobe, and languorously in the curve of her neck. She made low fervent sounds in the back of her throat. An urgency built within him. He thrust upward, trying to get more sense of closeness. She moaned and wiggled down, a feminine gesture that moved him quite deeply. Without a word or a sound she caught his rhythm. He began to feel the need to finish when a startling thought hit him, and he slowed down. The whores had tricks to prevent conception, but Claire would not have taken precautions. His body urged him to ignore the thought, told him they could take care of all problems afterward, but his conscience prodded him to a halt. He stilled. She followed and opened her eyes.

"Are you all right, Johnny?"

Damnation.

He tried to ease out; he wanted to with all his soul. But nature hadn't made him that way. A little devil rose up inside him. He pushed, and she answered. Together they finished, the end coming in passionate spasms, with her left trembling there in the grass and him up to his knees in cold water.

"Don't you feel wicked?" Johnny asked.

"No." Claire wrapped herself in the blanket, the scratchy quilt given them by the miner. Johnny sat naked beside her, his jeans beneath him, and Claire wondered how on earth he stood it, as she'd have been freezing without the covering. "Do you?"

"Not exactly." Johnny leaned against the bough shelter. "But I wondered if you did."

"Why?" Claire felt sleepy. She did not want to talk, but Johnny seemed worried. She propped her chin on her knees and watched the river. Waterwheel Falls thundered above them. They mesmerized Claire. White as the snows from which they melted, they cascaded over a vast slope of granite. An unusual falls, they flung themselves backward and upward before tumbling into this flat-bottomed valley. There the river transmuted, slipping through a pretty pine forest, its wildness transformed into placid beauty. "Did I surprise you?" she asked.

"Yeah."

"Well, I shouldn't have. I knew what you were up to."

He picked up a pine needle, and broke it in half. "Yeah?"

"Yes." He was still half aroused, and it seemed to Claire so natural to sit beside him and enjoy the forest. "You wanted to scare me. You thought I'd think you were a rapist."

"How come you're so smart?"

"Strictly God-given. Intelligence isn't a virtue. It's merely a blessing, no more worthy of admiration than height or eye color. It's what you do with your natural bounty that counts."

He chuckled. "You sound like you're reciting your catechism."

"I am." She lifted her chin and straightened her shoulders. "My father taught me. He didn't want me to be self-important."

"A very wise man," he said as he planted a swift kiss on her forehead. "But didn't he teach you to hold out for marriage?"

"No." She pulled the quilt over them both. Evening was falling. He'd brought some bread and jerky into their little nest, but she didn't feel hungry now. "He taught me to hold out for love. Advice I ignored first time around."

"I haven't told you I love you."

"True." Now her situation got tricky. She'd lied to him out there in the meadow, then compounded her lie with an act of true passion. She didn't know what he thought of her actions. She didn't know what she thought of it herself. She'd gotten caught in a trap of her own making. Having lied to Johnny about her affection, she couldn't now think of the proper rejection, especially since she'd once been married and obviously had sexual experience. "But I love you, and perhaps that's enough."

"I don't think so."

"You don't?"

"No, you shouldn't. You should wait for a fellow who loves you. But, this time it doesn't matter. You did good in spite of yourself. Because I do love you, you know."

She stared at his face. He seemed very serious, a fact that amazed and unnerved her.

He brushed a lock of hair back from her forehead. "You don't remember me, do you?"

"No." His touch was so tender she wanted to weep. What had she done? She hadn't meant to toy with his feelings. She'd simply gotten frightened, and tried to save him. "Should I?"

"I knew you when you lived in Bodie."

"Not well, I suppose."

"No, but I came to your father's funeral."

Outside of the shelter the winds were sighing. They pushed the moan of the falls before them, making the canyon sound haunted. She wasn't wearing the chain on her neck and she missed it. "I don't remember."

"I know that."

She studied his earnest expression. He had frank, regular features and the kind of eyelashes a girl would envy, but this time she saw something else there as well. She wanted to bury her face in her hands. Why hadn't she seen the emotion before, buried behind that raffish expression? She supposed because he'd kept it hidden, until she'd blurted out her terrible lie.

He stroked her damp hair. "I followed your life in the newspapers. I thought about you pretty often."

A kind of dull misery settled on her. Her legs ached from a hard day of hiking. Now that the excitement had subsided, she was sore and chafed from their lovemaking.

He touched a strand of hair on her neck. "I'll stand by you no matter what happens."

She wanted to bolt. She would have, too, except that it was warm under the blanket. "I'm not worried. I never got pregnant when I was married."

"It doesn't sound like you had too many chances."

"I didn't." She turned her back to him. She needed

to think, to plan her next move. This hadn't worked out the way she'd intended. He couldn't love her. He simply couldn't. "But it wasn't because I didn't want to be."

Chapter
Eleven

He couldn't leave her. He'd intended to, if his false rape had worked out, but that plan had gone all awry, which is why he'd decided to give up on planning. He'd take her down Tuolumne Canyon. He could dodge rattlers—he'd dodged dozens in his eight years at Bodie. Still, he hated the notion of endangering her. He'd never been all the way through this canyon, but he'd been to the narrows where the steep walls of granite confined the river and pressured it through a stone chasm that sunlight made into a haven for rattlers.

"Did Mr. Muir study the rattlers?" he said to her back. She pretended to sleep, but he knew that, and he couldn't just lie there and wonder how badly she regretted their lovemaking. "I mean, what did he think the rattlesnakes ate?"

It took her a moment to answer. He knew she was tense, by the tautness of her muscles, by her shallow breathing, and just from the logical fact that her nerves, like his, were probably jangling. "I never asked him."

"Oh." Which comment exhausted him on that subject. He wanted to tell her she shouldn't regret it. That no matter what happened, it would work out. Certainly he'd always remember what had happened there under the falls. That it had been glorious and magical to him, and that even if it were never repeated, he couldn't imagine regretting those moments. But unfortunately neither could he imagine any aspect of the experience that would make her happy.

"Is it that bad in the canyon?" she asked softly.

"I hear it's wretched." He stroked her shoulder. He considered lying, but discarded the notion. She was far too smart, and he didn't like lying. He often let people think what they wanted—their false assumptions were not his problem—but successful lying required planning, and he'd never been good at long-range thinking. "It's mostly the snakes that make it that way. Otherwise, it's just hot and rocky, though I often wondered, do the snakes eat the lizards? They're the only other creatures that like the hellish place."

She flipped onto her back. She wore the miner's shirt with no bottom, a combination he found extremely erotic. He lay prone also. She might be confident about her barrenness, he thought, but he had better get a hold on himself. He would have loved to give her a baby, but somehow he doubted she'd be happy about it. All Johnny's experience had been with whores. They'd taken care of the details of preventing conception.

He tucked Claire under his chin. She didn't react, and he sighed. Some aspects of life were a mystery to him, and he regretted anew his father's coldness. It was something he'd learned in caring for Hattie: People distanced themselves from the dying. It took someone special, like Alice Van Kessel, to love a child who might not outlive her. Johnny had wondered all of his childhood what he had done to make his father hate him. It had been the source of Johnny's physical prowess. He'd spent his summers, when he'd been almost well, building up muscles to make an impression. It was only much later, after caring for Hattie, that Johnny realized he'd done nothing to warrant that paternal distance. He'd simply been born with a defect, one his father couldn't accept.

Johnny kissed the top of Claire's forehead, grateful for that long year with Hattie. His father's weakness no longer hurt, but he still regretted its repercussions. He would have liked to understand better how much danger of pregnancy Claire might be in, how he could have helped her to safeguard against conception, and what he could do to reassure her he loved her, especially now that he might be a father himself.

She fell in love with him in Tuolumne Canyon. It wasn't just his courage in the face of the rattlers that did it. She now knew he wasn't a rapist. He didn't approach her sexually, though from what she could tell, he had an almost constant desire to.

She thought about this on their third day of hiking. They'd seen fifteen rattlers by now, several each evening and one or two in the morning, mostly sunning on rocks. There'd been the same warning each time, the startling buzz portending venom. And Johnny had laughed. She found it charming, and stupid, and, in the end, endearing, the way he kept up his courage in the face of those creatures.

He'd walked ahead of her as they wound down the canyon. Sometimes she rode Tiny, sometimes they both walked, but Johnny always protected both her and the horse, by staying in front and deflecting the rattlers. He tromped over the rocks and through the bushes, generally singing some barroom ditty. He said he sang to warn the snakes, but the dangerous beasts seemed not to have ears. They coiled and buzzed and sometimes lashed out and dropped out of the trees at astonishing moments. They never got Johnny, though they'd come close. By the end of the third day of hiking, every lizard, every turn of a leaf, every snake of uncertain nature left her nerves on edge and her heart aflutter, and every true rattler encounter drove home the point that she did not want to lose Johnny Christmas. And by the end of three days she realized she loved him.

She hadn't planned it. She didn't want it. She didn't even like to admit it. She thought herself foolish, and silly. But love, she knew, wasn't something you planned. Besides, of all her virtues, and she had many, her sense of adventure had gotten her furthest. While she thought of herself as quite proper in some ways, a truly staid woman didn't fight her wealthy husband in court, go on to become the state's third woman lawyer, outwit a lynch mob, or take off with a man accused of being a rapist.

There being no more pine bough shelters, they slept fully clothed. That day, they'd come out of the narrow inner canyon. When the riverbed had widened out, they'd dropped so far in elevation, the vegetation had changed. They slept under the stars, snuggled together under the quilt, with the river rushing beside them and the fear of snakes having somewhat abated, as they'd passed out of the hottest part of the canyon and into a more hospitable climate.

She thought about all those events on the third night. "Johnny," she whispered.

"Yeah?"

"They didn't follow us, did they?"

"Naw."

"But they could be waiting down in Hetch Hetchy?"

"Yeah."

"And anyplace after that?"

He rested the back of his hand on his forehead. "Yeah."

She sucked in a deep breath. He'd been right about one subject at least: She didn't know the first thing about him. So his offer had played in her mind for three days. "What would you do if I were pregnant?"

He made a small sound of grief in his throat. "Don't ask me that, Claire."

"I wanted a baby when I was married."

"Yeah?"

"More than anything else in the world."

He turned onto his side and rested one hand on her stomach. "Would you want one by me?"

"I don't think I'd mind one."

"Jesus Christ, Claire."

*   *   *

He turned over and looked at the stars, thinking about Claire Butler's comment.

"I mean it." She laid her hand on top of his. He could feel its softness. His was much harder, calloused from his years of firefighting. "I had a tough time in San Francisco, and not just with the law practice. You don't know what it feels like, having everyone whisper. 'Oh, she's the new lady lawyer.' The judges look down and ask for your license. 'You're so pretty, my dear, for this occupation. Shouldn't you have gone into teaching?' I blamed it on Chauncey. People sided with him because he was wealthy, and because of the false charge of adultery. But I don't think it mattered. I had the same problem in Bodie. Nobody wants a lady lawyer, either in marriage or as an attorney."

She was pretty. He had to admit he'd wondered himself: Why hadn't she just found a second husband? "Don't be foolish. You'll be a great lawyer."

"Oh, I agree—I'm my father's daughter. But I'm also a woman. What's going to happen when I conquer a man's world? Do you think there will be a husband for me?"

"Of course someone will want you. How silly."

She trembled and laced her fingers in his. "Don't make me beg, Johnny. I lied when I first said I loved you. But I'm not lying now. You're very special to me. And I could take care of a baby, no matter what happens. It won't be easy, but I know I can do it. I'll do my best to get you out of this pickle. If somehow I don't, I'd like a child to remember you by."

*   *   *

She wanted a baby. He thought about that as the sun rose. She was either a fiend or a genius. Of all the appeals she could have made, she'd voiced the one that had the power to move him most deeply. It had been a shadowed fact of his illness: He never wanted to father a baby and leave a wife with no husband to help her. It had been the reason he'd courted Louisa: He'd come to believe he'd conquered his illness. The thought had haunted his manhood: If he were to die, who'd know the difference? His mother, his sisters, perhaps the good people of Bodie. He'd probably be a small local legend whose star would dim as the town got tamer.

He threw one arm out from under the quilt. Now fate had brought him Claire Butler. She could succeed, he was sure, at whatever she wanted, including raising a child without him. Though it mystified him why she'd want to have his child, he found it a moving, seductive idea. If he survived, perhaps she'd come to Tahiti. And if the posse caught him and hanged him, he'd leave behind a child with a competent mother to raise him.

She wanted a baby. The sunshine poured between the cedar leaves. Its pungent scent sweetened the air. He couldn't fathom her reasons for having self-doubts. Perhaps there was some odd feminine logic that made her believe men wouldn't want her. He thought she was wrong and made stupid assumptions about what a man would want in a wife. He, for one, could get used to her status. It didn't make a man less of a man just because a woman accomplished something.

He turned over and felt the warmth of her body. The morning was already lovely, just as hot as it had been in the canyon, but cleaner and brighter and less oppressive. She slept in her shirt and thin pantalets, her wispy hair tangled and matted.

She wanted a baby. He nuzzled at the nape of her neck, held himself rigid, and whispered her name.

She snuggled backward. He stroked her shoulder, a tender gesture. He'd never made love to a respectable woman. The notion aroused him far more profoundly than any night of wild carousing ever had. "Are you sure you want this?" he asked.

She nodded. He nuzzled her earlobe. She smelled of nighttime and quilt and rumpled cotton, though she washed her shirt out every morning and let it dry as she hiked. He reached around and undid her buttons. "You're not lying, are you?"

He kissed the curve of her neck. A short breath caught in the back of her throat. "Why would I lie?"

"I don't know. I can't figure women. You told me you lied when you said you loved me. And Louisa lied when she said I raped her."

"I'm not like Louisa."

"I know."

He rolled over quickly and kissed her full on the mouth. He did not want to think anymore. He'd thought hard about this while they were hiking and all through the night while she was sleeping. He couldn't hate women because of Louisa. If fate had sent him Claire Butler, he'd chance whatever the future would bring. He'd been dreaming about her since that first day in Bodie. Maybe he'd dreamt about her far longer. She seemed like a dream as he kissed her. He'd just have to hope she knew what she wanted when she asserted she wanted a baby.

He drew away slightly. "If anything happens to me, I have a sister in San Francisco." Claire's lips were wet, and her eyes were glassy. "And a mother who lives in New York's Hudson Valley." She tried to kiss him, but he held back a moment. His body was ready, and he was more than excited, but his conscience niggled. "They'll help you. They'll drive you crazy, but they're both darlings. They'll give you whatever you need."

She nodded. She seemed wide-eyed, almost frightened. Johnny wondered again about her marriage. How could Lyman not have been attracted? If he had her with him, he'd plunder her daily. Any man who wouldn't would pretty much have to be crazy, he figured. He kissed her again, his passion building. He'd never had a respectable woman, and she'd never had a man who adored her. She might not remember him from before, but he'd been a boy in those wild days in Bodie. Now he had something he could give her. A love she'd remember forever.

Hetch Hetchy came into view that evening. Claire sucked in her breath when she saw it. Though she'd seen the valley's more famous cousin, that experience had not prepared her for this related wonder. Vast gray walls soared above the river, punctuated by two slender falls. The ribbons of white gave scale and movement to a landscape that might otherwise have been grave and forbidding. There were far fewer people in this remote valley than there had been in its more renowned neighbor. She wished they could stop and swim in the river, make love again, and try to make babies. The wide, flat valley seemed like a perfect refuge after the trials of the hot granite canyon.

Johnny walked before her, leading Tiny. She studied his shoulders. She'd never been much affected by masculine beauty, but there was something about that muscular chest, his swaggering posture, his sheer male bravado that moved her. He'd been happy today, supremely happy. They'd made passionate love in the morning. Though he'd always seemed carefree, this morning he'd seemed especially cheerful. Sometimes he'd watched for the posse, but mostly he'd seemed as if he'd escaped all his worries. He'd whistled and sang. Every once in a while, he'd kissed her. She'd tried to get him to be quiet, but he'd seemed so relieved to be out of the canyon, with most of the rattlers safely behind him, that she couldn't bring herself to restrict him. So she'd walked behind him most of the day, until they'd come to this spot this evening, with its beautiful view of the Hetch Hetchy Valley.

"Don't you think it's lovely?" she asked.

"Absolutely." He gazed out at the wide peaceful canyon. He looked wonderful after five days of camping. His skin had turned brown, his expression had softened, and he'd grown a short beard, a bit more golden than his fawn-colored hair. "Though I hear they've got better in the South Sea Islands."

"You think so?" She followed his gaze. "It's hard to imagine. The Garden of Eden must have looked something like this."

He squeezed her fingertips gently. A warm flush spread through her. "I've heard Tahiti's real pretty."

She wished he would caress her face. She liked standing above this valley with Johnny. Right at this moment their worries seemed distant, and she could imagine living in Bodie with him, a baby, and a little law practice. "I've never been outside California."

"No?" He sounded surprised.

"No. I'm that rare creature—a native of this wonderful state."

They'd reached a clearing where the trees thinned out. Johnny dropped Tiny's reins and kissed Claire's cheek. "Wait here a minute."

He reached up and grabbed the branch of an oak tree. Before Claire could question what he was doing, he hefted himself onto its lowest bough.

"My goodness." She watched Johnny, who was far more agile than she would have expected, climb higher and higher, until she lost sight of him among the scalloped leaves. "What are you doing?"

"Just looking."

Claire's heart constricted. She didn't think the posse had followed, but they could have used logic and doubled back. There were several routes to San Francisco. She and Johnny had taken the riskiest route, but it had been the most sensible choice from at least one perspective: It was the most direct route to San Francisco. If Flowers had been clever, he might have deduced their intentions and waited for them in this valley. "What do you see?"

"It looks pretty peaceful." The leaves rustled as he clambered up higher.

Claire's heartbeat doubled. She touched the chain on her neck. "Be careful."

He chuckled. The high tree branch echoed the sound. Half a dozen acorns spattered around her, thumping fuzzily as they hit the soft ground. Claire listened. She could no longer see him, so she looked out into the valley, which she could see fairly clearly.

"I don't see any sign of the posse," he said.

Claire's breath escaped her. "Do you think you could at this distance?"

"I think I'd see signs. I can make out quite a few buildings. There's no dust or movement, no signs of horses."

Claire wiped her hands on the miner's pants. They were grubby, but she'd grown to like them. They'd served her well in the past few days. As Johnny watched from the tree, she relaxed a little. Perhaps they'd make it, she mused. Once they got out of the foothills, they could ride like hell for San Francisco. In the wide, flat, hot central valley, very little would impede their progress. They could travel at night. They wouldn't have to follow the roads.

A few more acorns fell around Claire. One bounced on the toe of her boot.

"Now watch it!" She jumped aside and glared up at him. He smiled, a grin of pure boyish wonder. Claire's heart tightened within her bosom.

He leaned on a low branch and gazed down. "Do you like being with me?"

"Could be." She poked her nose in the air.

Johnny lowered himself and dropped down, landing next to the Clydesdale. Briefly Claire patted the horse's withers. She couldn't believe they'd gotten him through. After the rattlers, finding a route for the giant horse had been the hardest part of their journey. But Johnny had been incredibly patient, leading his animal over hot boulders, doubling back, or hiking up canyons, always seeking a way to save him. And now Claire was glad. Tiny had been worth the trouble, for he could carry them both with considerable ease. For the first time since they'd gone on the run, she began to believe they'd make San Francisco.

Johnny picked up the reins and followed the trail, though it was only a vague path where something or other, perhaps not even human, had traveled. He seemed less elated as they picked their way downward, no longer quite so boyish and joyful, but placid and quiet, as if the thought of success had sobered him.

When they came to a flat stretch, he waited a minute, walking next to her when she caught up and joined him. "You like this country, don't you?" he asked.

"Yes." She looked around at the trees, the golden sunlight. This was all of nature she'd ever known, the benign beauty of the Sierras.

"You've never traveled?" he asked.

"Not outside California. I've rambled all over these mountains. And I know San Francisco. But Chauncey didn't like leaving the city." Claire's heartbeat picked up a little. She could hear one of the falls. Though they'd traveled past dozens in the past few days, she never got tired of their beauty. "How about you?"

"When I first came West, I traveled all over. I've spent the last eight years in Bodie, though I like to visit the city, and I do it every chance I get."

She paused a moment and considered his comments. This was the first information he'd volunteered freely to her. "Do you visit your sister?"

"Yeah. She has kids, you know."

"Yes?"

"Cute little buggers."

They walked together in companionable silence. She thought Johnny would make a lovable father. He might be too irresponsible to be a good husband, but children would love his wry sense of humor, his physical courage, and his joy in living. She didn't find it hard to imagine him tickling a baby or bouncing a toddler or engaging in silly wrestling matches.

"So you like children?"

"Yeah."

He answered so quickly, her heart broke. "I'll get you off, Johnny. I know I can do it. Daddy always said I'd make a good lawyer."

He took her hand in his. "And what if you're pregnant?"

Briefly she considered his question. "There are no rules against pregnant lawyers." She wondered what a jury would think, and whether it would be good for a baby, spending its unborn days in such conflict. "Though I suppose it would be a bit of a scandal."

He chuckled.

"You think that's funny?"

"No. I think that's gutsy." He gazed down, his green eyes full of pride and bemusement. "And after?

What happens if you manage to free me?''

Her breath caught in her throat. She looked down at her dusty boots. ''I don't know.'' He'd asked a good question. What if she saved him? A tight lump formed in her stomach. ''My plans don't stretch quite that far.''

Chapter Twelve

❦❦❦

For once in his life, Johnny had plans. They included Tahiti. They included Claire. They didn't include how to tell her about them, so he decided to speak to her about it as soon as they left sight of the Hetch Hetchy Valley. They'd bedded down for the night in a haystack. In the foothills, the weather was warmer, so warm in fact, that they slept on top of the quilt. They made love again, and when they were finished, Johnny tucked Claire's head under his shoulder. He didn't quite know how to start. The day had been lovely. They'd not seen the posse. They'd ridden together on Tiny and talked.

Claire mainly told Johnny about her marriage. To his surprise and chagrin, she didn't blame Chauncey for his adulteries. She saw herself as an inadequate woman, unable to hold her husband's attention. She also talked about babies, and this surprised Johnny even more. Claire hungered for children. She hated that about her first marriage, that there'd been no conception, but she'd never considered remarriage, choosing instead her career as a lawyer. It made Johnny's heart ache as he listened. Claire had always been a bit of a tomboy, and her faith in her womanly charms had been completely shattered by her husband's rejection.

Which seemed to be one of the reasons why she was attracted to Johnny. She liked his lust for her, pure and simple. For his part, he found the freedom with which she rejected convention endearing. She wasn't a whore, he saw that quite clearly, but she wasn't much like Louisa either.

"Don't you wish we could stay like this forever?" He breathed in the straw-scented air. Her soft cotton shirt brushed the skin of his chest, and he could feel her still-hard nipple beneath it. The sky was black and silky above them. Far in the distance, a farmer's light twinkled, reminding him that civilization was only a few days' ride away. "The two of us and Mother Nature."

She smiled, snuggling closer. "We'd better slow down, or there won't be just the two of us."

"True. You know . . ." There was a faint glow in the air. Claire's hair charged with sparks as he stroked it. "If you turn up pregnant, I'll have to do a lot of explaining."

"I thought about that." She sat up, her eyes shining. "It might be very effective with jurors. . . ."

"Jesus Christ, Claire. The things you think of."

"I'm not saying it's why I'd get pregnant." She waved his objection away. "But it is a new angle I hadn't thought of. If the jury could see how much I loved you, they'd never believe you'd . . . you know . . ."

"Rape Louisa?"

"Yes."

"Come on, Claire, say the word plainly. They'll never believe I'm a rapist."

"Rapist," she repeated disconsolately.

He sat up and drew her into his arms. Coyotes yapped in the distance, a hungry, querulous chorus. The sound might have been eerie but for the crickets. They chirped with verve and persistence, a steady beat that kept the night cheerful. "Don't be a fool, Claire. If you show up pregnant, everyone will believe I forced you."

"Well, you didn't."

"I know that."

"And I'd never accuse you, no matter what happened."

"I know that, too." He cast about for his pants. He thought he should wear them in spite of the heat. It would be bad enough to get caught with Claire Butler, worse to get caught naked with Claire Butler. "But don't you see how hopeless this is? Even if you get me acquitted; for the rest of my life people will whisper: There's the man who raped Louisa Cantrall."

"So what are you saying?"

He pulled on his trousers. "Come with me to Tahiti."

"What?"

"I know you'll love it." He thought for a moment about giving her an elaborate description of all the reasons she should come with him. On second thought, he discarded that notion. If she didn't respond to a direct request, he doubted she'd be swayed by sweet talking. "It's pretty and natural. The kind of place you'd adore."

She stood, glared at him and then Tiny, paced in a little circle, and stopped. "You don't think I can save you?"

"I didn't say that."

She propped her hands on her hips, a parody of a fishwife, except that she was standing there half naked, her creamy thighs pale in the moonlight. "You think I'm a weak-minded female."

"Claire."

"Overemotional."

"Claire."

"Overinvolved."

"Now look—"

"Not able to think in a logical fashion."

"Okay." He pulled the derringer out and checked its lone bullet. "I do think you're a bit too excited. I'm just asking you to come to Tahiti."

"Before the trial?"

"Yeah . . ." he could argue with her, but that seemed pointless. "Yes, of course . . ."

"And never come back?"

"I don't know about 'never'. . . ." Her resistance probably made sense, he knew. He also knew it would take a strong man to marry a woman with three years' training in verbal combat. "twenty years ought to do it."

"You know," she said, her voice breaking, "that's the trouble with vigilantes: They're never around when you need them."

She'd know all the fine points of debate. "What

are you getting all huffy about?''

"Did you ever intend to turn yourself in?"

The technical side of the marital contract. "Of course not."

"How could you? How can you? If you don't turn yourself in, I'll lose my license for abetting a felon."

"You did not break the law. Remember, you're kidnapped." One hundred and three ways you never heard of to land your backside in jail. "You didn't know what I intended."

"I do now."

"And?"

"And you better be gone in the morning."

He supposed she didn't mean it, but she'd certainly gone from lovely to angry. "Or else?"

"I don't know or else, but I'm very clever." The charge in the air made her hair wispy. An occasional spark flew off as she talked. "Believe me, I'll figure it out."

He was gone in the morning. Claire regretted her temper, for he'd left Tiny, a fact that made her want to cry. A sob rose in her throat. She rolled up the quilt and sat it next to the saddle. Maybe she had gotten pregnant—she'd heard women got weepy. Or maybe she was just due for her monthly. It was an annoying and regrettable fact, but she got stupid when that event happened.

"Dumb," she said to Tiny, who was chewing contentedly from the haystack. "He's left everything with me." She plopped the scratchy covering next to the saddle. "Doesn't he remember which one of us is the outlaw? I can just walk up to a farmhouse for help.''

She pulled on her pants, tucked the derringer in the waistband, then saddled the Clydesdale, a considerable effort, as all his equipment was far larger than normal. Luckily Tiny was gentle. He waited patiently through the whole operation, then scarcely moved as she took a bounding leap for his back.

Once on, she gathered the reins and clicked the horse forward, sick at heart as she did. She wanted Johnny back. All his criticism had been correct. She felt stupid, irrational, weak-minded, and female. When Johnny had made his proposal, she'd been so shocked and frightened. Maybe she didn't want to go to Tahiti, but she certainly hadn't wanted him to leave. He was important to her. Maybe more important than her law license. Maybe more important even than babies, though his desire for children might be part of the reason she loved him.

But she had a deeper feeling about him. She liked his wildness. His sense of adventure was something they had in common. Because she'd grown up in these mountains, she had no respect for men in the city. Johnny'd survived eight years in Bodie, an impressive feat, and not one even her father had managed. And why she wanted to find him.

She urged Tiny forward, wishing she had more skill at tracking. Much as she enjoyed camping and fishing, she'd never liked hunting, and of course she'd never tracked down a human. She knew something about trailing fugitives, though. She'd listened to her father often enough. Outlaws were often caught by means of sheer logic. A clever lawman sized up his quarry and thought through the moves he would make.

Claire stared absently at the flattened grass that showed the direction Johnny had taken. Already the trail told a story. Johnny'd charged off in a fit of bravado, leaving behind all the provisions, the guns, the horse, the bread, beans and jerky, which meant— she smiled as she urged Tiny forward—she had only to figure where out there in those golden hillsides a horseless, unarmed, and hungry outlaw would figure he could come up with breakfast.

He missed her already. He missed her as he tromped through the brush in the cool gray morning before the sun rose. The fine high grasses whipped at his pants legs as he strode over the low hillsides that characterized the Sierra foothills. They didn't slow his progress, however. He liked the sensation of forward movement, and felt, here in the cool with a stomach that ought to feel empty but didn't, that he could walk all the way to San Francisco and not let anything stop him.

He knew this was not true, of course; still the illusion buoyed him and kept him cheerful, in spite of the ache deep in his chest. That was the damnable thing about women: They clung, even when they didn't mean to. He'd never stopped missing his mother. Hattie's ghost had stayed with him also, and Claire, he supposed, would haunt him forever. He'd thought about her for many years, even following her life through the newspapers. Now that she was gone, he'd have infinite questions about her. Had she had his baby? How would she raise it? How had she worked out as a lawyer? Was she right that no man would have her? What if she found a second husband? Could one man love another man's baby? And could anyone, no matter how high his status, really love Claire the way he did?

He missed her as he slogged down a streambed while the rising sun turned the world rosy. Why couldn't she just come to Tahiti? They must have some need for lawyers, to draw up deeds for banana plantations, or whatever they had on the South Sea Islands. Maybe they even had fire departments. In that respect Claire would be different from his mother. She wouldn't care if he risked his life, as long as she thought the cause was worthy.

He missed her as he crept toward a farmhouse in the distance, hungry for breakfast and ashamed of himself. He missed her as he crouched down and watched the henhouse. He could hear the mutter and cluck of the chickens as the farm wife collected their bounty. So much for eggs, the simpler theft. He thought he could get one of the birds, though. Johnny sat down in a small thicket to the side of a nearly dry stream. Except for his hunger, there was no hurry. Out here in the foothills, there was too much ground to be covered for the posse to easily find him. He peered out from behind the red branches of a small manzanita and planned. He could wait until the farmer went out, until the wife was occupied with her chores . . .

Which was what Johnny was doing two hours later when Claire showed up on Tiny. He didn't see her at first. She was following his tracks down the streambed, but he figured she'd spot him sooner or later, persistence being one of her virtues, so he stood up and watched her. She looked tiny on Tiny, a little blond slip of a girl. But she didn't look female in her miner's outfit. Rather, she looked like an overgrown schoolboy mounted on his father's workhorse. She reached him, looking sheepish, in a few minutes.

He kissed her as soon as she slipped down off the horse. A violent longing rose up as he did. He'd missed this more than anything else—her warmth and softness, the way she held him, fitting herself tightly to him.

He broke off the kiss. "Are you angry?" she asked.

"Naw." He held her close. He was glad to see Tiny and wanted to pat him, but she felt so perfect slotted to him that he just stood there, still concealed by the bushes, allowing his heart to slow down. "Embarrassed maybe. It doesn't say much for my skill as an outlaw that I can be tracked down by a woman."

Her hands were trembling. That fact surprised him. And pleased him. And made him want to stay with her forever.

"Well, I'm special," she whispered. "I know your habits."

"True."

He turned and patted Tiny's massive brown withers, glad to see the giant horse. He hated parting. He didn't know why exactly, but it was a leftover childhood habit, the last of his deep-seated terrors. It made him perversely and desperately loyal, to horses, to dogs, even to whores. He took Tiny's reins and walked down the arroyo, a sandy streambed that was mostly dry in late summer. He laced his fingers tightly in Claire's, glad for her presence, glad she had found him, but uncertain of what he should say. Tiny clopped behind them, creating a soft fall of hoofbeats. But Claire's cheeks were flushed, and her posture was self-conscious. He wanted to hold her, to touch her, to kiss her, to lay her down in the sand and take her. He also wanted to shake her, to kick her, to slap some sense into her head. He did none of these things. He simply kept walking.

The sun had gotten perceptibly higher, and his stomach noticeably hollower, before she lifted her chin and broke the silence. "Johnny, I'm sorry. I didn't mean to send you away."

He squeezed her fingertips briefly. "Don't worry about it."

"Well, I have to." She used her white cotton sleeve to wipe off her forehead. "You must think I'm horrid."

"Naw."

She ducked her head down. He couldn't tell what she was thinking, but he could tell she was struggling. Her blue eyes clouded over; a tiny frown tugged at her mouth. He let her tussle a little.

"I'm not good at planning," he said quietly.

"Johnny—"

"Let me finish. I'm not good at planning, but I can see this far at least: You're too much your father's daughter to spend your life outside the law."

They'd reached a small stand of oak, maybe two miles from the farmhouse. Johnny led Tiny to the shade and stopped. "Would you like to have breakfast?" he asked.

She nodded. He pulled the bread and jerked meat out of the saddlebags, handed them to her, then led Tiny to the small stream. As the horse drank, Johnny waited. The ache in his groin had faded away, replaced by the more subtle yearning that seemed so much a part of him in her presence. When the massive brown animal had drunk his fill, Johnny returned to Claire, who'd taken refuge in the shade of a handsome blue oak. Heat shimmered over the rolling, gold hills. Rock formations stuck up here and there. Parched slopes thirsted beneath the hot sun, but this didn't discourage life in the oasis. The little water hole brimmed with small creatures. Tan quail huddled beneath the bushes. Lizards sunned on rocks, and lines of red ants marched up the tree trunk. A black magpie perched on a rock.

Johnny checked for rattlers before he sat down. "I killed him."

"Who?"

"Your father." He could hear the sharp intake of her breath. He wanted to hold her, but thought he shouldn't. He might never hold her again in his life, but he needed to do this. He could outrun death. He could outrun the posse. He could even run away from Alice Van Kessel. But he'd never, even if he lived to eighty, outrun his love for Claire Butler. And so he needed to tell her the truth, now. "I didn't do it on purpose." The words tumbled out. "I hope to God you believe me." His heart was thumping so hard it hurt. She could kill him for this, and not only by her own hand—she could have him prosecuted for murder. She could certainly leave him, and he wouldn't blame her. "I wouldn't have hurt you for the world."

She sat there, wide-eyed, the piece of broken French bread in her lap. He noticed her breathing, deep and uneven, as if she were drowning or hurting, or both. He tried to touch her, but she drew back. "Why are you saying this cruel thing to me?"

"Because it's the truth." He touched the silver chain on her neck. "That's my bullet you're wearing. It's the reason I wanted to go to Tahiti."

Her hand shot up to her neck. He thought she might say something to him, but she simply sat there wide-eyed and silent.

He drew in a deep breath and continued. "The Colt had a match. That gun killed your father. I didn't quite know how it happened. There were three of us shooting—"

"Shooting at what?"

"At nothing. At ghosts. At whatever boys shoot at." He stood up and strode over to Tiny. "We were carousing. It got out of hand." Johnny checked the horse's cinch, then his leg feathers. "We tried to save him. You have to believe me. None of us meant to hurt anyone." He removed a burr from one of Tiny's hooves, studiously avoiding looking at her. How did you tell the woman you love you'd killed her father and kept it a secret? "But he died anyway, there in the snow, coughing the blood out." He set down the hoof and turned to face her. There were tears in her eyes, tears on her eyelashes. His own eyes burned in their sockets. "We thought no one would believe us.

We buried the guns and took vows of silence.''

She stared for a moment at the black magpie, his wings drooping, his bill wide open. Quietly she took the chain from her neck. She didn't look at the gleam in her palm, simply clutched the silver bullet, her knuckles becoming white with the pressure. ''And somebody found the match to the Colt and used it in the rape of Louisa?''

He nodded. She'd always been smart. She'd have brilliant children. He didn't think he deserved her, and he didn't know why he was taking the risk of telling her this. He had nothing to offer. No status. No honor. No way to prove he wasn't a rapist. He knew in his heart it was sheer male bravado that made him believe that a woman so golden, with such pretty blue eyes and such heartbreaking beauty, could not only love him, but believe him, forgive him, and accept the fact that he'd killed her father.

''Do you believe me?'' he asked

She stared down at the bullet. ''Why didn't you tell me? Finding the Colt might get you acquitted.''

He rolled the bread between his fingers, wondering how he should answer. She now held his life in her hands. He hated this weakness, this desperate position. He had no way to prove himself to her. Having made up his mind, though, he refused to turn back. He'd win Claire Butler, or he'd die trying. ''I loved you from the very beginning. I hated the idea of having you hate me.''

She touched his sleeve of red flannel. ''You'd have gone to your grave condemned as a rapist rather than tell me you'd killed my father?''

"No, but I'd have gone to Tahiti."

He thought he saw her mouth lift a little, and then her shoulders sagged downward. She stared at the bullet, at him, at the drooping black magpie. She stood up, looking dazed, and scraped against a tree branch. The quail scattered with a soft whir. She waved Johnny away when he tried to help her. Her hands were shaking, and he thought she was crying, but then he saw she wasn't. She simply stepped back, shuddered, and rubbed the pinkened spot on her forehead. He guided her to a rock and sat her down gently.

"Did he suffer?" she whispered.

"A little, though not badly by the standards of dying. He was shot in the chest. His lungs filled up with liquid. That hurts, as I can attest. But the end came pretty quickly." He thrust the crust of the bread into his pocket, then pushed back a lock of her hair. "I held him, Claire, so he wouldn't be frightened."

"I don't suppose you expect me to thank you?"

"I expect you to shoot me."

She pulled the derringer out of her waistband. "Now there's a thought."

He stepped back and faced her. She had only one bullet, but he wasn't sure she wouldn't try to use it. His chest had constricted so tightly that it felt like the old days, the bad days of childhood, when demons and fiends had twisted those muscles in a desperate effort to make his lungs work. She held the gun in one hand and the bullet in the other, seemingly weighing her choices. Trying to appear casual, he pulled the bread out of his pocket, but it was far too mangled for eating.

Avoiding her gaze, Johnny watched one of the lizards, a perky fellow, who darted about stopping sometimes to do little push-ups. It didn't help the ache in his chest, or make him want to hold Claire Butler less, but it did keep him from screaming or weeping. The worst of it was, she didn't cry, she didn't look angry, or puzzled, or hurt; she simply stared at the small silver bullet, as if she were seeing it for the first time.

Sweat trickled down the side of his forehead. He'd almost rather she had a tantrum than this dull expression of sickness and grief. The quail settled back into the bushes. The lizard twitched, and the ants kept marching. The magpie seemed bored.

At the end of this long eerie silence, Claire slipped the silvery chain back over her head. "Come on, Johnny," she wiped her hand on her pants. "I'm not really hungry, but I feel like walking. Maybe we can get to San Francisco that way."

"Do you hate me?" Johnny asked Claire.

They were walking Tiny through an arroyo that kept them hidden in the hot foothills. Claire tried hard not to look at the burly firefighter whom only an hour ago she'd considered her lover.

"I don't know, Johnny."

He'd unbuttoned his shirt, the heavy wool flannel being far too hot for this elevation. An expanse of flat muscle peeked out from beneath it. The sight made Claire weary and weepy and crabby. She wanted to rest her head on his chest, and she damned well knew she couldn't. Finally, after all these years, she'd met the villain, the bastard who'd murdered her father, and he turned out to be her lover and—she shuddered now to think of the possibility—maybe even the father of her baby. "I don't know what to say. Why couldn't you have just left it a secret?"

"Because I love you, and it didn't seem moral to keep it a secret when you were falling in love with me."

"So, what do you want me to say? 'Oh, gee, it doesn't matter, I forgive you for killing my father.' "

"It was an accident, Claire."

"Oh, Johnny. How could you?"

"I told you before. I was full of the devil. I didn't give a damn about dying. I'd spent my whole life in a dance with that demon. Ah, Claire, I wish you'd believe me. We didn't mean to hurt anyone."

An accident. She wanted to weep, to scream, to rage and to kill him. Judge Randolph Butler, her father, one of the state's most prominent lawyers, had been killed for a lark by carousing boys. The news came as a shock, though she hadn't actually thought much different. Claire had known her father had died by a bullet, and probably not in a conventional gun battle, but other than fragments and irrelevant details, she'd had no real knowledge of what had happened. Her ignorance hadn't haunted her really. She'd spent several summers in Bodie and knew that death could be randomly meted out in the wild mining camp, over the stupidest of reasons—the twitch of a gun hand, a drunken remark. Still, it came as a blow, the actual knowledge, especially on top of the fact that Johnny had pulled the trigger. Johnny, who'd held her; who'd seduced her; who'd asked her to defend him. Johnny, the one man she'd loved besides her father.

"What were you thinking?" she asked.

"Nothing, I told you."

"No, I don't mean when you killed him, but when . . ." She let her voice trail off. How could she express this? She could scarcely frame the idea to herself. "We could have created a baby together."

He didn't answer, simply kept walking, leading the giant, gentle-faced horse. He'd been right that day by the waterfall. She'd fallen in love with a total stranger.

"How many men have you killed all together?"

"Two. Your father and one before that in Montana."

She lifted one eyebrow and frowned. "You're not even much of an outlaw, are you?"

"No, not really," he answered calmly. "After I killed your father, I hung up my guns and let people's assumptions protect me."

She fell back into a sulk. The ground was dusty, and the day had gotten hot. From the shade of a tree, these hills could be pretty, but in the bright midday light they seemed only barren. "Did you ever make money by stealing?"

"Never stole a cent in my life."

"Then where does it come from? The money."

"My mother."

The answer surprised her. He'd spoken about her

as a distant figure, someone from his childhood, his past. "Your mother?"

"My mother has money." He kept his face averted, his eyes to the ground. He had a strong profile, square-jawed, though not brutal, and he seemed less boyish when viewed from this angle. "She's a grande dame of social New York, monied for four generations at least."

This answer surprised her more than the other. She'd had experience with people from a wide range of social strata, from the humblest of Digger Indians to the socialite friends she'd had in San Francisco. She never judged people by status, but she had a certain astuteness about it. Johnny had always seemed like a dispossessed farmboy, a type often found in the West. He had none of a wealthy man's affectations. Except for his sheer physical beauty, he'd never struck her as being privileged. "You don't seem like you come from money."

"In some senses I don't. You might as well know: I only know a little readin', writin', and cipherin'."

"You're joking?"

"Nope. Too sick for schooling. My family never expected anything from me, excepting, of course, that I'd die. I surprised them all by surviving. Not that mother wasn't delighted. She never begrudged me my grown-up boyhood. Those—" he gestured back toward the Sierras, a line of blue hills in the distance—"are the childhood she couldn't give me."

She saw in his expression not self-pity, but stubborn pride, the look of a man who'd defeated his demons and didn't care to dwell on his past. "Your lungs don't bother you anymore?''

"Not in five years at least. They got gradually well in the West. I don't know if it was the mountains, or the fact of my freedom, or if I simply outgrew my illness, but my lungs got stronger over the years. I can swallow smoke. I can ride up these mountains, or walk in the dust''—he scuffed up a small cloud and breathed it—''and just inhale it. I can't tell you what that means to me. When I was a boy we had a long hallway. I used to sit in the middle and cry with frustration. I couldn't walk from one end to the other.''

She glanced down at his bulging thigh muscles. "It's hard to imagine."

"Asthma's rather a nice illness that way. I looked pretty normal. And in the summer I built up my body, trying to make up to my father for the fact that I was born such a weakling."

Some of the anger had seeped out of her now. It wasn't that she felt sorry for Johnny. He didn't seem to want pity, and she didn't feel it. It was simply that anger seemed pointless. Her father had died for a foolish boy's wildness. A wonderful life had ended suddenly and violently, but he had died in a way he would have wanted, up in the mountains next to the sky. He might have been a prominent jurist, but he loved the risks of mining camp life, and never backed down from its dangers. She strongly suspected he'd have liked Johnny Christmas, a reckless boy who immediately regretted his folly. "Is that why you wanted to go to Tahiti? You think if you divulge your alibi, you'll get the death sentence for my father's murder?"

"Pretty much. Yeah. That and fear of your hatred."

They plodded through a narrow arroyo, the sun baking the landscape. She knew they'd make better time if they rode on Tiny, but she didn't want to suggest it. The intimacy of it repelled her: sitting so close to her father's killer. She pushed that thought aside and tried to work through the problem with logic. She was still his lawyer. She would have to advise him. "I can see how you'd fear that, but really, I don't think it would hurt to be honest. There's no statute of limitations on murder, but there is on manslaughter. If your friends will stand by your version of what happened, you'll probably never be charged with the killing, and you could cast doubt on the rape charges."

He readjusted his hat and tightened his grip on the reins. "I'm not turning my friends in."

"Johnny—"

"No dice on that. We keep their names secret, or we go to Tahiti. I'm not getting anyone else in trouble."

She resisted an impulse to touch his sleeve. He was so stubborn in certain ways. If he didn't exactly have high social status, he certainly had a strong sense of morals. "It would help you a lot if they'd testify."

"It might. Then again, it might just get them convicted for murder. Can you promise different?"

"No lawyer can guarantee winning." A hot wind picked up the dust. She could already feel her lips cracking. "He—or she, as the case may be—can only promise to do a good job."

"Does that mean you will defend me?"

"I didn't say that."

"So what are you saying?"

She ran her tongue over her mouth. She missed San Francisco. Camping was fun in the Sierras, but here in the hot central valley, she mainly longed for a bath. "I'm saying I believe you're not guilty. And if I can believe you, why not a jury?"

He studied her from beneath his long lashes as he plodded forward in the dry heat. She expected a question, but he didn't ask it. He watched the horizon, glanced at the ground, slowed down a little, and fiddled with Tiny. "What makes you believe me?" he asked finally.

She shrugged. "You have no motive. No one hated my father, not even the bad men he sentenced. He stood for something in Bodie. In the whole mining district. Justice and honor. No one would have killed him on purpose."

He smiled slightly. "You thought a lot of Judge Butler."

"I thought the world of my father."

He stopped, glancing again at the horizon. "Then let me ask you this—would he have wanted you to defend me?"

"That's not a fair question."

"Why not?"

"Because it just isn't."

He stared at the bullet, a heavy weight over her heart. "I stand by it."

"Johnny, that's low." The heat seared her lungs. She felt sweaty and grimy, almost dizzy with panic. "That's a rotten tactic."

He lifted her chin, as if to kiss her. "So let's just say I learned from an expert."

She'd stopped breathing completely. She wanted to run, or to hit him. To cry, scream, or pray. She wanted her father. "I guess you did."

"So answer the question."

Hot tears sprang to her eyes. "You know the answer already. He'd say defend you. He'd have defended the devil if he thought it served the interest of justice."

Chapter
Thirteen

~~~~

They didn't make love that evening. Claire side-stepped that problem quite neatly by announcing she had her monthly in a tone so cold Johnny knew instinctively he couldn't touch her. Then, she threw herself down in the sand and wept. Johnny sat beside her, trying to stifle the pain in his chest, a sensation so raw and aching that for a moment he thought his childhood illness had seized him.

"Ah, Claire."

She was weeping profusely. He stroked her hair, so gold and pretty, and touched the faint pink scar on her forehead.

She brushed the gesture away with a wave. "It's all right, really." She sat up and wiped her eyes with her sleeve. "It's only natural." She stood up and walked shakily toward the massive brown Clydesdale. They stopped in another shallow arroyo whose sandy cliffs hid them from the surrounding country. Johnny studied her as she circled the horse. Fat droplets coursed down her cheeks, tears without sobs, thick, wet, and silent. Reaching Tiny, she made a swift movement, drying her tears on her shirtsleeve, then removed the quilt. Without glancing at Johnny, she returned to the edge of the arroyo and used her hands to dig out a shallow depression.

Johnny posted himself on the small cliff above her. He watched, frustrated and helpless, as she lay down in her clothes and turned her back to him. She looked so fragile. He wanted to hold her. He hadn't expected lovemaking and didn't know why she'd mentioned her monthly. She must think him a total bastard, he figured. Not that he didn't want her, of course. He was aching for her right at this moment, and felt like a scoundrel for wanting a woman as she wept for her father, especially considering who'd killed him.

He readjusted his sitting position, taking the Colt out and holding it lightly. She was still crying, he could tell by her shoulders. They weren't shaking, but every few seconds a little convulsion escaped her. Johnny wanted to join her. They could have hung him and he would have felt better than watching Claire Butler mourn for her father.

He balanced the barrel in the palm of his hand. He deserved to be punished. He'd cut short a man's life, though he hadn't meant to. He'd robbed a beautiful woman of her father's guidance and the mining district of one of its stalwarts. He would have voluntarily gone to the gallows to bring Judge Butler back, but he didn't have that power or option.

He slid his fingers over the gray metal. ''I suppose this means you won't defend me.''

''I didn't say that.''

"Claire . . ."

She scrabbled out of her little hollow and climbed up the cliff to join him. She sat down cross-legged and glanced at the gun. A tiny tremor ran through her. "I've been thinking about what you told me." She toyed with the silvery chain on her neck. "Do you still want me?"

"Of course." He touched her hand shyly, glanced at the horizon, and pushed the Colt back into his waistband. "But I can wait until you feel better."

"Oh." She bolted to her feet and paced to the cliff. "No. I didn't mean that."

"What do you mean then?"

"Do you still want me to be your lawyer?"

"Jesus Christ, Claire, how can you ask that when you're lying there crying your eyes out because I killed your father?"

"I'm not crying only because of my father."

He couldn't read her expression. The sun was setting behind the coastal mountains, and the glow of the sunlight washed out her features. "What then?"

She pushed a dirt clod around with her toe. "I'd rather not tell you. You'll think I'm silly."

"Try me."

"Well, for one thing, my monthly." She wiped her hands on her pants. "I thought you were special. I wanted your baby."

That came as a shock. He'd scarcely even expected forgiveness, much less that she'd still want his baby. "Well . . ." Now, he really felt awkward. He wouldn't have minded helping her out, but they had only two days until San Francisco. He'd grown up with three sisters, but the girls had their secrets, and no one he'd been with in Bodie had been trying to make babies. So the timing of the female cycle escaped him. "We could go to Tahiti."

"That's not what I meant."

"Oh."

"Johnny." A determined look came into her eyes. She touched the place on her shirt that covered the bullet. "You must know how things stand between us. And I wouldn't want to mislead you. I'm not sure I can even forgive you, much less . . . you know . . ." She gave an eloquent shrug, dismissing his hopes. "But if you want me, I'll still be your lawyer."

He was really confused. She wanted his baby, but not his lovemaking. She harbored a grudge toward him for his having killed her father, but still wanted to act as his lawyer. "Are you out of your mind?"

"No. I don't think so."

"Why would you want to defend me except—you know—except—maybe you have some feeling for me?"

"Because anything less would be failing my father."

He'd always thought lawyers had peculiar ethics, and knowing Claire Butler confirmed it. "But I killed him."

"I know."

"So, thank you."

"Don't thank me until I've succeeded. If you were smart you'd change lawyers. You don't know how much I hate you."

"I told you before: I'm not very smart."

"You were smart enough to seduce your own lawyer."

"Is that what you think?"

"I don't know what I think. I used to believe I was a sensible woman, but now I feel like a weak-minded..." She walked down into the arroyo, opened the bags, and fished out a notebook and pencil. "Technically, it's a conflict of interest, but I can still represent you if you give me permission."

"If you hate me so much, why should I want you to defend me?"

"Because I've got something to prove. And the least you can do after killing my father is be the means by which I prove it." She sat down cross-legged and started to write. "No one would be able to say I'm not a good lawyer if I could acquit the man who killed my father." She looked up from her work and gazed straight-faced at him. "What do you think?"

He glanced at the horizon. He was pretty sure they'd shaken the posse. Now Flowers would wait in San Francisco. "And why shouldn't I just go to Tahiti?"

"Because you said you loved me, and now you can prove that." Her voice was like a caress, soft and seductive.

"But you don't love me."

"So much the better." She ducked her head and toyed with her pen. "A lawyer's not supposed to have feelings. Like gunmen."

He plunged into the arroyo, grabbed her up by the shoulders, and shook her. "Goddamn it, Claire, I'm not a gunman and I want to know: Can you love me after what I've confessed?''

If she was rattled, she didn't show it. She stood her ground without protest, pen in hand. "I haven't the faintest, but I can defend you, and I'd like the chance."

"Do you think I raped Louisa Cantrall?"

"No, I don't think so."

"Then why can't you say it?"

"I will, if you let go."

Slowly he eased his grip. The sun had gone down, and the air had turned cooler. Her vivid blue eyes had darkened to violet. "I don't think you're a rapist."

"And you'll defend me no matter what happens?"

"No matter what happens."

"Beyond reason and logic. Better than anyone else."

"Better than anyone else."

"Because this is my life we're talking about."

"I know that, Johnny."

He wanted to kiss her. He wanted to take her, lay her down and make love and afterward abduct her, if not to Tahiti, then to a meadow in the Sierras. He didn't care if he was risking his neck. Claire knew the truth and wanted to save him. She hated him, true, but that didn't matter. He had a certain male pride, a faith in himself, that given time he could change her bad feelings, but first he had to win back his freedom, and she had promised to help him.

He stood, strode over to Tiny, vaulted onto the back of the Clydesdale, and let out a war whoop. A jackrabbit scurried into the bushes. A badger tunneled into his burrow. Claire glanced at the horizon, then scrambled to the top of the cliff. Johnny ignored all three of them. He gave a low whistle and kicked Tiny. The massive brown horse bunched his bulky muscles and charged, sand spraying in great sheets behind him. Claire watched from the cliff, hugging herself.

Tiny drove down the dry creek bed like thunder. Johnny could almost hear the fire bells clanging. For eight years this had been heaven, racing behind a shiny brass steamer on the way to some blazing cabin. He laughed. He might never return to his mining camp life, but Claire knew the truth and wanted to save him. A hope, long since abandoned, revived. He tugged on the reins and cantered back to their camping place. Claire stood silhouetted against the horizon, a small, lovely woman against the low, flat plain of the central valley.

He moved the Clydesdale close to the ridge. "Are you frightened?" he asked.

"Yes." In spite of the warmth, Claire seemed to be shivering.

"Good. I wouldn't want an overconfident lawyer."

He held out his arms. Claire looked quizzically at him. "Come on," he shouted. "Hop on."

She glanced at the quilt.

"You won't need it," he continued more softly. "I'm in charge now. We're all through with thinking. We're all through with planning. We're all through with running. And I guess we're all through with lovemaking."

She leaped for the Clydesdale. Johnny reached out and grabbed her and pulled her aboard.

He snuggled her tightly to his chest. "We're riding like hell for San Francisco."

Johnny turned himself in two days later. Claire could barely stand to see him in jail. She knew his side of the story, so she concentrated on the change of venue and won him a trial in San Francisco.

His sister showed up on the first day of the trial.

"Laura Hammand, nee Van Kessel," the pretty young woman said as she offered her card, leaning over the mahogany guardrail that separated lawyers from spectators. "You're Johnny's attorney?" she asked.

Claire nodded, taking the small rectangle of ivory paper and noticing that it was richly embossed with feminine printing. "Pleased to make your acquaintance."

"The same, I'm sure." Johnny's sister smiled at Claire, then sank into the first chair behind her. An elegant woman in a black-trimmed gray suit, she was more fair-skinned than her brother, with a more slender build and a sprinkling of freckles, but much the same smile, relaxed and infectious. "Is that the prosecuting attorney?"

Claire nodded. Tall and swarthy, Bartholomew Sanders dominated the courtroom, not with swagger or bombast, but with the confidence, splendor, and high-toned self-assurance discreetly displayed in the cut of his suit and the coiled energy with which he was reading. Claire studied her papers, avoiding his gaze.

A clink of metal caught her attention. Johnny appeared in the door of the courtroom. Claire's heartbeat doubled. He was flanked by two bailiffs and shackled in leg chains. They'd replaced his red shirt with one of gray muslin. His hair had been cut, though not very neatly. His newly shaved face was unevenly colored. To Claire he still looked handsome, though unkempt. In spite of his confined condition, he carried himself with the same pride and vigor as ever, which made the shackles a double insult.

He smiled when he saw her, lopsided and boyish, and walked awkwardly to his place in the courtroom. Once he was seated, he said very softly, "You look pretty, counselor." He turned and blew a kiss to his sister. "You, too, sweetheart."

Laura Hammand squeezed her brother's shoulder, but Claire sat frozen, tears pricking her eyes. "Excuse me." She pushed out of her chair and strode the length of the low, shiny table reserved for attorneys and client.

"Did you arrange this?" She jerked her head toward Johnny's ankles.

Sanders turned a paper over and lay it on top of some others. "You mean the leg chains?"

Claire paused a moment, shocked by his gesture. She wasn't trying to read his trial notes, though it occurred to her that maybe she should. She smoothed the front of her navy-blue suit. "Since when does a prisoner stand trial in shackles?"

"It's standard procedure."

"I don't believe it. I've been in plenty of courtrooms and I've never seen it."

The bearded attorney rose from his chair, unfolding

himself to maybe six feet. From the side of the room, Johnny's chair scraped. Sanders glanced that way briefly. Fear, then disdain, flickered in his eyes. All lazy elegance and towering grace, he pulled back his suit coat and rested a casual fist on his hip. "And how many proceedings have you seen exactly?"

Claire tried to peek at the rest of his papers. "This is my first appearance as an attorney, but I cut my teeth in my father's chambers and I know the routine well enough. Shackles aren't standard. You're trying to make my client look guilty in front of the jury."

"Shackles are standard with an escapee."

"He didn't escape." She lifted her chin and matched his posture, still wondering about his papers. He didn't seem to have many notes. By contrast, hers were neat and compulsive. "He ran from a lynch mob."

Sanders tugged on a snowy shirt cuff. "Whatever."

Claire studied him gravely. It occurred to her that she had a problem. This man was an expert, both shrewd and ruthless and comfortable with pure male aggression. She, by contrast, was small, frail, and female, had a client whom she both loved and hated, and was learning the ropes in a capital case while being haunted by the ghost of her father. Cold reason told her she ought to give up, to find someone else to act as his lawyer. But she wasn't a quitter. She'd learned that with Chauncey. In fact, she was probably a little too stubborn for her own good. "I'm bringing a motion to have them removed."

"Go ahead." Sanders sat back down and poured

himself water from a porcelain pitcher. "I can't prevent you."

Claire bit her lip and sat down next to Johnny.

"Good work," he wrote on her paper. She'd trained him to do that in their preparations, write her notes so as not to distract her. She drew a little smile on her paper, though the cartoon was mostly bravado. She could feel Johnny's tension, his warmth and alertness, and a part of her ached to reach over and kiss him. She straightened his shirt collar instead. He smiled, and the world went a little bit crooked. She'd be lucky to get through the day without crying, she told herself. Claire picked up the pen she'd inherited from her father and drew a tiny star on her notebook. She felt vulnerable and very nervous. In a few moments the judge would come out, and she'd speak her first words as a trial lawyer. Her pulse clicked as she mentally practiced. Stand up to acknowledge His Honor. Keep away from the bench unless you have permission. Stay in eye contact when selecting the jurors. And most of all, ignore the charge that's flowing between yourself and your client.

She reached out and straightened her jumble of law books. She knew in her heart she'd made a horrible error. She could sense Johnny's presence, his vibrancy and being, even his friendly warmth toward his sister. She had to ignore it, as well as the hatred. She swallowed and touched the chain on her neck. For the first time in her life Judge Butler's daughter, the former wife of the banker Chauncey Lyman, incorrigible tomboy, and the state's third woman lawyer, completely regretted that she was a woman.

*   *   *

Johnny saw Claire the next day in jail. She conducted their interviews in a side room, after having had almost as much trouble making the arrangements as she had that first time in Bodie.

"That prosecutor's going to beat me." She threw herself into an oak Windsor chair. She'd grown prettier since they'd come to the city. The time outdoors had turned her skin golden. In her tailored gray suit, she looked serious and mannish, but as always she softened her outfit with a slight show of ruffled white collar.

"How's Tiny?" Johnny asked.

"Didn't you hear me?" She pulled notebooks and lawbooks out of her green carpetbag and stacked them on the rugged pine table. "That Sanders is going to beat me in court."

Johnny grabbed a ladder-back chair, sat it next to her, and straddled it backward. "You're too pessimistic. I thought you were wonderful in there yesterday."

She pushed back a silky lock of blond hair. "He knows every trick in the book." She opened a leather-bound volume and ruffled through its yellow pages. Frowning, she propped it up on the stack and stared, as if she really believed the musty papers held magic. "Oh, Johnny, I'm frightened."

He leaned forward and brushed the pale tendrils that seemed to always escape her ladylike hairdo. "Don't be morose." He closed the distance between them and kissed her. She had a clean taste, like fresh mountain water. He wanted to tangle his hands in her hair, but she wiggled away with a huff.

"Johnny, I'm serious. You could get the death sentence. They've added conspiracy, jailbreak, and assault to the charges. The only reason there's no charge of kidnapping is I haven't been a cooperative witness."

"And no charge of murder."

"No, I've managed to still keep that a secret."

"See, you've beat two out of six already. I'm a fortunate man. Now, how is my horse?"

"Tiny's fine. Don't be supercilious." She closed the book softly and fingered the chain on her neck. "God, Johnny, what'll I do if you're convicted?"

He wanted to kiss her, to hold her, to make love on this table. "Would you be so very sorry?"

She toyed with the chain on her neck, then jumped up from the chair and walked over to the window, looking out of the small, barred embrasure. Her reaction surprised him, as he hadn't been entirely serious. But he'd take to his grave the stricken expression she wore now.

"There's always Tahiti," he said.

"Be serious."

"I am." He picked a fleck of white paint from the chair he was straddling. "Come away with me, Claire. I've got money enough. They're not so civil in San Francisco that a policeman or two can't be bought."

"Johnny, I can't."

"I know that, my love."

The sunlight fell on her golden hair. She'd perfumed herself in the scent of old roses—heady, spicy, rich, and enticing. He ought to be sorry he loved her, he knew. He could be on the ocean this very moment, feeling the salt spray on his face. But he couldn't regret his love for Claire Butler: their days on the river, the lilting surprise of their lovemaking, or the magical, wonderful feeling he'd had before he'd confessed to her that he'd killed her father. Maybe they'd never make it as far as Tahiti, but he'd come closer to the Garden of Eden than he'd ever expected to do in his lifetime.

"I know I'm a coward." She touched one of the thick metal bars. "If I had courage, I'd follow."

"I'm not asking, Claire." He pushed out of the chair and strode to the window. From there he could smell the sea air. "We'll try this your way."

She turned and touched the gray muslin shirt. "But you're gambling your life on my skill as a lawyer."

"That's right, counselor, so you'd better be good."

"Then you have to trust me a little bit further."

His chest ached, and he longed to touch her. He hated being confined in small spaces. They made him desperate, almost claustrophobic. He wanted to ramble out in the mountains. He had the wild thought that he could take her, but there were deputies behind the doors and rows of prisoners who could probably hear them. "I've trusted you with my life."

"I know." There were tears in her eyes. "I know." She walked back to her law books and touched one of the pages. "But that's not enough. I need to know more about Father. I need to know who was with you the night . . . when . . . the night Father died."

"No dice."

"But, Johnny—"

"You said you wouldn't bring up the murder."

"This has to do with the rape." She picked up her pen and arched her eyebrows. He'd learned to be frightened when she got that expression, because he knew it meant she was trying to look like a lawyer. "Somebody framed you using that gun." She pointed the pen for emphasis. A few drops of ink spattered the paper. She opened the notebook and wrote down the date, with a little notation beside it. "I need to know who was at Father's killing in order to track down whoever raped Louisa."

"We've discussed this already." He walked to the table and stilled her hand. With her, a pen could be a potent weapon. "That information won't help you."

She glanced at his hand, the pen, the law books, the paper. She set down the writing utensil and laced her fingers together. "I don't know who you're protecting. But I don't think your talking will hurt them."

He tightened his grip on her wrist. An old friend's life would rest on her answer to his question. "Can you promise me that?"

She dropped her eyes and stared at the law books. They were musty, probably twenty years old, and he guessed they had belonged to her father. She picked up the closest—a book on criminal law—and ran her hands over the binding. "No, not absolutely. If the authorities viewed it as murder, they could be accessories after the fact."

"Then I stand by my decision."

"Oh, Johnny. Please." She jumped up from the

table, straightened her suit, paced to the window, then returned to the law books. She slumped down in the chair and buried her face in her hands. "Please . . ." She spoke very softly. "If you love me. I promise I'll help if I get them into trouble."

She look so unhappy. Perversely that cheered him, as it made him realize how much she cared. All of life's cruelty and beauty seemed one at this moment. He remembered how he'd felt with his mother, watching her sit by his bed while he suffered. He had hated it more than his physical illness, seeing the fear and pain in her eyes.

And now he had Claire. He'd never wanted to hurt her, and he was sorry now he'd told her he loved her. If she lost this case, his death would haunt her forever. But he couldn't betray Lefty and Tucker. Granted, he no longer loved them; the years had taken a toll on their friendship. Tucker had even been in the posse, both on the night of the attempted lynching and during the debacle in Tuolumne Meadow. But that didn't matter. He'd taken an oath. Johnny had none of Claire's fine sense of honor. He did have a strong sense of friendship, however. No man, much less a woman, would make him betray his long-ago comrades.

He took her in his arms and folded her into his chest. "I do love you, Claire—you must see that— but I'm not going to endanger a friend with my follies."

"That's stupid." She tried to draw back, but he held her firmly. Maybe his silence made her doubt the truth of his story, but he wouldn't give his friends' names to her without a fight. "They can't care about you. They'd have come forward already."

"You don't know what they think." He pressed himself to her, all heat and passion. "They're probably frightened."

She stilled. "You're not?"

He wanted to kiss her. He didn't care about the propriety of it. He needed to feel her against him. "Of course I'm frightened." He ran his lips over her neck, and she shivered. "God, how I'm frightened." Maybe he could just unpin her hair. "But this is my problem only. There's no point in bringing down others simply because I've got troubles."

She pushed him away. She picked up a law book and clutched it to herself. For a moment he thought she was going to throw the massive tome at him. "I'm a very good lawyer, you know."

He moved slightly back, eyeing her warily. "I've never doubted that for a moment."

"I'm going to figure this out." Her knuckles were white on the binding. "I don't know what you're hiding or who you're protecting, but I'm going to find out what happened that night. And when I do, you'll all be sorry. I'm not my father's daughter for nothing."

Chapter
Fourteen

~~~~

Louisa Cantrall testified the next day in court. Prim and polished, she wore a black suit, with her hair pulled back in a bun. Johnny's scarlet ladies had come in from Bodie. Madam Cleo and the girls ranged in the back seats, decked out in fine silks and bright red satins. They whispered and giggled when Johnny appeared, causing a stir in the row of white-shirted men on the jury.

Bartholomew Sanders led off the questions. "Now, Miss Cantrall, are you familiar with the accused, Jonathan Van Kessel?"

Louisa glanced briefly at Johnny, blushed, then swung her gaze back to the prosecuting attorney. She had a long, pale face and a pinched expression. She took a deep breath before she answered. "Yes. We met at a picnic on the Fourth of July."

"Did you like him?"

"Yes." Her sallow coloring deepened, but she kept her gaze fixed firmly on Sanders. "Everyone loved Johnny Christmas."

"I see." Sanders smiled. He glanced at Claire, then back at the whores. "I see. Did you believe him an honorable man?"

"Yes." A row of white buttons marched down from each shoulder. She looked like a soldier doing her duty. "He had a wild reputation, but he seemed decent enough once you got to know him. I thought he had . . ." She fingered the lace on the edge of the kerchief. "Potential."

"Did he court you?"

"Yes."

"How long and how often?"

"Objection." Claire sprang to her feet, running her finger over the list of objections contained in a horn-book she'd borrowed. "Compound."

Judge Percival Riley drew together his bushy white eye-brows and peered down from his high dais. To Claire, the gesture seemed oddly paternal. She wished her father could see her.

"Technically, you're correct," the square-jawed judge said, "but I might point out we'll be here for days if you nitpick us to death by objecting to the form of the question." He looked over at Sanders. "Counselor, rephrase for the sake of our new lady lawyer."

"Did the defendant make improper advances?"

"Objection." Claire remained standing. "He's leading the witness. He didn't go back to his previous question."

The judge scowled. "You can't run this courtroom, young woman. Sit down." Claire hesitated, then did as he asked. From the back of the courtroom the whores made small catcalls, but the judge raised his winglike black robes and silenced them with a rap of his gavel.

"Now, close up that book," he said to Claire.

She hesitated, then shut her little textbook.

"The first objection's well taken. The second you won't find on your list. And I'll give you a lesson. You don't need to tear up the background questions. We're just trying to find out what happened."

"Of course." Claire cleared her throat and arched one eyebrow. "But the question's vague. Who knows what's improper between a man and a woman?"

"Somebody does." The judge smiled at her. "That's why we have the crime of rape." He waved his gavel at Sanders. "You may proceed."

Claire reached for the textbook, unsure of herself. Johnny put his hand over hers.

"Excuse me, Your Honor," Sanders said smoothly. "Would you instruct the defendant that there's no pawing his lawyer in court?"

"Not fair!" Claire shot to her feet. "He scarcely touched me." She could feel all eyes in the courtroom on her. Johnny grinned, winked at her, then turned himself forward. A visible ripple moved through the jury. Catcalls and boos issued forth from the whores. Claire felt like trembling, but steeled herself rigid. This wasn't going at all the way she wanted.

As the hubbub died down, the white-haired judge laid down his gavel. With calm movements he picked up the pitcher perched by his elbow and poured himself a full glass of water. He sipped thoughtfully for a moment, studying Johnny, then set down the tumbler. "I'll tell you right now, Mr. Van Kessel. I don't believe in lady lawyers. Seems to me that's a contradiction in terms. But Miss Butler is still Judge Butler's daughter and—far more important—she's an officer of this court." He leaned forward, black-robed and forbidding. "You do not touch her while she's in my courtroom."

Johnny stood up, his chair banging back. "I've never hurt her, not once in my life. Louisa neither, I swear it."

Judge Riley seemed shocked. Cheers and whistles came from the back. The judge picked up his gavel, but Johnny silenced the whores with a gesture.

The judge scowled and pointed the gavel at Claire. "Control your client, young lady."

"He'll behave." She tugged on Johnny's elbow. He grinned and sat down. "I promise," she added, completely abject. She could feel Johnny's thigh brush against hers beneath the table, an unnerving distraction and one she ignored. Evidently the judge could not see Johnny's act of defiance, and motioned for Sanders to resume the questions.

The prosecutor stood up, striking a pose, the one with his fist on his hip. "Did the defendant ever make improper advances?"

"Yes." Louisa had pulled out a lace-edged hankie, which she twisted and crimped as she answered. "That night . . . the very night it happened. We were speaking of marriage. . . ." She shot Claire a venomous look. "Johnny—"

Sanders held up his hand, cutting her off. "Can you

describe the defendant's actions?''

"Objection." Claire stood again.

"Counselor?" The judge looked her a question.

"Relevance. The rape happened later."

Sanders stalked past the end of the table and leaned on the railing enclosing the jury. A dozen mustachioed faces turned toward him. "Surely this goes to motive. It shows the defendant was thwarted. It also shows the character of the accused."

"Overruled." The judge spoke to Louisa in the witness stand. "You may continue."

Louisa picked at the lace. "He tried to touch me—intimately."

Sanders pulled out a thick black fountain pen and drummed it softly against the railing. "Can you be more specific?"

Louisa knotted her fingers, the handkerchief trembling. "An upper part. Reserved for husbands."

"And did you allow this?"

"No," she said quickly, "and he left, making threats."

"What kind of threats? What were his words exactly?"

"He said . . ." She smoothed the white square flat in her lap. "I can't remember exactly, but near as I can recall, he said, 'Someday you'll get your comeuppance.' "

Sanders returned to the table. He paused a moment, then made a series of checks on his paper. "What happened next?"

"Well, I went to bed early, a little distressed. And

I awoke to find him above me. He was holding a gun to my head.''

"Stop." Sanders waved her to silence. "How did you know it was him?"

"His size and his clothes."

"Could you see his face?"

"No. He had it covered with some kind of sacking, but he was wearing his red flannel firefighter's shirt, and there's no mistaking those shoulders."

Johnny grinned and straightened. Louisa blushed, looking away. Claire kicked him under the table, cursing the peacock male ego that did not give him the sense to hunch when he should have.

Sanders picked up a silverplate pistol from a clutter of objects on his side of the table. He crossed to Louisa and handed it to her. "Is this the weapon he used? Please look carefully."

She held the gun with two fingers and studied it closely. "Yes," she said after a pause.

"What happened next?"

"He took me by force."

"Did he achieve penetration?"

"Yes." She spoke so softly Claire almost did not hear her.

"Can you repeat your answer?" Sanders asked gently.

"Yes," Louisa said more loudly. "Yes. He completed the act." She tightened her grip on the butt of the pistol. "Took what I'd denied him out on the porch."

Sanders picked up a folded square of flower-sprigged cloth from the polished surface of the attorney's table. He approached Louisa and held the material up. "Is this what you were wearing?"

"Yes." She averted her face. There were tears in her eyes.

Sanders did not pause for an instant. He shook the fabric out, revealing a nightgown, and held the garment before her. A small brown splotch stained the bottom half. An audible gasp passed through the jury. A small chorus of boos came from the ladies ranged in the back.

"Is this your blood?" Sanders asked softly.

Louisa nodded her head for an answer. Claire thought to ask for a verbal response, then rejected the notion. If Louisa's answer was vague, that was better for Johnny. Sanders bunched up the flannel, handed it to the clerk, then sat down and announced he'd finished his questions.

Claire stood. She glanced briefly at Johnny, then sized up Louisa. She was telling the truth, Claire was certain, but some feminine instinct told her that spotless Louisa was not quite as good as she seemed. For one thing, she glared at Claire with a look of pure venom—not just pride or strained composure, but jealousy and hatred, woman to woman.

Claire dropped her eyes to her pen and her law books. She felt a bit like a traitor. Her instant dislike of Louisa had been considerably softened by the sight of the bloodstain. Claire struggled to frame her first question. The jury, the judge and Louisa waited. It ran through Claire's mind that she could not do this.

She glanced quickly at Johnny. He grinned. She fixed on the day beneath Waterwheel Falls. She'd bet her life that he wasn't guilty, but guilty or not, she was his lawyer and she owed him all the skill she could muster. She squared her shoulders, straightened her suit coat, and walked slowly to the witness stand. She picked up the nightgown and inspected it closely. "Is this the first time you've bled during sexual relations?"

Louisa stiffened. "Yes," she shot back.

"Objection." Sanders sprang to his feet.

"No!" Louisa's voice lifted an octave. "I mean . . . Oh!"

The jury looked stunned, then sullen and silent. A chorus of cheers arose from the back. The judge rapped his gavel, but the cheering continued.

The prosecutor spoke above the tumult. "Assuming a fact not in evidence. As far as we know, Miss Cantrall's a virgin."

Claire had arched an eyebrow and turned to the judge when, to her horror, a strong voice boomed out. "I object also." Johnny's words rang through the courtroom. "I want to talk to my lawyer."

"That was sneaky, Claire." Johnny flung himself into a chair, his manacles clanging as the wood banged the wall. He stared at his beautiful lawyer, wondering how someone so pretty could be so ruthless. "Louisa's a schoolmarm."

Claire paced to the window of the tiny holding cell. "What's her job got to do with my trial tactics?"

He wanted to shake her, to pace and to shout, but he knew that kind of behavior would likely not help. He thought of Claire as a brilliant woman, but her sense of ethics escaped him. He grabbed both sides of the table. "Look, Louisa was raped. Not by me, I'll grant you. But that doesn't mean she should be raped by my lawyer."

"Would you rather go to the gallows instead?"

"No, but there's always—"

"Don't." She cruised to the table, satin rustling beneath her wool skirt. "Don't be such a dreamer." She glanced at the slotted doorway. A shadow moved past the shaft of light. Claire grimaced, sat down, and picked up her notes, perusing them with a great show of interest. The scent of roses filled the small room. Johnny could see the rise and fall of her bosom, a rapid rhythm matched by his own. She sat there in silence, ice-cold and rigid, as the guard at the doorway passed by several times. Johnny thought of the mountains, her ethereal beauty, and the silvery water of the Tuolumne River. His heartbeat slowed down. Hers must have also, for her visible struggle had ceased. "Don't be stupid, Johnny," she whispered. "You can't escape anymore."

He touched her hand gently and whispered back, "If I could, would you come with me?"

She twitched away, clearly impatient. "Don't even think it. That's not a choice, and you know it."

"So what are my choices?"

"Let me shred up Louisa, or you can go to the gallows."

"No."

"No, what?"

He scooted closer, the manacles making a hash of his movement. "Don't hurt Louisa. She's been hurt enough. There's no one in that courtroom to defend her.''

"What do you care?'' Claire slipped her pen out of her breast pocket. She unscrewed the top and examined the nib. ''She may have been raped, but she's still a conniving, hypocritical—''

''I do care, Claire.'' He stilled her hand and took the pen from her. ''I'm an innocent man. There must be some way to show that without destroying an innocent woman.''

She stared at him in abject frustration, then stood and paced back to the window. The afternoon sunlight created a glow in her hair, making it preternaturally bright in the gloom and dimness. ''There might be if you'd help me.'' She touched the ruffle poking out of her suit dress. ''Tell me more about what went on between you. Did you really court her? Were you two to be married? Did she have other suitors? Was she making them jealous?''

He pressed the pen down and made a deep black mark in the paper. He didn't know how to answer. He'd asked all these questions himself. Louisa had been a bit of a tease, but he couldn't imagine the mind of a rapist, or why a man would slip over the boundaries that held decent men to civilized standards. ''I've told you before, four or five times.''

''Tell me again.'' She waited.

He scribbled on the top of the paper. He didn't know why he resisted, but there was something in the tone of her voice, something in the way she seemed to be trying to control him, that made him balk at her query.

"For heaven's sake, Johnny, don't be such a Christian. The woman means nothing to you."

He made a large letter *C* on the paper.

"Or does she?"

He wrote out a *B,* then a *J* and a *K.* He drew a large heart around them. The tone of her voice caught his attention. She had a look on her face, fierce concentration, and it suddenly dawned on him why she was asking. "You're jealous."

"Don't be absurd."

"I like that." He grinned.

"Please, Johnny," Claire said as she looked out the window, "stay on the subject." She touched one of the bars, then ran her fingers over the solid brickwork. "Do you want to spend your life in this place? Are you trying to protect her?" She turned, her eyes filled with pleading. "Oh, Johnny, why won't you let me help you?"

"She means nothing to me, Claire. You know that. But do you really have so little conscience that you're going to defend me by destroying her honor?"

"You're not paying me to have a conscience."

She could make her voice so damnably flinty. "So raise your fees. I'll pay a bit more."

"That's not the point."

"What is the point, Claire?"

She returned and sat down next to him. "The law isn't perfect." Her gaze skittered over the figure he'd made, her initials and his enclosed in a heart. "Each side has a spokesman. It's supposed to make the process a little more fair. I'm speaking for your side, that's all."

"Who speaks for Louisa?"

"No one, exactly." She stared at his initials. "The prosecutor speaks for the people."

"Then listen to me, my new lady lawyer." He wanted to pace. The ankle bracelets were far worse than handcuffs, for they bound a man more tightly and truly. "The law isn't perfect, and neither are you." He screwed the top back on the pen. "You're hurting her because you're jealous." He lowered his voice and glanced at the door. "You're brilliant, Claire. You can win an acquittal without hurting Louisa."

She looked as if she were ready to cry.

He flashed her the broadest smile he could muster. "Don't hurt Louisa." He pushed back a strand of her golden hair. "Because I already know from the death of your father that freedom's not much fun without a clear conscience."

The jury convicted Johnny in less than two hours, and the judge sentenced him to be hanged. Claire accompanied him back to the holding cell and burst into tears as soon as the guard shut the door.

"Oh, God, Johnny, what have I done?" She tried to be calm, but she'd developed the hiccups, and her question was punctured with silly shudders.

Johnny grinned and put his arm around her shoulder. "You've lost your first case. And I'm really sorry."

She pushed him away and threw herself into a chair, pulling a hankie out of her pocket. "How can you stand there and smile? They're going to—" She stopped. She couldn't say it, couldn't imagine how such a disaster had happened. A judge, a man much like her father, had sentenced an innocent man to the gallows. A deep tremor racked her. "Johnny, I'm scared."

"Look," he said as he pulled a chair up beside her, took the cloth, and brushed her cheeks gently. "I'm not dead yet. I've been closer than this and survived."

"Yes. Well . . ." She touched his hand. A wave of frustration rose up inside her. She glanced at the walls. "This isn't Bodie."

He shrugged, but his gesture did not console her. The gloom of the cell closed in around her. It was damp and oppressive and smelled faintly of urine, which her rose perfume didn't quite mask. "It isn't fair. You did not rape Louisa and because you had scruples, you're going to go to the gallows."

He stroked back a strand of her hair. She felt so foolish. She should have let him go to Tahiti.

He cupped her chin in his hand. "I know you're disappointed," he said. "I had an advantage: I never thought justice was fair."

"I wish it had been justice that failed." She touched the side of his mouth. Dear God, could they really wipe out those dimples? Obliterate Johnny for a crime he didn't commit, in the name of the law? "It was me. I was too inexperienced."

He caught her hand and kissed the tips of her fingers.

She leaned into his chest, strong and wide and covered in rough muslin. "I wanted so badly to prove I could do it."

"Ah, Claire, don't be so hard on yourself. You did a good job. You had a tough client."

"I had a client I loved. That was the problem. I behaved like a woman. Silly. Mush-headed. Female."

He pulled her tight, stroking her hair. She could feel the deep boom of his heartbeat, a strong, steady cadence. Her own heart felt like it was breaking. They would never again make love. They would never get another chance to make babies. They would never catch fish or swim in the Sierras. Tears dripped with ridiculous swiftness, but at least she kept herself silent. Her cheeks might look like Waterwheel Falls, but she would not give the guards the satisfaction of hearing feminine sobs escape the small jail cell.

"I talked to my sister," he said quietly.

"Oh?" She had an ache in her chest, and her eyes felt prickly.

"She wrote to my mother."

There was a little catch in his heartbeat. Claire straightened. He took both her hands in his and spoke softly. "We could get to Tahiti. She'll send me money. The guards can be bribed, I'm certain of that." He stared at her intently. "Would you come with me, if I can arrange it?"

She froze. The chain on her neck felt suddenly heavy. "Oh, Johnny. I couldn't."

"Why not? You have no family. Wouldn't you like one?"

"I have an uncle, but that doesn't matter." Her blood rushed, but her hands felt icy. She couldn't blame him for wanting to bolt. This place made her crazy, and she could walk out anytime she wanted.

"I'm the third woman lawyer in California. I can't run off with an outlaw."

"You did it before."

"We were escaping a lynch mob."

"You didn't mean the things you said?"

"I did mean them, Johnny. I will never forget you, but I can't abandon all that I've worked for to follow you to some South Sea island."

He stood, his neck muscles bulging. For a moment she thought he would strike her, but he hobbled to the window that led to the outside. "What would it take to convince you?"

"Nothing. There's really nothing."

"We could raise beautiful children. We would always have money."

"I'm sure we could."

"I know I haven't made much of my life, but I could prove myself to you, if only you'd let me." He grasped the small bars of the window. "I was a good firefighter. That may not be much in your estimation—"

"Don't—" She tucked her hankie into her pocket and straightened her suit coat. "That's not the problem. I'm not nearly so snooty as you seem to think. My father was a judge, and I had a wealthy husband, but I'm not so blinded by wealth, class, or status that I don't understand the nature of goodness. You're a fine and decent man. Any woman would be lucky to have you. It isn't you, Johnny, it's me."

"Which means?"

She touched the place where the bullet was hidden. "You may have killed him, but I'm still his daughter.

I'll always love him and I'll never forget him. I don't want to avenge him by hating his killer. I want to spend my life taming Bodie, and I want to spend it being a lawyer.''

Chapter
Fifteen

They returned Johnny to Bodie for hanging. Claire filed an appeal and wrote to his mother. She didn't allude to his planned escape, but she did pour out her heart about Johnny. How much she loved him. How angry she'd been about her father but how she'd nonetheless told Johnny she thought she could help him if only he'd trust her and accept her protection. How she had failed at the trial level. But Alice Van Kessel never wrote back, and she was far from Claire's mind two weeks later when the bell on the door of her law office jingled. Claire looked up from the brief she was writing. A gust of cold wind blew through the room. A plump woman with gray-streaked hair and a self-assured bearing walked through the door and closed it behind her.

She shivered in spite of her thick, fur-collared jacket. "Are you Claire Butler?" she asked.

"Yes." Claire stood, moving away from her desk.

"Alice Van Kessel." The woman fished a calling card out of her black leather pocketbook. "Jonathan's mother.'' Claire accepted the card, but studied the woman. She looked much like Johnny. Same eyes. Same complexion. Same smile and dimples. She dressed in a manner appropriate to her class and station, in a burgundy skirt and black fur-trimmed jacket, topped by a hat with an elegant feather neatly secured by a silver buckle. She had a pleasant expression, however, frank and good-hearted. Claire knew instantly: This woman had raised Johnny Christmas.

Claire bounded forward and hugged her. Alice Van Kessel hugged back, warm and unaffected, though Claire could feel her hands tremble through her fur jacket.

''Oh, I'm so glad to see you,'' Claire said, squeezing her again. Mrs. Van Kessel smelled like winter, dust, stagecoach, and horses, faintly softened with the fresh scent of lilac water. ''I expected an answer, but not in person. When did you get here? Have you seen Johnny?''

''May I sit down?'' Mrs. Van Kessel rubbed her gloved hands together, looking longingly at the pot-bellied stove.

''Of course.'' Claire pulled a chair toward the stove. She opened it and chucked a log inside. ''Let me make it warmer. I often work in a chilly office— the slight asperity makes me think better.'' She gestured the woman into the Windsor chair. ''I'm sorry. Would you like some coffee?''

''Why, thank you.'' Mrs. Van Kessel sat down. She pulled off her gloves and unbuttoned the top of her jacket, then held her hands toward the stove as if to toast them.

Claire poured two cups from the enamel spatter-ware pot she kept simmering. She wanted to question Mrs. Van Kessel, but held herself in check as she poured. No matter how curious she was, she should be civil: another lesson she'd learned from her father. Attention was the stock-in-trade of a lawyer. It never paid to hurry a client, especially one on her first visit. Claire handed a porcelain demitasse embellished with roses to the woman who'd raised Johnny Christmas.

Mrs. Van Kessel accepted the cup graciously. Claire took her own cup back to the oak desk that served as her table. The afternoon sun cast long shadows on it, making canyons and chasms in the litter of papers. Claire had to move them to find a place for her drink. "Have you seen Johnny?"

"No." Mrs. Van Kessel took a shallow sip of the dark liquid. "I just arrived on the stage this morning. I'm staying at a hotel. I wanted to see you. Your letter concerned me. They're planning on hanging my son. You, I gather, are still trying to save him."

Claire sipped her coffee slowly. Faced with this woman, she rather regretted the letter. In the frustrating weeks after the trial, she'd poured out her heart to this stranger. Now, however, that action seemed foolish, another example of how she'd handled her problems in an illogical fashion. Still, Mrs. Van Kessel seemed friendly. Claire read no judgment in her kindly expression. Like Johnny, like Johnny's sister, Alice Van Kessel seemed frank, good-hearted, straightforward. "You gathered correctly. I'm trying to help him, and I'm having trouble. He's got his own sense of morals and he's trying to impose them on a situation that's too complex for such scruples."

Mrs. Van Kessel sighed. She took another tentative sip of her coffee. "Do you mind if I ask a few questions?"

"Of course not."

"My daughter thinks you love Johnny." Turning away from the stove, Alice Van Kessel set the fragile cup down on the table corner. "Do you?"

Claire fingered the porcelain cup, toying with the rose on the side. She thought about lying, then discarded the notion. She hadn't spoken of love in her letter, but she'd probably made herself clear enough. "Yes."

Standing, Alice Van Kessel picked up one of Claire's law books and riffled through its yellowing pages. "She also says you're a pretty good lawyer."

"I hope so."

She studied the gold-embossed leather binding. "But you don't know how to control him."

"She's right on all counts."

The older woman set down the book and pushed up her collar, snuggling more deeply into the rich fabric. "I also gather from what you wrote me that he has trouble accepting your help."

Claire's coffee was going cold in her hands, but she was reluctant to discard it and too worked up to drink it. She didn't know what Alice Van Kessel wanted: whether she'd come to help Johnny escape, to pay off his debts and fire his lawyer, or simply to say good-bye to him. "You might explain my problem that way."

"May I ask you two more, very personal, questions?"

"Of course."

"Didn't you think it foolish to try to defend a man you're in love with?"

"Stupidest thing I ever did in my life."

"I'm glad you admit it." The older woman slipped out of her jacket and tucked her leather gloves in the pocket. She pushed the cup off to the side and pulled a pencil and notepad out of her pocketbook. "We'll get along better that way. And do you think the fact that he killed your father affected your representation?"

Claire took a sip of her coffee. It had gone a little tepid, but she wanted a moment to think of her answer. Robbed of its heat, the liquid seemed bitter, but the acrid taste was nothing next to the pain caused by this question. "I don't know really." She set the cup in the saucer with a soft chink. "I'd like to hate him; that would truly be better." She glanced at the law books, the pen, and the table. She touched the chain that hung on her neck. "But I'm a little too much my father's daughter to punish a man who feels truly remorseful."

Alice Van Kessel was writing swiftly, as if she'd made up her mind about something and wished to make a note of her thoughts.

Claire drank the dark liquid down to the bottom, then put the cup back in its saucer. "Can I ask *you* a question?"

"Of course."

"Why did you come here? I mean, if it's something

illegal, perhaps you shouldn't tell me. . . ."

Alice Van Kessel paused in her writing. "Let me ask you one final question: Do you think Johnny defiled this woman?"

"No. I don't believe it. Not for a minute."

Mrs. Van Kessel's hat feather trembled a little, the only visible sign of emotion, but Claire could almost see her muscles relax. "I have faith in my son, but justice should not rest on a mother's indulgence." She clasped her pen a little more tightly. "We're hardly objective."

"No," Claire pushed her coffee away. She wanted to hug this plump, kindly woman. Alice Van Kessel might be a wealthy society matron, but right at this moment she was simply a mother, casting about for a way to save her lost son. "But then I'm not really objective either. At least, in this particular case."

"You were not in love when you accepted his case."

"True."

"And I gather you're going to try an appeal?"

"Trying, though he does not make it easy."

"That's my fault, you know." Claire looked quizzically at the middle-aged woman. She shrugged, scarcely wrinkling her beautiful suit coat. "It's a long story. But I'm glad Johnny's found a woman who loves him. And it's only fair that I help him, though perhaps not in the way he wanted."

Johnny, too, had written Alice Van Kessel. He didn't tell his mother about his planned escape—his sister would have to speak for him there, as his letters might be read by his jailer—but he did pour out his heart about Claire. How much he loved her. How she'd tried to help him. How angry she was about her father. That she had faith in the legal system and how she still wanted to save him, though he questioned her tactics and sense of ethics. Alice Van Kessel never wrote back. Her silence puzzled Johnny. For the first time in his life, his mother had failed him, and her desertion was much on his mind when Sheriff Frank Flowers banged on the door to his jail cell in Bodie.

"You've got a visitor, Johnny."

Johnny lifted himself off the cot. His feet had been chained since San Francisco, and the manacles rattled as he approached the door. "Claire?" he called out.

"No, Johnny, it's me."

He hadn't heard that voice in ten years at least, but he recognized it immediately. "Mother?" He tucked in his shirt and straightened his hair. Sheriff Frank Flowers opened the door. Alice Van Kessel stepped into the rectangle of sunlight, as beautiful as he remembered. There was gray in her hair now, and she'd gained some weight since he'd last seen her, but all he saw was the wide, frank face that had seen him through such misery and illness. Even her scent evoked his hard childhood—a lilac perfume she wore for him always, to brighten long days spent without sunshine. She smiled, the lopsided smile she'd passed on to him.

"Mother!" He scooped her into his arms and hugged her, the chains clanking around his booted ankles.

Sheriff Frank Flowers pulled out his bulldog. "Settle down, Johnny. I suppose I can trust you with your own mother, but I'd be less nervous if you'd take it easy."

"Sure." Johnny set down the woman who'd raised him, the woman who'd saved him so many times, the woman who'd been a miraculous refuge from all of life's battering monsters. "Just let her stay with me. I haven't seen her since I was eighteen."

Sheriff Frank Flowers looked from Johnny to Alice Van Kessel, as if considering the proper action.

"If you'd be so good, Sheriff." Alice Van Kessel nodded regally. "I'd like come coffee."

Flowers scowled.

Johnny grinned. "I'll be a good boy, I promise."

The sheriff let himself out and the door clanged, that deep, hollow echo peculiar to jails. Johnny crossed his arms, leaned on the wood wall, and waited for the footfalls to fade. His mother perched on the edge of the bed, her leather-gloved hands clasped in her lap, her feathered hat bent toward the dying daylight. As they waited in silence, Johnny wanted to hold her. Of the many regrets in a life filled with errors, no regret, not even killing Judge Butler, remotely approached what he felt at this moment. He wanted to hold her. To kiss her. To reassure her that he hadn't done what he'd been accused of. That these chains meant nothing. That he'd been a decent man since he left her. He loved life and did not want to die, but he'd never die in front of his mother. Someway or another, he would escape that. She'd saved him too often to lose him that way.

Flowers' booted approach broke the silence. "I hope you like your coffee black." He opened the door, British bulldog in one hand, a spatterwear cup in the other. One eye on Johnny, he advanced to the cot. "Be careful, ma'am. The rim's apt to burn you."

"Why, thank you." She accepted the cup without rising, as if serving her were a privilege. Johnny wanted to talk to his mother, but held himself in check as Sheriff Flowers studied Alice Van Kessel. She was a piece of work, and nobody knew better than Johnny the entrancing effect she could have when she wanted. A great joy shone from her always. She was an accessible woman beneath the great lady, so much an earthy Dutch housewife that five generations of upper-class breeding had not altered the essence of Alice Van Kessel.

She curled her fingers around the cup. "Has my boy been behaving?"

The sheriff waved his snub-nosed revolver. "In a manner of speaking. He fled from the lynch mob. But he turned himself in. Of course . . ." He let his gaze wander off. "You know what happened after."

"Of course," she said. Flowers, the kitten, poked its nose through the door. Grown to adolescence since Johnny had left Bodie, the black-and-white foundling still lived in the jail. Flowers, the sheriff, in an act of compassion, had let the furry creature remain. "That's why I'd like a private moment."

The sheriff's fat mustache drooped down. He perused the plump woman with the ladylike gestures. "You'll give me your word you won't help him escape?"

"Of course."

His gaze skimmed off the kitten, off Johnny, and off Alice Van Kessel. "This is not the Grand Central Hotel, but I'll be civil, just to show you we're not so bad in Bodie as you might have heard in the Eastern papers."

"Thank you," she said with just a hint of disdain.

"You behave now, Johnny." The sheriff slammed the jail door behind him.

"I will." Johnny cricked his knees and motioned to the kitten. "How are my sisters?"

"Fine." His mother set down the coffee while perusing the jail cell. "The babies are growing. One of your nephews looks just like you."

"And you?"

"Older. Not very much wiser."

The kitten trotted to Johnny, then rubbed against the irons that held him, purring steadily as it did. "I didn't do it, you know."

"I know that."

"Did Laura write you?"

"Yes."

"And?"

Alice Van Kessel stood up. She walked the brief length of the jail cell, peered out the slot in the door, returned to the cot and pressed the thin mattress, walked over to Johnny, and hugged him. "I'm not going to help you run to Tahiti."

Johnny stiffened in shock. He'd never once in his life ever considered that his mother might desert him this way. "Is this about money?"

"No, not exactly." His mother was crying. He

could feel the tears on his shirtfront. "It's about this woman Claire Butler."

"What about Claire? Are you jealous I've found someone to love me?"

"Don't be absurd." She pushed away and returned to the cot. The sheriff must have taken her purse, she decided, and dabbed her eyes with her coat sleeve.

"Well then, what?"

"She says she still loves you, even after all that's gone on between you."

An odd feeling came over Johnny, as if the world had become a little unreal. He thought that he'd loved life better than he did Claire, but right at this moment he wasn't so certain, because this pronouncement about Claire's feelings made him almost forget his mother's betrayal. "I'm glad to hear that."

"I'm glad of it also, though it left me with a tough decision." She picked up the spatterwear cup, as if the coffee could make her stop shaking. "You have to stop running."

He picked up the kitten. He couldn't believe what his mother was saying. All his life, she'd fought for him. It was the only reason he hadn't been bitter about a bleak and desperate childhood.

"Listen to me." She set down the cup. She hadn't been able to keep the coffee from slopping over the side. "I always tried to be a good mother."

"You were. You were perfect."

"No. I wasn't." She steadied herself by touching the jail wall. This time she kept the tears from slipping. She looked at Johnny holding the kitten, took a deep breath, and clasped her hands tightly. "I was overprotective. That's why I let you come West. I know that last attack was a sham. But a boy needs to escape his mother, and sometimes the better the mother, the more a boy needs to escape her.''

He couldn't be angry. He'd never be angry with her. She'd not only given him life in the first place, but also she'd saved his life over and over. He simply couldn't understand what she wanted. ''What's all this got to do with Claire?''

She stood, walked back over, and hugged him again. ''You need to figure that out for yourself. I just came to tell you I love you. I know you could not have hurt that woman. I'll give you the money for a good lawyer, but I won't help you run to Tahiti.''

''You'd let me die?''

''I certainly hope not.''

''That's what will happen.''

''Not if you come to your senses.'' She stroked the kitten, which had started purring. ''You're a wonderful boy, and I have to admire the man you've become, but I don't think it's your friends you're protecting. Or even this Louisa Cantrall. Claire told me how you protected her feelings in the courtroom.''

He let go of his mother. She was almost as furry as Flowers, the kitten, in her fur-collared jacket and feathered hat, and he missed her warmth as he moved to the cot, but he wanted to think about what she was saying. He'd never been smart, but he had common sense. He might not have gone to college or had expensive tutors, but he knew a lot about people. ''Who do you think I'm protecting?''

''Yourself. Your own sense of manhood. You can't

seem to let Claire Butler protect you.''

''I let her defend me.''

''To some degree, yes.'' Flowers snuggled into her lap. ''But you don't seem to trust her. You won't let her do what she thinks is best.''

''She has peculiar morals.''

''So do all lawyers.'' She scratched the kitten's head. The purring hum became louder. ''In their hands, the law is a weapon. They make the rules. They shape them and bend them. They're different from mere mortals, who have to live by the Ten Commandments.'' She paused in her cuddling and gazed straight at Johnny. ''The point is you're at the law's mercy. You need to let your lawyer help you.''

Johnny hobbled to the slot in the door, the chains a frustrating restraint as always. ''You're right. But it doesn't seem manly. Turning my friends in. Attacking Louisa. Hiding behind the skirts of a woman.''

''Johnny.'' She stood and advanced holding the kitten. ''Does it seem more manly to let your mother get you out of this pickle?''

Chapter
Sixteen

❧❧❧

Claire came to see Johnny the next day in his jail cell. Flowers, the sheriff, nervous about his infamous prisoner, refused to let her use the side room. Johnny's hanging had become an item in Bodie, with the town's whores threatening a boycott and the men in town getting edgy. A necktie party wouldn't be fun without the subsequent cooperation of the town's fancy ladies.

Claire thought about that as Sheriff Flowers led her down the narrow, dark hall of the jail. How much the whores loved Johnny. What a mistake it had been to let them into the courtroom. And how she'd been misled by her own foolish heart into assuming a jury would see Johnny as an innocent man just because she did.

"Brought your lawyer, Johnny," Flowers said gruffly as he opened the door to the cell. Claire stepped in, clutching a pencil and notebook. The door clanged behind her, and Claire stepped forward. Johnny lay on the bed, Flowers, the kitten, asleep on his chest.

"Hello," he said softly.

"Hello," she answered. She looked around for a seat, slid down to the floor, fluffed out her skirt, and propped the paper on one of her knees.

Johnny didn't get up from the cot. He stared at her from beneath lowered lashes. He looked different, though she couldn't say why. Maybe it was his several weeks stubble, or his paleness of skin, or that he was thinner, though she didn't think those qualities accounted for the funny feeling he brought to her stomach. All his boyish bravado had fled. Instead he looked reckless, hungry, and wolfish. She reflected briefly that had he truly been an outlaw he'd have wanted to kill her, and she couldn't have blamed him.

She wrote out the date on the top of her notebook. "I've filed an appeal, but that's just pro forma. I've applied for a stay and I'm bringing a writ. That gives us two bites at the apple."

"I love it when you talk like a lawyer."

Claire didn't like his hungry expression. She teetered the book on the top of her knee and reminded herself that she was his lawyer, and that all that raw masculine beauty was just a distraction she should ignore. "All that's just tactics. I need new evidence if I'm to succeed."

He grazed his fingers over the small cat's whiskers. "My mother says I ought to trust you."

"She's a smart woman."

"The best."

She drummed with the pencil, watching him closely. Something was going on inside his head. "Are you going to help me find out who raped

Louisa? And who was with you when you killed my father?''

"Maybe." He lifted the kitten, dangling the black-and-white mass high above him. In the weeks of their absence, the cat had grown longer, but it still had floppy, kittenish habits, and now it hung happily over the palm of Johnny's hand. "But I've got a condition."

She waited. He lowered the kitten to the floor, then crooked his finger, indicating he wished Claire to come to him. She grabbed her notebook and looked at him questioningly.

"Scared?" he whispered.

She glanced at the door, and considered. She was, maybe, a little frightened. She hadn't seen him alone since he'd been brought back to Bodie. Now he was not only a convicted rapist, but an innocent man doomed to death by hanging. The latter fate was completely her doing, brought about by her failure to save him. "Not exactly."

"Then what?"

What? She put down her pencil and notebook. She didn't fear him. She loved him. God help her. He'd killed her father. Spent his life as a wastrel. His current ambition was flight to Tahiti. And still, she loved him. She could barely fathom the reasons. If she'd believed in such nonsense, she'd have called him her soul mate, but she thought of herself as a logical woman. Unfortunately, he brought out the female side of her, that swooning, unreasonable part of herself that loved wildness and freedom and sheer male bravado. He'd worked his way into the fiber and weft of her being, and now he'd live in her heart forever. "I love you," she said.

He grinned and turned sideways, the manacles clanging together. "Come here," he whispered.

She glanced at the door, then scooted over. She couldn't hear Flowers or any prisoners. She certainly hoped they couldn't hear her. "What condition?" she asked.

The kitten hopped into her lap. Johnny took her by the chin and turned her face sideways. She could feel his warm breath as he whispered, "I want to make love before I tell you."

"What!" She blushed and glanced at the door. Luckily she kept her voice low. "Johnny! How—?" The kitten scrambled out of the way. "Where?" She scrambled onto her feet and brushed her skirt quickly. "Are you out of your mind?" she whispered fiercely.

"There." He sat up with a clang and jerked his chin toward the wall by the doorway. "And, no. Except for the fact that I'm listening to my mother, I'm pretty sane, to my way of thinking."

He kissed her, lifting her easily at the same time. The shackles hampered his freedom of movement, but he moved her quickly against the wood wall. He balanced her on one thigh and hipbone, showering kisses over the side of her neck.

"Johnny." She spoke low and intently. "If the Sheriff comes in, he'll be sure you're a rapist."

"I've been convicted of that crime already."

He was touching her breasts, urgent and fervent, and she was torn by conflicting emotions. She wanted to laugh because he still loved her after she'd failed him. She wanted to hit him, because she was so frightened the sheriff would hear them. But mostly she wanted to kiss him, to hug him, to touch him, to take him inside her, because this was her Johnny, and chances were good she might lose him—if not to the hangman, then to Tahiti. But good sense prevailed, and she didn't kiss him.

"Stop." She pushed his hands down toward her waist. "The sheriff will hear you, and we'll be in big trouble."

"I don't care, Claire. You can tell them I raped you. But give me this chance." He pressed himself against her, hot, hard, and urgent. "If this appeal doesn't work, they're going to hang me. I want to remember why I'm taking this gamble."

She pushed his head back. Those green eyes had darkened to emerald, and his brown hair tumbled over his forehead.

"Tahiti?" she asked.

"Nope." He cupped one breast in his hand, bent his head, and kissed the curve he'd created. "Mother won't help me. She says I must trust you."

A sense of shock traveled through Claire. Though she believed in herself, the possibility that he could escape had always been there. Now, suddenly, it wasn't. She tried to fight down the swift rush of pleasure his kisses created. "There must be some other way," she said in a panic.

"There probably is, but I have to say I agree with her logic. What's the point of living if I have to keep running? Especially if you won't come with me."

"I'm not so sure . . ."

"I am." He pulled her blouse out of her skirt and ran his hands up her bare back. "Besides, you can do it. I'm sure you'll be brilliant. It's just that I have to help you."

"Johnny." He lifted her skirt up, pulling the wool from between their legs. "Stop," she whispered fiercely. She had to think more logically. He was going to trust her. There'd be no more chances. If this writ didn't work, they were going to hang him. He was gambling his life on her skill and logic. He shouldn't be driving all thought from her mind, she told herself. He covered her mouth with his own. She felt she was drowning in wildness and sensation, his hand on her breasts, his hip pinning her to the wall, the thrust and hardness of their body's juncture. She suppressed a moan. He suckled an earlobe, his hot breath feathering her neck.

She stilled his hands and listened intently. She supposed there was an odd logic to it. She could not hear the sheriff. The cell next to Johnny's was empty. They could make love in total silence, and if, God forbid, the law should hang him, they'd have shared this one last moment, created this last memory, together. She bared her neck and let him kiss her. Her suit felt hot and confining, but she supposed they could not do this unclothed. She helped him bunch her skirt at her waist. He pushed her pantalets down, then freed himself from his pants.

"Ah, Claire." He drove himself between her thighs, creating a hot, wet, spiraling pleasure in her that made her want to take him inside.

"Johnny." She crushed her lips to him and lifted,

wriggling her pantalets down past her knees. "I love you." His kisses were searing, adoring, hot, and demanding, as if death itself waited outside that door. In some ways it did, she knew, and that made him more precious to her. Not only the fact that he might die, but that he'd risk his life in order to give her a chance to act as his lawyer and himself a chance to snatch back his honor.

"Marry me, Claire," he whispered. "Promise me no matter what happens, if I go to my grave I'll go as your husband."

He paused, tense and expectant. She dropped her pantalets to one ankle and nodded. "On my honor."

He smiled. "I might better make a better bet with the devil than to take the word of a lawyer."

She kissed him more lightly, their clothes grinding between them, both of them cold and exposed in only their privates, the rest of them covered and buttoned. "I promise on the grave of my father. I'll get you out. We can be married. I'll follow you, if you want, to Tahiti, but just let me get you out legally. I promise, Johnny, this time I won't fail you."

He pushed upward and kissed her, balancing her on one thigh as he did. She would have thought the position would hurt her, but she was wider, softer, wetter, more giving than she'd ever imagined love-making could make her.

Then the rhythm commenced, the great waves of passion, and she forgot the walls of the prison, the gentle clank of his shackles, the fact that she was his lawyer, and gave herself over to the small, wayward, abandoned spirit that found refuge and comfort in the arms of this man.

They finished quickly, pushed by fear of the sheriff's discovery, and by something deeper, more urgent and frantic, that plunged them forward with immoderate haste and into spasms, both sharp and delightful, but without the deeper, more languid finish she'd experienced in their more leisurely lovemaking.

Johnny eased his weight back. She struggled off his thigh, trembling and gasping, trying her best to make her breath quiet. He leaned against the wall, his chest heaving though he also managed to struggle in silence.

"Jesus Christ, Claire." He kissed her forehead and zipped up his pants. "I may go to hell for taking you that way, but it certainly feels like I've gone to heaven."

"So tell me about Louisa." Claire sat on the floor by the side of the cot. Johnny lay on his side, propped up behind her. He wanted to touch her. He wanted to hold her. To kiss her. To take her into his arms and cuddle her softly, fall asleep with her beside him, and dream they were sleeping under a log in the Sierras. That he was far away from here and safe from the hangman. Safe from the posse. Safe from the law, the lynch mob, and Bodie.

He did none of these things. Because he wasn't safe. He was still in Bodie, and the last he'd likely see of the mountains were the shallow hills of the Eastern Sierra visible from the gallows on Main Street.

"Louisa." He touched a wisp of hair on the nape of Claire's neck. Now he'd have to hurt Claire, talking about this long-ago romance. "She was right. There was a courtship."

"Did you love her?"

"No. Not exactly." He brushed her white ruffled collar lightly enough that she couldn't feel it. "But after Hattie, I couldn't . . . take pleasure . . . in the whores anymore. And I'd lived a lot longer than I had expected. So, I thought I'd try a respectable woman."

She made several notes on her pad, her hand seeming steady as she wrote. Only a catch in her voice betrayed her. "Did you make love with her?"

"Never." He picked up Flowers, who'd fallen asleep under the bed. "She wouldn't allow it. She regarded sex as the province of husbands."

She didn't make a note of his answer. "But she must have had other suitors."

"I gathered that from the trial." He winced in memory of that day. It still amazed him that Claire could have done that, extracted Louisa's imprudent answer. "I had no idea. Though it doesn't surprise me. She seemed pretty desperate to get married. I don't really see why that matters. Virgin or not, she still has the right to say no to the next man who asks her to . . . you know . . ."

"Well, I have a theory."

"Want to discuss it?"

"No." She wrote down more answers. She must have had some kind of system, for she put little stars by some of her comments; circles and arrows by some of the others. "I want to keep asking you questions.

Now, tell me about the night you killed my father.''

He turned onto his back, holding the kitten. This part of the task was far harder. Without revealing the names of his friends he'd confessed to the killing on the stand and explained about the Colt's disappearance. As Claire had promised, he hadn't been prosecuted for murder. But, of course, he had Claire as his lawyer, plus they had six other reasons to hang him. ''Can you promise me, if I say who was with me, that my friends won't get in trouble?''

She put down the notebook and turned to face him. ''No. I can only say what I already have: that if they don't regard it as a conflict of interest, I'll do the best I can to help them.''

Johnny buried his face in the cat's fur, struggling with his sense of conscience. He wanted out desperately, but it still didn't seem right to betray his buddies. He'd killed two men in his life, but he'd never broken his word to a soul.

He felt Claire's hand on his forearm. ''Johnny. Listen to me. I'm not your mother; you don't have to escape me. Sometimes between a man and a woman, each has to concede to the other. When we ran from the lynch mob, it was you who saved us, because out in the mountains you were the expert, and I was just some little tomboy who caught one trout and was proud of her efforts. But now we're back in civilization. You're caught by the law and I am the expert.''

He lifted the kitten away from his eyes. ''Is conscience really a matter of experts?''

''No. But the law is. And I'm your lawyer. In this,

you just have to trust me. No one will get hurt who doesn't deserve it.''

He looked around at the jail cell.

''All right. I've failed you so far. But, if you're going to ask me to defend you, you have to give me the tools to do it.''

He sat up in the cot and let down the kitten. His chest hurt, not as with asthma, but with a heartsick feeling. He knew so well himself what this nightmare had cost him. He hated burdening anyone else. ''It was me, Tank Tucker, and Lefty Lebow.''

She grabbed her notebook and scribbled the names, drawing stars and arrows around all her scratchings. When she finished, she studied the paper. ''Funny names.''

''They're both firefighters. We often give each other nicknames.''

''Yes?''

''Yeah.''

''Are they big?'' She chewed on the end of her pencil. ''Can you describe them?''

''Pretty big. Yeah. Actually, Tank Tucker's bigger than I am. Lefty's a little bit smaller.''

She leaned on the cot and kept scribbling. ''Do they still live in Bodie?''

''Yeah.''

''And are you still friends?''

''With Lefty, yes. With Tank, not so much. For the last three years we've been rivals.''

She looked up, surprised. ''For what?''

''For the captaincy of the fire department.''

''I see.'' She wrote down his answer.

"Well, I don't." He picked up the poor ignored kitten. Flowers purred as Johnny scratched him all over. "That's not a reason for an old friend to frame me."

"No." She tapped her pencil against her pink bottom lip. She could be very pretty, even when distracted. "Maybe not. But there could be other reasons."

"Like what?"

She flipped through her notebook. Somehow she'd managed to fill up several pages. "Why don't you let me do a little more work before I get involved in speculation."

"I don't see why Tank would frame me."

She put down her notebook and picked up the kitten, kissing its forehead and scratching its ears. "I know you don't, Johnny."

"I suppose you think I'm stupid."

"I don't think that at all." She dropped Flowers gently and touched Johnny's hand. "You're clever, resourceful, and honest. In short, a good man." She stood and straightened her jacket. Their lovemaking should have left her disheveled, but she'd tidied herself, and if he hadn't been there himself, he wouldn't have known that an hour ago they'd made passionate love against the far wall. "But I'm a good lawyer. In some ways, that's different from simply being a righteous person."

"That's what Mother was trying to tell me."

"Your mother was right."

He looked down at the shackles and around at the jail cell. His fate shouldn't depend on obscure rules or dimly grasped logic, he said to himself. "I still don't understand it."

"Of course not." She picked up her notebook but couldn't seem to meet his gaze. She touched the chain on her neck. "You're a good man, Johnny. You look at the world with a clear conscience. A lawyer's world isn't so simple. Sometimes we're paid to stand up for evil, and sometimes we just have peculiar talents."

He took her elbow and moved toward the door. Once more, he wanted to kiss her. He missed her more deeply each time she left him. "Like what?"

She touched his chest, then pushed a few wisps back off her forehead. "We look at the world through the eyes of the wicked."

Chapter
Seventeen

∽ର୨ର∽

Louisa lived in a little white house about three blocks down from Claire's office. Claire stood on the porch, clutching Flowers, the kitten. She knocked, hoping and praying this tactic would work.

"Who's there?" Louisa's pedantic voice wafted to the outside. Claire didn't answer, fearful of Louisa's reaction. She held her breath and waited. High-heeled boots clicked across a wood floor. Heat blasted out of the parlor as the pinched-faced teacher opened the door. She stepped back in shock, then shoved the door to close it. Claire pushed out her foot and stopped it. "Wait." She held out the kitten. "Do you know this cat?"

"No." Louisa recoiled, confused and indignant, but kept her eyes on the squirming furball. "Of course not."

"It's Johnny's." Claire pressed the kitty to Louisa's bosom, then dropped it on the flower-sprigged ruffles of a dowdy, though feminine, wrapper. "If they hang him, you're going to orphan the poor little thing."

"Are you a candidate for the asylum?" Louisa plucked the kitten far away from her body and looked as though she wanted to throw him. "After all I've been through, why should I care if I orphan a cat?"

"Because it belongs to an innocent man."

To Claire's surprise, Louisa pursed her lips together, pulled the kitten onto her ruffled bosom, and trembled. "That's not what the jury decided."

"But what do you think? Do you really believe Johnny did it?"

Louisa glanced down the street at the snow-sprinkled mountains, then stepped back from the door, gesturing for Claire to follow. "No one's ever asked me that question exactly."

"You identified him at the trial."

"I didn't exactly." She led Claire through the parlor and into the kitchen, where a potbellied stove warmed the corner. "I said my assailant looked a lot like Johnny. And he had Johnny's shoulders and Johnny's clothes. And I know Johnny wanted to do it."

"Wanted to rape you or wanted to finish what he thought you'd begun?"

Louisa set the kitten down and opened a back door, pulling a can from a small shed. "Is there a difference?"

"I think there is."

The slender schoolteacher climbed onto a stepstool and pulled a flat saucer out of the cupboard. "Johnny wanted to love me, but I made conditions." Climbing down, she poured out some milk for the kitten. "I don't know when his desire turned to hatred."

"Maybe it didn't. At least not for Johnny."

She knelt down next to the cat and stroked its fur as it drank. "I don't know what you mean."

"Was there somebody else?"

Louisa pressed her lips firmly together. "That's none of your business."

"Yes, it is." Claire crouched down and stilled Louisa's hand. "Because the way it stands, you're sending an innocent man to the gallows."

Louisa stood and bolted straight for her parlor. Claire followed. There were pictures and papers on her dining table, the kind of bright scrawls made by children. "What makes you think Johnny doesn't deserve it?"

"Were you and Tank Tucker lovers?"

Louisa looked stricken. She sank into a chair next to the table and studied Claire for a long moment. She looked almost pretty in the thin, blue light of the Sierra winter. Claire felt a brief stab of pity. With her pale face and pinched expression, there weren't many lights in which Louisa would be pretty. She tightened the bow on her wrapper. "How did you know? We pretty much kept it a secret. A woman in my position . . ." She waved her hands at the paper.

Claire wanted to kiss her. Suddenly it all fell together in her mind. She had only to figure out how to prove it. "Louisa." Claire sat down in a chair and pulled it toward her. "I know you once loved him, but you have to think clearly. I believe it was Tank Tucker who raped you."

"No." Louisa covered her face with her hand. "I don't believe it." A little meow wafted out of the kitchen, but Louisa didn't hear it. She sat immobile, with a grief-stricken expression. Heat radiated from the corner stove, making a sensual contrast to the cold mountain autumn that seeped through the drafty windows and corners. Claire waited. Flowers trotted out of the kitchen. The black-and-white furball bobbed to Louisa and swatted at the hem of her dress. The schoolteacher moved her feet to the side. "Why would Tank do something so heinous?"

"Could he have been jealous of Johnny?"

"I don't know why." She lifted the ruffled skirt of her wrapper. Flowers pounced, then tumbled over. "He didn't want me."

"He didn't want you? Or he didn't want to be married?"

Louisa bent down and picked up Flowers. She puckered her lips and held the kitten close to her bosom. She must have had milk left on her fingers. Flowers ignored her distress and licked her hands nonchalantly.

"He didn't want to be married," she said. "And he wasn't gracious when I suggested there was more to love than skulking about."

"Did he know about Johnny?"

"No." She stroked the kitten, and Flowers started in purring, a steady sound, loud and contented. "I don't think so. I was quiet about Johnny also. Though I didn't make the same mistake twice. I held back . . . from Johnny, and I broke off with Tank." She shot Claire a look. "I was tired of being a spinster."

"Could Tank have seen you and Johnny out on the porch?"

"I don't know." She leaned back into her chair. Tears seeped out from beneath her lashes. "I was . . . spooning . . . with Johnny. It was dark. No one could have seen us unless they were lurking . . ." Her eyes flew open, and she looked at the kitten. "Oh, Miss Butler. How would Tank have gotten the silverplate Colt?"

The jail's wooden floor creaked beneath Claire's leather boots as she waited for Sheriff Flowers to open the cell door. Flowers, the kitten, squirmed in her hands. Claire tried to make herself look patient as the burly lawman unhitched the keys from his belt and unlocked the small chamber that imprisoned Johnny.

"Fifteen minutes," he said as he opened the door, "and not one minute longer."

Claire opened her mouth to protest, but the sheriff scowled. He readjusted his gun belt and frowned at his namesake. "I don't want people talking. You were a little long in here last time."

Claire held her objection, uncertain of what the sheriff meant by that comment. What if he'd heard their indiscretion? Could he ban her forever as Johnny's lawyer? She pushed her nose into the cat's fur, scooted far into the cell, and waited.

Johnny sat on the cot, leaning against the wall, his feet still shackled, but his hands free. He was holding a notebook and seemed to be sketching. The door clapped shut behind her with a thud. It flashed through Claire's mind how much had changed since that first visit. Then, she'd been frightened. Now, she was frightened as well, but her fears were for Johnny, not for herself.

She glanced out the slot in the door. She didn't see the sheriff's shadow, but she hadn't heard the retreat of his footsteps. Clutching the kitten more tightly, she crossed to Johnny, broad-chested and handsome even in the worn prison outfit.

"What are you drawing?" she asked casually.

"It's a contraption for Flowers," he said as he held out the paper. "The sheriff won't let me have hammer and nails, but I thought if I designed a little shelter, you could have someone build it."

"Very nice." Claire sat next to Johnny and passed him the cat in exchange for the sketch. He'd drawn a little round house perched on a post. Instructions and numbers crowded the corner. She wanted to break to Johnny *the news*, but she wasn't sure the sheriff had left. "Do you want to explain how it works?"

"It's to keep him safe from the coyotes." He scratched the kitten's black ear. "Since there are no trees in Bodie, I thought this might help him escape them."

Claire studied the sketch and written instructions. Johnny's spelling was awful, and he wasn't artistic, but he had an obvious love of mechanical gadgets. His kitty contraption was clever and detailed. "Couldn't Flowers just live in the house?"

"Scrawny fellow like that?" Johnny held the kitten up by the scruff. The lanky creature hung loosely, completely at ease. "Naw, I don't think so." He glanced at Claire and lowered the cat to the floor. "Flowers would rather be dead than cooped up for life, but this little refuge might help him survive.''

Claire looked away. She couldn't hear Flowers. She remembered again the sheriff's time limit. ''I know who did it,'' she whispered so softly she hoped only Johnny could hear her.

''Yeah?'' Johnny flashed her a look, but to Claire's surprise, he didn't stop his play with the kitten. He watched the cat coolly and wiggled his fingers. ''Who?''

''Tank Tucker.''

''Naw.'' Johnny tore a corner off his drawing paper, crumpled it into a small ball, and tossed it. The kitten chased the makeshift toy across the floor. ''I don't think so. He'd be courting a murder conviction. We were rivals in the fire department, but no man would do something so stupid just for a chance at a captain's position.''

''Maybe not by itself.'' She smoothed down the skirt of her dark blue suit coat. She didn't like bringing Johnny this news. She was saving his life by destroying a friendship, not to mention the fact that it might hurt him to learn of what had gone on between Tank and Louisa. ''But what if in the process he avenged himself for the loss of his mistress?''

His hands dropped between his knees, the notebook dangling from two fingers. ''He and Louisa?''

''Were lovers.''

He tossed down the sketchbook, stood, and walked to the cell door. Pausing, he peered out the tiny window. Flowers jumped on his boots. ''It seems strange to me.'' He bent down and picked up the kitten, allowing the gangly creature to stalk up his muscular arm and onto his shoulder. "How did you get her to admit it? Did she lead him on in some way?"

"I don't really think so." Claire picked up the ball he'd made and rolled it from one hand to the other. "I'm not sure what made him do it, but I don't think rape's just a matter of thwarted lust. After all, I slept next to you for three days, and you didn't take me against my wishes."

He shot her a look, the kind that seared her. "It's not that I didn't want to."

"That's exactly the point." The kitten was watching. It purred loudly enough that Claire could hear, but kept its bright gaze fixed on her paper. "I don't think he did it out of . . . you know . . . sexual frustration. I think it was something darker, more evil."

"Like what?"

"I don't know exactly." Claire tossed down the paper. Flowers launched off Johnny's shoulder, landed on the floor with a plop, pounced on the ball, and batted it quickly, but the paper toy stuck to its claw. The kitten flew into the air and shook its paw briskly. "I thought a lot on the subject of motivation. One tends to, you know, when kidnapped by a man who could be a rapist."

"And?"

"You were . . . virile . . . enough, but I never believed you could have hurt someone weaker. I still can't explain it." Flowers landed, twisted, and rolled on its stomach, the paper still stuck to a sharp claw. "Maybe it was how the prostitutes loved you. Or the fact that you had a strong sense of honor. Maybe it's just a feminine instinct. All men lust after women and scheme and plan to get what they want. Sometimes they engage in aggressive seduction. But rape is somehow different than that. It's like when Chauncey charged me with adultery. It must be more a function of anger than passion. More a lack of conscience than an excess of feeling.''

''You finally believe I'm innocent, then?''

''I always believed it. It's just that now I can prove it.''

He hobbled across the room, pulled her up off the cot, and kissed her, shutting his eyes and hunching his shoulders. It wasn't just a sexual kiss, but a loving and hungry one, as if he wanted to claim her with more than his body, but had nothing better with which to express his devotion. She froze. She did not want a repeat of the previous visit. Johnny would hang if Sheriff Flowers banned her. She pushed at his broad, warm chest muscles. He stopped, eyeing her closely, then returned to the slot in the door. Flowers, the kitten, had freed itself from the papers and was lying on the floor and munching it, purring loudly. Johnny curled his fingers around one of the bars.

''Are you sad?'' Claire asked. ''I thought you'd be happy. Were you and Tank Tucker very good friends?''

''No.''

Her suit coat felt clammy in spite of the air, which was crisp and unheated. ''Do you feel betrayed by Louisa?''

''No. Not at all.'' He walked slowly over and held her, his heart thumping inside his chest. She circled her arms around his waist. She wished she could hold him forever. He stroked the pad of his thumb over her earlobe. "I was just wishing I had not killed your father."

For a minute, Claire was taken aback. In her worry over how she'd free Johnny, she'd forgotten the haunting fact of the killing. She squeezed Johnny tightly. "Don't punish yourself. I'm just sorry he did not get to meet you. He would have liked you far better than Chauncey Lyman."

"You think so?"

"Oh, yes." She stroked the rough muslin, hoping that someday he'd return to his flannel. "I know so."

"He wouldn't have thought you deserved someone better?"

"Well." She touched his broad shoulder, the flat, hard plane of his muscles. "He was like all fathers in that way. No one would have been good enough for his daughter. But he would have thought you came closer than most."

"Really?"

"Sure." She heard the sheriff's boots in the hallway. Suddenly she remembered her limit. "Listen." She cursed herself. She'd done it again, let the woman get ahead of the lawyer. "This is grounds for appeal. Not just a writ of errors, but habeas corpus. Maybe complete reversal."

He kissed her forehead and lifted her chin. "There are only three days to the hanging."

"We'll get a stay. I can do it. I promise."

He picked up his sketch of the Flowers contraption. "Good. Because I miss Tiny. And Flowers really wants to go home."

* * *

Johnny had more on his mind than Flowers' home. He trusted Claire and respected his mother, but he still didn't like the idea that his life depended on some goddamned lawyer, even if that attorney was Claire. He thought about this as he sketched the gallows. There had to be a way out of Bodie. Had to be an escape from this jail. He was rather put out with his mother, though he had to admit she'd been right about one thing: Once he'd let down his guard, Claire had discovered the rapist. She might even win his appeal. Still, it seemed a hell of a gamble, sticking around and risking his life just to prove he loved Claire, though she would have done the same, and more, for him.

He peered at the dark wooden ceiling. He wanted desperately to look out a window. The darkness oppressed him, even more than the shackles. He supposed that was the point of a jail cell: to kill a man's soul and make him reflect on what it was like to be dead and buried. But though he'd tried and tried to figure one out, he hadn't come up with a plan. He'd sent for Cleo, who couldn't help him. He'd explored every inch of the cell. There'd never been a breakout from this jail, for the simple reason that it was built like a coffin except for the small hole in the door.

He'd even considered having the gallows rigged and smuggling himself out in an actual coffin. But that plan would require that he bribe the hangman, and he didn't have access to his mother's money. For that he damned his dear, loyal mother and her fit, so late in life, of sentimental delusion.

Still, he tried to see the point she was making. It was true that he ought to stop running. And maybe Claire would get him out legally. But if she didn't, he'd try to keep planning—or at the very least, to give a great deal of thought to how to get out of a tight situation.

Claire's heart pounded freely as she mounted the stairs to Louisa's house. She clutched the handle of her dark green satchel and knocked.

Someone peered out the window from behind a lace curtain. The sallow schoolteacher opened the door. "You brought it?" she asked.

Claire reached into her bag. Light snow flurried around her. She felt perfectly warm in her suit coat and cape, though her thick wool gloves made her movements clumsy. She pulled out a fat envelope.

"You can change anything I have written," Claire said as she handed the long tan rectangle to Louisa. "You just have to initial the parts you do over."

The tall schoolteacher studied Claire's offering. Her muttonchop sleeves made her look formal and underlined her serious expression. "Do you want to come in and wait while I read it?" She gestured Claire into the house.

"No," Claire said quickly. "You should read it in private. If you don't mind, though, I'll wait on the porch."

"I'd rather you didn't." Claire thought she saw the schoolteacher pinken. "I don't like to leave you out in this weather."

"Well." Claire glanced at the street. This end of

town was sparsely settled, but she preferred no one ask what she was doing at Louisa's anyway. "All right."

She entered the parlor, the door clicking shut behind her. Louisa sat down at her paper-strewn table. She rustled through the childish rubble, then picked up a pair of reading glasses. Perching the gold rims on her thin nose, she perused the declaration Claire had prepared.

Claire watched for a minute. "Take your time," she said. "Ask all the questions you want."

"I'm reading." Louisa studied the paper intently. Claire had hated making so many concessions, but she needed Louisa's cooperation. This woman held the keys to Johnny's freedom. Getting her signature on this paper was the only objective that counted.

Claire turned and looked out the window. A snow-dusted bluff defined Bodie's limit, with the houses scattered up the enclosing slope. The mining camp had seen better days, or worse, depending on one's point of view. The great boom was passing. The Standard Mill employed fewer men than it had only a season ago. Weeks went by without a killing. When the mine died, so would the town. But somehow Claire knew Bodie would always be precious to her. Someday the gold in the heart of this mountain would be buried too deep for practical uses, but this mining camp and its wildness and harshness would haunt Claire's memory forever. "I love this town," she said softly.

"That's nice." Louisa turned the page of her declaration. "I hate it."

From high on the bluff, the Standard creaked, the mechanical pulse of the town. The wind sighed. Gray clouds scudded over, bathing the hillsides in traveling shadows. The heat from the stove radiated in waves. Claire tried not to wonder if Louisa would sign the statement.

"You did a good job," the schoolmarm said quietly. "You're a good writer." Claire thought she could hear the scratch of the pen. She had not known until this moment that her chest had been hurting, but a painful press crushed her ribs and lungs. Turning, she walked slowly toward the pinched-faced schoolteacher.

Louisa held out the formal-looking paper. Wet ink gleamed on the bottom. "What happens now?"

Claire accepted the declaration. She glanced at the definite, feminine writing. Louisa had signed clearly and firmly. "I have to go to Bridgeport to file it. I'll be back in a couple of days."

Louisa removed her glasses and pinched the bridge of her nose. "They won't hang Johnny in the meantime, will they?"

"No." Claire moved away from the window. The parlor was stifling, and Claire could scarcely get enough air. "The commissioner has granted a stay, but I have to file these at the County Courthouse. The sheriff has promised he'll wait."

"How about another lynch mob?"

Claire's heart turned over. She didn't like to think of this part. "That's always a risk, but I think they'll wait also." She blew gently on the wet signature. "They're pretty placated by the guilty verdict."

"And what about Tank? Can we have him arrested?"

"No." Claire stopped. She glanced at Louisa. The sallow schoolteacher looked paler than normal. "We could ask the sheriff, but I doubt he'd do it. We have to get Johnny's conviction reversed first. It's probably better for both you and Johnny if Tank doesn't find out what we're doing." Louisa stood up. For the first time, Claire felt sorry for her. "Are you frightened?" she asked.

"A little."

Claire glanced around the parlor. It was dark, cluttered, and swamped in papers, with pillows and afghans strewn over the chairs. A shotgun gleamed in one corner, however, a blunt, anomalous masculine object in otherwise wholly female surroundings. "Has Tank come around?"

"No." She closed her glasses and secreted them in her dress pocket. "But I'm still nervous, now that I know he's the rapist."

Claire walked to the table. She laid down the court paper and folded it carefully over, sealing the creases into perfect thirds and tucking the finished product in an envelope. "Would you like to stay in my house while I'm gone?"

"I don't know. Maybe. Thanks for the offer."

Claire paused. She wished she could say something wise to Louisa. The schoolteacher seemed lost and pathetic. Claire regretted having to pry into her secrets and hoped Louisa would find it in her heart to forgive her. She touched the chain on her neck, bent down, and scooped up Flowers. "Thanks for your help."

Louisa shrugged. "What will you do when this is all over?"

Retrieving her satchel, Claire dropped the declaration inside. "Practice law in the bad town of Bodie."

"And Johnny?"

"I don't know." Claire closed her satchel and walked toward the door. "He's talked about the South Sea Islands, but . . ."

Louisa followed. "But?"

"But," Claire said as she twisted the cool metal doorknob. What did she want when this was all over? "But . . . if I'm lucky, maybe he'll stay."

Chapter Eighteen

Claire studied the judge as he read the papers she'd prepared on Johnny's behalf. She straightened herself in the stiff-backed wood chair. The odd little jurist was a bantyweight representative of Western justice, with a scraggly beard, a scruffy appearance, and a voice like a boar-bristle brush on a washtub.

She wiped her palms on her wool skirt. She'd brought along Patrick Reddy, Bodie's most experienced attorney, prepared her papers, and practiced her arguments. She wanted desperately to believe in this process. For all she'd grown up as a judge's daughter, she still found it strange that a man's life could depend on the skill of his lawyer; and that she, Claire Butler, like a true gunslinger, might actually cost a client his life.

The judge looked up from Claire's papers. "You're the attorney of record?" he asked.

She nodded. The prosecuting attorney stirred to the side, then seemed to think better of whatever he wanted.

"You wrote these?" The judge peered from above his white collar.

"Yes, Your Honor." She picked up her pen, ready for questions.

The ruddy-cheeked judge glanced at Patrick Reddy. "You might want to use her from time to time, Patrick. She does a nice brief. Though from what I hear, you shouldn't trust her with clients."

Claire blushed, but Reddy seemed unaffected. "She did what I would have done in her place."

Claire swallowed. Reddy's praise made her feel miserably self-conscious. She had not done at all what a male lawyer would have.

The judge leaned over his mahogany dais. "What I'd like to know, counselor, is why you didn't present this defense at the trial."

Claire clutched her pen and composed herself, determined to present this argument better than she had the first time in San Francisco. "I didn't have all the evidence then."

"Why not?" The judge had three law books open before him. He picked up the biggest and scanned it. "The trial ab initio is the proper forum. If your client were dead, all these pretty phrases wouldn't help him a bit."

"I know that, Your Honor." Claire stood. She'd figured out this much about being a lawyer: Judges expected grit in attorneys, and her female status did not exempt her. "But there were complications."

"Such as?"

"Well," she said as she picked up an outline and read her first point, "as you noted in your opening remarks, the trial had to be moved to San Francisco in order to avoid a vigilance committee.''

The judge leafed through his book for a couple of pages, then read part of a page to himself. ''Were these witnesses unavailable there?''

''No.'' She forced herself to make her voice bigger, more calm. ''But there were other problems.''

''Such as?''

Claire took a deep breath. She didn't like using this argument, but she had to explain Johnny's long silence. ''My client didn't trust me. He didn't like having a female attorney.''

''Then he shouldn't have hired you.'' The judge shoved one of the books to the side. ''We have better things to do with the taxpayers' money than hand out new trials to foolish defendants.''

''He probably was a bit foolish, Your Honor.'' Claire looked at her notes. It was one of the techniques Reddy had taught her: make a plan and stick to it. ''But I think we're losing sight of the point. He's innocent of the crime he's charged with. That's the point of the declaration.''

''It's part of the point.'' The judge picked up Claire's papers and flipped them to the signature page. ''But he's been convicted, and by the same witness who now wants us to believe she's recanted.''

''She isn't recanting. She was merely mistaken the first time around.''

Pausing, the judge took a small sip of water. ''It seems as though she's recanting to me.''

''She never said she recognized Johnny. Her assailant was masked. She identified him by the slope of his shoulders.''

"But she knew Mr. Christmas quite well, I gather.''

"An acquaintance.''

"A courtship, I see from your opponent's papers.''

She glanced at the prosecuting attorney, who until this point had not said a word. She wondered why he hadn't, and then the chilling truth hit her—he knew he was winning. This had been another lesson of Father's: If the judge is on your side, keep your mouth shut. Let the other attorney bear the brunt of the judge's anger and don't spoil your own chances of winning. "A courtship," she said.

She flipped through to the prosecutor's papers. Her hand was steady, but her heart was pounding. Johnny wouldn't die right away if she lost here, but he'd spend weeks, maybe months in the Bodie jail awaiting a ruling from a higher court. And, of course, if she kept losing . . . "A courtship," she repeated. "Yes, Miss Cantrall put it that way, but that doesn't necessarily make her so familiar with the slope of his shoulders that she could identify him with a mask on.''

"No, I suppose not.'' The judge smiled at Claire. He scratched his scraggly beard with one hand. "Now quiet while I make up my mind.''

Claire shut her mouth, but remained standing. The prosecutor lounged in his chair, Patrick Reddy continued doodling. Claire felt sick to her stomach, but thought it would look stupid to excuse herself while awaiting a ruling. She sat down in her chair. So this is what the law came down to. A person like her to argue for a client. Another person as an opponent. And a third person with life-or-death power. Not some awesome, paternal power, but a human being, crude and imperfect. She thought about Johnny, trapped in that jail cell. She still didn't believe the law could kill him.

"Denied."

"I'm sorry?" Claire shot to her feet. Reddy did also. The word had come from the judge, but she didn't believe it. "I don't believe I heard you."

"Your motion's denied."

Reddy spoke up. "The reason, Your Honor?"

The judge held up the paper Claire had prepared. "There's no evidence here that could not have been raised before the first trial."

"But, Your Honor—" Claire began.

"Enough." The judge slammed one of his law books shut on the dais. "The law's not a circus." He closed another one with a thud. "The people of Bodie want justice." He sneezed, then closed the last one. "We've scheduled a hanging, and a hanging they'll have."

"But that's not right." Claire knew she was shouting, but she couldn't help it. She wanted to strangle the judge. "He didn't do it."

"Enough." He rapped the gavel on the mahogany dais. "I've made my ruling. Your sex won't protect you from a contempt citation."

Reddy was scribbling frantic notes to her. Claire glanced at one, then nodded. "Then stay the sentence. Delay the hanging while I'm appealing your ruling."

"Motion denied."

"But—" She could scarcely get out her next sentence. Her head hurt, and her throat had gone dry. "But—" A sense of horror rose in her. She couldn't say this, could not even think it. Johnny was an innocent man, living, breathing . . . She pushed her next thought aside. Johnny was also her client. His life depended on her quick thinking. "Mr. Christmas could die while I'm appealing your ruling." To her surprise and relief, her voice came out calm.

"I'm well aware of that, counselor." The judge leaned back in his chair. To Claire, he looked suddenly tired. "And lest you think I'm inhuman, I'm doing this partly to help Mr. Christmas."

Claire wanted to sink into her own chair, but pride and fear kept her standing. "I don't see how this helps Mr. Christmas."

"As you noted before, the good people of Bodie are fed up with justice. I don't think they'll put up with much more delay. Mr. Christmas is going to die anyway. It's more apt to be done right if he dies legal."

Claire returned to Bodie and did something foolish. She visited Johnny. She brought the denial, a preacher, his mother, and a wedding cake baked by Louisa.

"That schoolteacher's mighty good-hearted," Sheriff Flowers said while inspecting the fluffy white frosting of the cake Claire was holding in her clammy hands. "I ought to cut it, but I don't suppose Johnny's victim would sneak him a file. Hold up your arms."

He patted the silver-haired preacher, searching for guns. "You came to bring the prisoner his last rites?"

"I believe," the preacher said, looking bored and disdainful as the sheriff completed his search, "that I came for a wedding."

Sheriff Flowers drew down his bushy eyebrows. He glanced at the preacher, at Claire, at Johnny's mother.

"Johnny and I are going to be married." Claire wanted to smooth her cream-colored dress, but the cake required two hands to hold it. She wished the dress were as white as the frosting, but she wasn't a virgin, and it couldn't be helped. Still, this was Johnny's first marriage. For his sake, she thought she should wear something akin to white.

"I see." The sheriff turned, leading the group down the hall. His metal keys jangled as he opened the door. "You know, Johnny," he called out loudly, "you sure got a way with females. I don't know what was wrong with Louisa, but it looks like she was the only one who resisted."

Johnny stood up as the little group entered. He was thinner and paler than Claire had seen him. She wanted to cry at the difference, but his grin still showed the same boyish dimples. So she lifted her chin, stepped into the dark cool square of the cell, suppressed a shudder, and held the cake tightly. Johnny glanced at her dress, at the sheriff, at the preacher, at his mother.

"You look very pretty," he said to Claire. Manacles clanking, he moved slightly forward, took her by the elbow and drew her nearer. "And you lost my appeal?"

"Yes." Now Claire really wanted to weep. The tiny room seemed like a coffin, and she didn't see how he could stand it. He guided her a couple more feet, the hand to her elbow completely steady.

He took her by the shoulders and squared her in front of him. "And this is my consolation."

Claire blushed. The dress had been abjectly old-fashioned, and she wasn't sure he would like it. "You really do think it's pretty?"

He nodded, then ran his hand across the gray muslin that stretched across his ample chest muscles. "You don't have to do this. I know I asked, but I was foolish."

She clutched at the cake to keep it from dropping. The whole plan depended on Johnny's going through with the marriage. "You no longer want me?"

"That's not what I mean." He looked at the sheriff, his mother, the preacher. "It's not really fair. There's nothing for you in this marriage. When I let you defend me, I wanted to help you, not ruin your career as a lawyer."

"I don't think I'm going to make much of a lawyer. Look how badly I failed my first client."

"You didn't fail, Claire." Johnny took the cake from her. Claire held her breath as Johnny set the heavy pastry down on the cot. He turned and faced her, taking her hands. "You've just lost one case. What you did took guts, and everyone knows it. I'm sure you'll get clients after a time." He squeezed her hands, turning them over, holding them in his much larger palms. Claire held her breath, and tried to think quickly. She needed Johnny's cooperation; he had to assent to this marriage. But right at this moment all her clever logic suspended itself and she wanted to weep at his courage. She felt shallow and craven, devious and unworthy, and it occurred to her what a frail thing the law was compared to the power of a man with a conscience.

He grinned, flashing those dimples. "But one thing about being my widow. You'd have money for the rest of your life."

He glanced at his mother. Alice Van Kessel had tears in her eyes. Trembling beneath a hat of gray feathers, she said, "Of course. And even without the marriage, as far as that goes. But I'd be honored if you'd make it a legal union. I'd like having a daughter-in-law who's a lawyer."

Claire wanted to kiss her. Johnny's mother could certainly think on her feet. She turned to the sheriff and gave him her prettiest look. "Could Johnny and I just have a brief moment together?"

"Johnny," Claire whispered, "there's a knife in the cake." The others had gone, and Claire stood less than two feet from the bulky firefighter. "We've got it rigged so it'll come out and we can cover it back up with frosting."

"What?" Johnny whispered, "What are you saying?" He touched a ruffle at the edge of her shoulder. She'd removed the bullet, and he must have noticed. He ran his thumb over the dress's high neckline, grazing over her chin. She shivered. She missed him so much—not just his touch, but his presence, his smile, the sense of excitement she felt around him.

She leaned up and kissed him. "We thought you could use it to help you escape."

He drew back as if burned, his gaze raking her figure, as if he couldn't decide whether to eat her, strip her, kiss her, or hurt her. Then he put his fingers into the cake and pulled out the crumb-covered knife. He studied it for a moment, wiping his fingers on his pants, turned, and rammed his fist into the wall.

"Johnny!" She tried to touch him. She could see that his knuckles were bleeding.

He pulled away and fled into the corner, turned around, and slid to the floor. He crooked his knees and grabbed the ankle shackles, jerking them toward his body with a vicious tug. He tore with his hands, his muscles straining, though he must have known he couldn't budge them. He pried with his fingers, then pulled again, his knuckles still bleeding, sweat on his forehead, making no impact on the implacable metal. He leaned down, as if to bite them, and then something in him gave way. He dropped the thick chains with an oath, shut his eyes, and rested his head in the corner, his chest heaving as if he'd been running. "So we're faking a wedding?"

"No." She pulled a handkerchief out of her pocket, seeing her plan in a different light. "Not exactly," she said in a small voice.

"Which means?"

She wanted to help him, but didn't know how. He looked so bloodied, bowed, and defeated. "The preacher is real."

An expression of horror dawned in his eyes. Manacles clanging, he jumped to his feet and threw himself against the cell wall with a violence that made Claire jump back. "You'd do that, Claire?" He seemed to have gone a little bit crazy. Sweating and bleeding, he muscled the wall with his shoulders. Then he quit suddenly and dropped to the floor. "You'd really do that? You have so little morals, you'd marry me just to help me escape?"

"No." She crumpled the bit of lace in her hand. She wanted to throw the wedding cake at him but knew she wouldn't, though she couldn't help thinking he deserved a cake in his face. "No. It's not what you think."

"What is it then, Claire?"

She sat down on the cot and smoothed out her dress. She wadded the kerchief to keep from trembling. "I love you, Johnny. It will be a real marriage."

He studied her from beneath lowered lashes, his head resting against the corner. "I'd like to believe you."

"Believe me, Johnny." She dropped to her knees and began to crawl. When she reached the corner, she sat next to him. She tried to rest her hand on his thigh, but he jerked away with an oath. "Please." She wanted to feel his warmth, his heartbeat, his breathing, all the vivid, wonderful signs of his living. "Please, Johnny, believe me."

She felt his thumb graze over her earlobe; then he stroked her hair lightly. His breath slowed down, and his body heat cooled. Some of the tension leached out of his posture. "Does my mother know?"

"Yes." She took his hand gently and dabbed at his

knuckles. "And so does Louisa. Your mother is giving us money. Louisa is giving her blessings."

"And what about you, Claire?" He buried his face in the curve of her neck. "What do you mean, it will be a real marriage?"

"Tahiti?" she said in a small voice. She could feel the groan more than hear it. "I don't care, Johnny." She wanted him to hold her forever. He seemed so weary, so tired and defeated. She would have done anything to help him escape. "I'll be your wife. Nothing else matters. I've pretty much failed as a lawyer anyway."

He pushed her away and stood up. Manacles clanging, he strode to the cot and studied the cake.

She looked down at her dress. There was blood on the hem and dirt on the front where she'd been crawling. "What's the matter? You asked me to marry you. You don't want me now that I've lost your case?"

"Come here, woman." She stood. She didn't know what to make of him now. He had an expression, fierce and determined, as if he'd been fighting with some terrible monster and had made up his mind to defeat him. She approached cautiously, suddenly frightened.

He grabbed her, pulling her toward him. "I love you, but if we're going to do something this foolish, let's do it in another direction." He stroked her hair and kissed her forehead, grazed his thumb over her earlobe.

She flattened her palms against his broad chest. Even five weeks in the jail cell hadn't affected those strong, corded muscles. "Which means?"

"You're going to help me, but you're doing it my way." He kissed the curve of her neck and cupped his hands over her buttocks. "I have a plan."

She should have pushed him away, but she liked the heat and hardness, his vibrant, masculine presence. "And it doesn't involve the knife in the cake?"

"No." He nuzzled her warmly, nipping the tender flesh of her earlobe.

They could make love again against the far wall, but both the sheriff and preacher were waiting. She pushed away slightly. "Or your mother's money?"

"No." He gripped her more tightly, bumping playfully against her pelvis.

"Or even Tahiti?"

"Maybe." He tilted her chin on his finger. "We'll discuss that part later. But, for now, my plan involves your skill as a lawyer."

Johnny stared at the knife the women had smuggled to him. He was tempted to use it. He could call Flowers over, get the drop through the window, escape the jail, and be free forever.

Or he could gamble on Claire's skill as a lawyer.

He sat down on the cot and pulled out his drawing, the one he'd made of the gallows. Now that he had money from his mother, he thought he knew how to escape. It would be easier, of course, to escape from the jail, but that wouldn't give Claire her chance to free him. He thought she could do it, though this plan made him nervous. He would have preferred to free himself.

He slipped the knife into his boot. The way he saw

it, he owed her. He'd shaken her confidence in herself
as a lawyer. She thought she'd failed him, and had
agreed to the marriage because she had no more confidence in herself. But he didn't see the situation that
way. She'd argued and scrapped and risked her life
for him with a resourcefulness he'd come to admire.
He had yet to return the favor. He did not condone
her odd sense of morals, but he did understand it was
her code of honor, the prickly pride of a verbal gunslinger, as fiercely protective as a cat with her kittens.

She'd done what she'd promised. She'd fought her
hardest, far more fiercely than he'd expected. And he
had yet to return the favor. His mother was right: He
couldn't escape her. And he didn't want to. He'd re-
neged on his offer of marriage, but it wasn't because
he didn't want her. He loved life, but he loved Claire
also. He'd made up his mind to have both of them.
He thought she could free him, using her skill as a
lawyer. If she didn't, he'd go back to old habits, trust-
ing his instincts and his mother's money. They'd
never failed him yet in this life.

Chapter
Nineteen

Claire shivered inside her heavy wool coat. The wind cut through the fabric and ruffled the capelet that hung from her shoulders. She could see Johnny through the frame of the gallows. The sheriff was loading him into the buckboard, a tiny, distant, insect-size figure, made to seem smaller by the hugeness of the crowd. The whole town had turned out for the hanging. They sat on rooftops and stood on railings, a dark mass of bodies flowing in both directions down the wide, dusty street. A few moments ago they had been talking, a somber and judgmental assembly, intent on justice, at least as they saw it. But they had fallen dead silent when Johnny had appeared in front of the jail. The hush didn't fool Claire, however. They'd dance on his grave in a swift minute, but death itself, that awesome moment when life ended forever, commanded respect, even in the bad town of Bodie.

Suppressing a shudder, Claire tucked her hands in her pockets. She nudged Louisa's elbow and nodded in the fire station's direction. Louisa followed her gaze and grimaced a little. Tank Tucker stood in front of the wooden building. Smiling, he tipped his red leather helmet at Claire, then turned and strutted in front of his companions, the volunteer firefighters who kept Bodie from burning.

Claire looked at Louisa questioningly. "Do you still want to do it?" she whispered.

"Yes." Louisa tucked her arm in Claire's. "Especially now. Look how he's preening. I'll never have peace if he's not brought to justice."

Claire locked elbows with Alice Van Kessel and glanced at her allies. Louisa looked grim. Johnny's mother looked frightened. Cleo and her girls were fighting back tears. Claire tightened her grip and tried not to tremble. Arm in arm, the three women moved forward, followed by the madam and her trembling whores. Patrick Reddy moved also, standing behind them. Though not part of the plan, he seemed to have some sense of its essence. A low murmur rose from the crowd. Claire and her followers parted the miners, a graceful phalanx of black-coated women, and arranged themselves in a wind-whipped circle just beneath the foot of the gallows. The mutter grew louder as Claire and Louisa climbed the steps to the platform.

"Hey!" A gangly man with a bushy white beard bounded onto the scaffold. "Git off there. This is no place for ladies."

Claire ignored the old man and faced the buckboard, which was wending its way along Main Street.

"Hey." The bearded man tugged on Claire's arm.

He wore a wide belt with odd instruments on it. "What ya doin' up here?"

"I'm Johnny's lawyer," Claire said. "This is his mother and his accuser. We have something to say to the crowd."

"I don't care who you are, sister. I'm the hangman, and this is my gallows." He pointed to the rope. It hung thick, stiff, and snakelike from the heavy crossbeam. "I'll thank you kindly to climb down."

A sound of assent came from the miners. Claire tried not to look at their faces, but couldn't ignore the tone of their voice. They were rowdy, confused, and more than a little impatient.

She glanced up Main Street again. By now she could see Johnny. He stood in the bed of the wagon, his hands bound behind him, but his feet unfettered. Sheriff Flowers was standing beside him, a Parker shotgun cradled in his arms. Tiny pulled the lumbering buckboard, driven by two men with badges. Flowers, the kitten, sat neatly between them. Claire could have cried at the sight of the cat. She wanted to run and hug Johnny for comfort, as it seemed too pathetic that this was his solace, the tiny creature whose life Fang had saved.

Claire clutched Louisa's elbow instead. A deep shout went up from the crowd. To Claire's surprise, the firefighters moved out, a long parade of red-shirted men, in shiny black pants and red leather helmets identical to those worn by Tank Tucker. They wended their way through the muttering miners and halted beneath the newly built gallows. Once there, they surrounded the whores, making a living wall of protection around the women.

"Hey! What's going on here?" The hangman did a jig of distress. Evidently astonished, the crowd of miners fell back. They stilled for a moment, then shouts broke their hush, and jostling disturbed the pattern of faces. A fistfight broke out by the fire station. For a brief moment public peace hung in the balance. Then a deep boom interrupted the incipient fracas.

"Make way!"

Another low-pitched boom rang out. Smoke curled from the sheriff's weapon. The assembled men parted before the oncoming buckboard, once more solemn and silent, their lust for blood evidently abated by the sound of the gunfire and the sight of their victim. As the buckboard creaked to a halt, Sheriff Flowers cradled his shotgun in the crook of an elbow.

"Get off there, counselor." Flowers seemed tense, though he held his gun lightly and refrained from pointing the barrel at Claire. "This is no time for grandstanding." He shifted the gun just a little. "And don't make any moves I think are suspicious."

"Now, wait just a minute." Johnny moved forward. He tried to move in front of the sheriff, but Flowers restrained him.

Johnny shrugged off the stocky lawman. "Don't I get to make a last statement?"

Flowers' gaze darted over the crowd. Most of the miners looked hostile and uneasy, evidently disturbed by this new proceeding. Flowers' gaze swung back to the women—Claire, Louisa, Alice Van Kessel—and then to the whores who circled the gallows and the line of firefighters who guarded the ladies. He gripped his gun tighter.

"Sure," he said lazily. "You can pray, or confess, or even kiss them." He jerked his chin toward the assembled women. "But don't draw out your farewells. You can't avoid the entrance to hell. There's nothing more stupid than prolonging a hanging."

Johnny grinned. Claire couldn't believe he could do it, but he conjured up that lopsided smile. "I'd like my lawyer to say a few words."

The sheriff glanced at the sea of sullen faces, then again at the women barricading the gallows. "All right." He rocked back on his booted heels. "I suppose she's entitled."

Claire tensed. The miners seemed to draw closer, though she supposed this was just an illusion, the product of her fear or imagination. She tried to slow down the thump of her heart. This was no time for sorrow, no time for terror. She'd written her argument out on small cards, but once she saw the pale, grim expressions of all those around her, she left the square papers in her coat pocket. She drew a deep breath and disentangled herself from Louisa.

"You're about to hang an innocent man." Claire spoke in a voice she had practiced—measured, commanding, authoritative. They'd shut down the mines for the hanging, and the breeze carried her words without interference. Her brave speech traveled over the miners and bounced off the bluffs and low mountains that surrounded the basin and sheltered the bad town of Bodie.

At first the miners seemed attentive. The afternoon

sunlight gilded their faces, making them look more alive and romantic than Claire remembered. A glimmer of hope rose in her breast. These were the kind of men she'd grown up with.

"Most of you know Johnny Christmas: firefighter, carouser, miner, and gunman. You've seen him, as I have, on good days and bad. You've seen his wildness and also his kindness. You know the things he might do and the things he wouldn't. You think he's a bad man and know he's a killer, but how many believe, when you think hard on the subject, that the Johnny you know would rape a woman?"

No answer rose up from the crowd. They sulked in the street, their Sunday suits topped by pale faces, hanging on each word she said, as if they were a jury and she were a lawyer, which, Claire thought as she drew her next breath, was not far from the truth. "I've brought Louisa to make a statement. I think you'll find a mistake has been made."

No sound escaped the dark mass of humanity that pressed toward the gallows, but a dissonant pattern of movement swirled through the assembly.

"What's she doing up there?" a miner shouted nearby. "Is she trying to interfere with our hanging?"

"It's true." Louisa's voice was softer than Claire's, but she still managed decent projection. "I was mistaken."

The miners farther away did not seem to hear her, but a murmur ran through the men who were closer. Flowers moved slightly, though Claire could barely discern it.

"Get those women down from the gallows." The

low command rumbled out of the back. ''A necktie party's no place for women. We came for a hanging and we deserve one.''

''Yeah!''

The one-syllable sentence ran through the throng, passing from one man to another, then taken up at the edges by voices in chorus.

''Hang him!''

Claire recognized the voice as Tank Tucker's. She glanced at Louisa, who looked panicked and frightened. At the edge of the gathering, another fistfight broke out.

The deep boom of a shotgun rang out. ''Quiet!'' Flowers's voice thundered against the mountain. ''We're going to have an orderly hanging, but listen to what the women are saying.''

He nodded to Claire.

''Johnny didn't rape Louisa Cantrall.'' She spoke the word plainly, though it hurt her feminine nature to say it. ''There's a match to the silverplate Colt.'' This was a gamble, an outrageous ploy, but some instinct told her that a coward like Tank would have squirreled away for his furtive pleasure the evidence of the crimes he'd committed. He played into her hands by looking up, fear and a question in his expression.

Claire locked her gaze with his. She could sense his tension, so she kept talking. ''And I know where to find it.''

Tank melted into the crowd.

''Get him!'' Claire shouted to the nearest firefighter. ''Grab Tank.'' She stood on her tiptoes. ''And search his cabin.''

The man looked at Johnny, who nodded.

Three red-shirted men charged, muscling their way through the miners. Tank Tucker disappeared behind the fire station. Claire's pulse beat so quickly, she felt as if she were running, though she remained on the platform, standing next to Louisa. The crowd seemed mesmerized for a moment; then a low growl went through it, a murmur of anger. ''What's she doing? Get on with the hanging.''

''No. Let her talk. She's helping Louisa.''

The murmur turned into a rumble, complete with chants and shouted opinions.

Claire pulled her derringer out of her pocket, curled her finger around the trigger, and pointed the barrel at Johnny. She did not say a word, but stood at attention. The wind whipped her skirts. She could smell the green wood of the freshly cut gallows. The sheriff cocked his shotgun. Johnny half smiled. He looked so handsome Claire wanted to kiss him. She figured, however, that this would not help him. Instead, she waited. Amid the din and ruckus, her stillness attracted attention. One by one the disputes settled down, and the crowd congealed back into a mass of dark-suited bodies and expectant faces.

''I swear to you on the grave of my father''—she said this so loud everyone could hear her—''I'll shoot him myself if he's guilty.''

A deep silence fell over the little valley that sheltered the bad town of Bodie. The crowd drew inward, becoming a darker mass still.

A clear voice rang out. "Bullshit!"

"We came for a hanging!" resounded another.

"Get those women down, Sheriff."

The shotgun echoed again. "You'll have your hanging. I promise. But it doesn't seem right to hang the wrong fellow." The bearded hangman jumped down from the gallows and clambered into the flatbed wagon. Johnny raised his fettered hands.

"Hey!" someone shouted from one of the rooftops. A red-shirted firefighter appeared on the top of the Miners' Union building. He waved his arms above his head, and a glint of light flickered in his upturned hand. The hangman froze, as did Sheriff Flowers. The crowd turned to follow their astonished gazes. Three more red-shirted figures rounded the building. Between them, Tank Tucker struggled, his own red shirt torn at the shoulder. The firefighters muscled him through the muttering miners.

When they reached the foot of the gallows, one of them pushed Tank upward. Louisa shrank back, but Claire moved forward. She turned her gun on Tank and gestured him toward the buckboard. "Here's the man you want, Sheriff. And there—" she pointed to the man on the top of the Miners' Union building— "is the weapon that proves it."

The good men of Bodie held a trial for Tank Tucker. They didn't dispense with justice altogether. They formed a committee and held an impromptu trial right there. The broad-shouldered fireman confessed to Louisa as she held the silverplate Colt to his head. He sweated profusely and begged her forgiveness, but she didn't relent, telling him coldly that if she had her way she'd make him bend over and see what it felt like to have a hard object shoved deep inside you.

Claire protested the mob's decision to declare him guilty, of course, arguing passionately that they allow the legal process to run its course. She became so distraught, the sheriff freed Johnny and ordered him to control his lawyer. He succeeded briefly. She started another verbal harangue, however, when the crowd decided to avenge Louisa by hanging Tucker right then and there. When nothing would stop her stream of objections, Johnny plunked her over his shoulder and carried her off to the fire station, Claire keeping up her tirade during the brief journey.

When he reached his old workplace, he whacked her bottom, then dumped her into the hay in the back of the stall reserved for Tiny. She yelped as she fell, then righted herself and sat up in the straw, gulping deep breaths. She listened. He listened also. The wind had died down. The crowd had gone silent. Only Tank's sobs reached the small building. Claire's hot looks seared Johnny, but he stood there unflinching, hatred and feeling crackling between them. Claire struggled to get control of her breathing.

A crack and a thump fractured the silence. Claire winced, and so did Johnny.

"I'm sorry." He wanted to kiss her. He knew she was hurt, though he didn't follow her reasons exactly. To him, this result seemed perfectly just. But he could see by the look on her face that Claire considered Tank's hanging some kind of personal failure. "I didn't mean for things to come out this way.''

She looked shocked and distraught, her hair disheveled. "I suppose you're happy?"

He sat down beside her. "Why wouldn't I be?"

She tucked up her knees, crossed her forearms, and buried her face in her sleeve. "No one deserves to die in that manner."

"Especially me." He grinned, irrepressibly lifted by his narrow escape.

"Be serious, Johnny." She slumped back against the hay bale. "He deserved a fair trial. Due process of law. All the protection the law can give him."

"Don't get yourself all worked up." He picked a bit of straw off her sleeve. "He got enough process. Everyone could see he was guilty."

"Sure." She shrugged off his gesture. "And a few months ago everyone knew you were guilty."

Johnny stood. His freedom struck him. He'd been so long in jail cells, he'd forgotten the pleasure of being able to move around as he wanted. "You don't think he did it?"

"Yes, I think he did it." Leaning back, she covered her face with her forearm. "That's not the point, Johnny. I'm sure you can see that."

"No, I can't. I'm real simpleminded that way."

"You don't feel bad for your friend?"

"No. I don't." Flowers trotted into the station. Johnny bent down, scooped the little furball into his hands and nestled it on his shoulder. "He didn't show me any mercy. Louisa either."

The tone of his voice must have touched her. Claire sat up and looked at the cat. "I'm sorry." She patted the spot on the ground beside her. "Sometimes I'm too much the lawyer."

"I'm damned glad you're so much the lawyer." He sat down beside her, hugging her shoulder, a brotherly gesture and not what he had in mind, but his newfound freedom felt strange. For months they had been bound by the threat of the hanging, the pall of injustice. He wasn't certain of his new status. "And look, now you've won your first case."

She leaned into his chest, seemingly grieving. "This is not what I wanted."

"Don't feel bad, Claire." He stroked her lightly, a gesture of comfort, though part of him had a livelier interest. Flowers purred in his lap, concealing that interest, though the hum of warm cat seemed to increase it as well. "I owe you my life."

"Yes. Well. I suppose so." She touched his wrists where the handcuffs had left marks. Her hands seemed to be trembling. One small tear slipped over her cheekbone. She didn't mop its silvery track. As if in a trance, she disengaged slowly and stroked the fuzzy head of the kitten. "Don't get me wrong. I'm happy I saved you, but I've never had a life on my conscience."

"A life?"

"Tank." She picked up the kitten and buried her nose in its fur. The cat purred, sublimely indifferent to why it was getting all this attention. "I killed him as surely as if I shot him."

"You feel bad about Tank?"

"Of course I do." She touched her ruffled collar, the place on her neck where she'd worn the bullet.

"I should have known better than to appeal to a mob. I don't know what happens when I'm with you, Johnny. I love you and I'm glad not to lose you, but I can't believe I sank so low as to give a man up to a lynch mob."

"If you hadn't done that, I'd have been dead."

"Yes. Well. The law isn't perfect."

Pulling away, he felt for the knife in his boot. "I never thought I'd hear you admit that."

"You think I'm being silly?"

He studied her gravely. He'd risked his life for the sake of this woman. Seeing the force of the mob and their anger, he'd realized how truly hair-raising his last plan had been. Had Claire failed to convince them that Tank Tucker was guilty, it would have been he, Johnny, who'd have died on those gallows. He pushed back a frail wisp of her hair. "I never think you're silly, Claire, but I don't always follow your thinking, and your morals confuse me completely."

"You think I'm a shyster?"

"I didn't say that, but, yeah. I think you're a shyster."

"You just said you liked that."

"I like it about you when you're helping me, but it seems completely immoral when you defend Tank Tucker."

"Yes. Well." She stood, clutching the kitten. "What kind of logic is that?"

"It's how the common man thinks about it." He missed her already. He wanted to grab and kiss her, make love to her the way he'd done in the river. He no longer carried the label of rapist. He could be forward. Bold. Even aggressive. But instinct told him to check that approach. He knew Claire Butler by now. Machiavellian and subtle herself, she had to be lured, not assaulted. "Lawyers should only defend innocent people."

"But that's not our function." She dusted the straw off her bottom. "The judges decide who's an innocent person. We all like to think we'd make good judges, but in the end it's a complex process."

"Speaking of that." He held out his hands. He still felt the weight of the fetters, even though they were gone. "Does the law still think I'm guilty?"

"You're still convicted, but I can appeal it." She straightened her jacket and lowered the kitten, letting it drop a few inches to the floor. Her face had the strangest expression—a mix of grief and nostalgia, as well as inexplicable longing. "I don't think you'll have any trouble now that Bodie has had the hanging it needed." She straightened, picking more hay off her skirt. "You do want that, don't you? To keep me as your lawyer?"

"Yeah." She looked like the damsel in the fairy story, the one who turned straw into gold. "Sure."

"I mean . . ." She pushed her hair back off her face. "There's always Tahiti."

Tahiti? "Yeah. I suppose so, but . . ." The reference confused him. Now that she'd freed him, they could get married. They could spend the rest of their lives in Bodie. "I mean . . . it's good to have choices."

"Exactly." She gave one last sorrowful look at the

kitten, then bent down and kissed Johnny's cheek. "It's good to have choices."

The day after Tank Tucker's hanging, Claire answered a summons from Alice Van Kessel. The request came written on creamy vellum, a full folio, folded just once. In it, Johnny's mother asked Claire to meet her in the reading room of the Grand Central Hotel, for the avowed purpose of touring Bodie.

Claire knew better, of course. Still, she blinked back her tears when she saw the plump matron. She hadn't talked to Johnny since the day before, but it didn't surprise her that he'd sent his mother. Matters had changed so completely between them that a go-between seemed a clever idea. Mrs. Van Kessel held out a leather-gloved hand. Her cheeks had been reddened by the crisp mountain air, and she looked snug and happy in her fur and feathers.

She gave Claire's hands a squeeze, civil yet warm. "I want to thank you—"

"Yes. Well . . ." Claire pulled away. She touched the top button of her black wool coat and patted the package concealed in her pocket.

"Shall we walk?" Johnny's mother linked an elbow in Claire's, stepped onto the porch, and headed down Main Street, leading her gently away from the gallows and toward the bluff edging the town. Claire was glad to walk in that direction. She still couldn't speak of what had happened. She was glad she'd saved Johnny, but the hanging appalled her. She preferred not to think too much about it.

Their backs resolutely set to the gallows, the two

women strolled past the row of white, false-fronted buildings that gave Bodie's main thoroughfare a respectable air. In spite of the lynching, or perhaps because of it, that atmosphere had turned festive. Pasty-faced miners smiled at Claire and murmured apologies to Alice Van Kessel. Claire lowered her gaze to her boots as she answered, too distressed to enjoy her apparent good fortune. The miners of Bodie thought her a good lawyer, but she regarded that as a mistaken opinion. It was true she'd saved Johnny, but she'd failed her own ideals completely. For the first time since she'd lost him, she was glad her father wasn't there, and that realization left her heartbroken.

Fortunately for the pace of their progress, Alice Van Kessel kept striding forward. Chin up and plump bosom pushed forward, she answered "No need" to every proffered "I'm sorry" and beamed at the smiles directed at Claire. She marched past the business district, slowing only near the outskirts of town. There, at the far edge of the good side of Bodie, stood Claire Butler's little white house. Its neat sign swung gaily, squeaking in the autumn breezes. Claire's heart lifted briefly when she saw her name and the word "Attorney." She might not deserve her title, but she still liked the idea of being a lawyer. The sign she'd hung had weathered the summer and might even survive the cold winds that generally lashed Bodie in winter. Maybe, she thought, she could shake this desolate feeling and leave her haunting failure behind her.

As they passed the house, Alice Van Kessel slowed down. She glanced at the sign from beneath her black feathers. "Johnny tells me you're setting up a legal practice."

"Yes." Claire pushed her wool collar up to her ears. She'd eschewed a hat, and didn't regret it. The dry autumn air made her pale hair wispy, but she didn't care that she might look disheveled. The wild bite of winter nipped her nose and made her remember why she loved Bodie. "Maybe."

Mrs. Van Kessel stopped, studying the house as if to judge it. She glanced at Claire, then at the gallows. She turned away from the scaffold. "You feel bad about the hanging?"

Claire shoved her hands into her pockets and looked away from the sign. She'd had such high hopes at the start of the summer. "I feel horrid. I always thought . . ." She stopped. She couldn't cry in front of Johnny's mother. "I don't know . . ." The hot sting of tears pricked her eyes. "I knew what I wanted before I met Johnny."

Mrs. Van Kessel turned her toward the mountain, resuming again her resolute stride. She did surprisingly well considering her age and her plumpness and her Eastern background. When the two women reached the last of the town's buildings, she slowed down again, a little winded. "Can I ask you a very personal question?"

"Yes," Claire answered, almost eagerly. She wasn't sure why she'd responded that way. She should have been wary of Alice Van Kessel, but she'd never had her own mother. It seemed pleasant and natural to have a woman to turn to for guidance.

Johnny's mother pushed back a black feather, looking away as she did. "Might you be in a family way?"

The question surprised Claire, though she supposed it should not have. Like Johnny himself, Johnny's mother was both bright and instinctive. "What makes you think that?"

"I don't know." The matronly woman lifted her skirt and climbed up the slope. Bodie sat in a hollow bowl surrounded by low arid mountains. Birds darted through here in the summer, but in autumn these buttes were more austere. Their golden glow had mellowed to brown; their barren hillsides looked solemn and silent. She wished Johnny's mother could see them in summer, as this was the bleakest of seasons. Alice Van Kessel didn't seem daunted, however. She gazed up at the morning sky, clear blue as usual and with a shimmer and depth of unspeakable beauty that drew the soul and plucked at the heartstrings. "It's quite beautiful here."

"I know," Claire said softly.

"A lovely place to raise children."

Claire brightened a little. "I'm glad you think so."

Mrs. Van Kessel paused, evidently reconsidering the hike up the bluff. She turned back, glanced at the gallows, and grimaced. She snugged her elbow back into Claire's and led her along the plane of the slope. "Have you spoken to Johnny about your condition?"

"No." Claire's heart hammered wildly. She loved the idea of a tiny baby. She also loved Johnny. She wasn't certain, however, that he loved the idea of her having a baby. Heck, if she were honest with herself, she wasn't certain he loved *her* anymore. "I'm still not certain I'm pregnant, so I'd rather not speak to him yet on this subject.''

Mrs. Van Kessel picked her way over the barren slope, her wool skirt rattling against the dry sagebrush. ''You're not thinking of raising the baby singly?''

''Maybe.'' Claire was glad it was autumn, for the sage was no longer scented. She'd tended toward sickness the last few days and hadn't liked the odor of spices. This morning the mountains exuded freshness, a state that spared her morning-churned stomach. ''I don't know what's fair in this situation. I never met another woman lawyer, much less one who had children.''

''You do know my son loves you.'' Mrs. Van Kessel bent down and picked up a rock, a little sliver of pyrite.

''Yes.'' Claire shoved her hands in her coat pocket and felt for the packet concealed there. ''But that doesn't mean I'd make a good wife. I have practically no feminine virtues. I was responsible in a way for Tank's lynching, by pleading his case in front of the mob. But I did save my client.''

Mrs. Van Kessel handed the stone to Claire. ''Is this gold?''

''Fool's gold.'' Claire turned the stone until it glittered. ''It's prettier, really, than the real metal.''

''Oh.'' Alice Van Kessel looked disappointed. ''I wanted to take some gold to my grandchildren.''

Claire picked up another handful of stones. ''So take them. They'll never know.''

''No.'' Mrs. Van Kessel looked shocked. She

tossed the rock into the bushes. "I don't think so. That wouldn't be right."

"See what I mean?" Claire scattered her pebbles. "I'll probably make a terrible mother and drive Johnny wild with frustration, because I've got no morals and he'll think the poor baby should be brought up honest."

Alice Van Kessel laughed, pleasant and easy, relaxed like Johnny. "You're much too hard on yourself."

"You think so?"

"I do." Mrs. Van Kessel snagged Claire's elbow again and started marching up toward the mill. "Johnny told me your former husband put up a reward when you'd been kidnapped."

Claire scuffed at the ground. "He was probably jealous." She touched the packet. "Just because he didn't want me didn't mean he wanted anyone else to have me."

"Perhaps he was sorry for how he'd hurt you."

"Chauncey? I doubt it."

The two women fell silent as they skirted the town. The Standard Mill roared on Bodie Bluff, a dark, clanking, infernal machine that poured both madness and life into Bodie. As they walked, Claire wondered if Mrs. Van Kessel was right about Chauncey. She considered it an amazing notion that her former husband might ever be remorseful. They dipped down below the mill before Mrs. Van Kessel broke their mutual silence. "Would you not want the baby?"

"Of course I'd want it."

"Then you'd better have a talk with the father."

"No."

"Claire . . ."

"I don't think so." She reached into her pocket and pulled out the tissue-wrapped packet. It felt light in her hand, too fragile to have survived so many adventures. "Here." She shoved it forward. "I have something for you. I want you to give it to Johnny."

The middle-aged woman opened the tissue and held the silvery object in the flat of her palm. She drew down her eyebrows and glanced Claire a question.

Claire shoved her hands back into her pockets and shivered. She'd worn that necklace so many years. She felt odd without it—odd, but much lighter. "It's the bullet—that—it—that killed my father."

"You want Johnny to have it?"

"Yes."

Mrs. Van Kessel frowned. Her black hat feathers shadowed her eyes as she studied the bullet and the necklace that held it. "I very much doubt he would want it."

Claire turned, heading down the bluff parallel to Bonanza. She could see the jail and the squat row of houses where in former days Kid Christmas had taken pleasure. "Then perhaps you can keep it. I can't bring myself to throw it away, but I wouldn't want my baby to see it."

"I can imagine." Mrs. Van Kessel followed, the bullet and necklace clutched in her hand. "It's certainly gruesome, but I don't want it either. I wouldn't want my other grandchildren to see it. After all, these children would be your baby's cousins. They might meet each other someday.''

''I doubt it.''

Mrs. Van Kessel looked stricken, and Claire added, ''I wouldn't keep you from seeing the baby, but I doubt very much we'd come to visit.''

''I don't understand.'' Claire felt a grip on her elbow. She tried to shrug off the touch, but Alice Van Kessel held her firmly and kept up with her furious pace. ''You consented to marriage that day in the jail.''

''That was different.''

''It was?''

''Absolutely. I was trying to free him.''

''Let me get this straight.'' She tugged on Claire with a small huff. ''You'd marry Johnny to help him escape, but not to give a name to his baby?''

Claire slowed, feeling a brief stab of both guilt and pity. ''That makes sense to me. I was the one who wanted the baby. I should be willing to raise it. I love Johnny and I respect him, but I'm not sure he wants this baby.''

''He might surprise you.''

''Oh, I know he'd propose, but I married once for the wrong reasons. I'd never be happy. Johnny'd never be happy if we married to give a name to our baby.''

''And the baby?''

''Babies need love, not pieces of paper.''

''Johnny's right about one thing. You're an admirable woman in many ways, but you've certainly got an odd sense of values.''

Claire stopped. She turned and looked at the other

woman, her cheeks flame red from the brisk walk. "Mrs. Van Kessel, listen." Claire wanted to kiss her for her kind concern and at the same time shake her for her obtuseness. "This is very, very important. I like Johnny. In fact, I love him. I think he'd be a good father. I've forgiven the fact that he killed mine. But I have no desire to tame him. That's the best thing about him—his wildness, his freedom, his sense of adventure."

The black hat feathers trembled. "Would marriage to you be so very stifling?"

Claire hugged her. She just couldn't help it. "I don't know what our marriage would be like. I told you before. I never met a lady lawyer, much less one with a baby. Last I knew, he wanted to move to Tahiti. Bodie's my home, and I think I'll like being a lawyer. I liked freeing Johnny."

"I know." She patted Claire's coat sleeve. "And he's very grateful."

"Then how can I tell him his newfound freedom is just an illusion?" Claire's hands were cold, and she shoved them deep inside her pockets. "How can I explain to the town's foremost carouser that he's free from jail, but trapped into marriage?"

Chapter Twenty

~~~~~~

Claire wrote the appeal, sent it off to the California Supreme Court, and waited for Johnny's marriage proposal. She felt sure Johnny's mother would tell him. Though Claire still wasn't sure she was pregnant, Mrs. Van Kessel was far too protective to keep her suspicions secret. She felt equally certain Johnny would propose. A man who couldn't abandon his horse would never desert his baby. So she had written out her refusal and practiced it in front of a mirror.

She needed to practice. She missed Johnny so much it hurt. As the weeks went by, she became more and more teary. She cried each time she repeated the speech. So she practiced and practiced. And tried to keep busy, because, much as she loved the idea of having a baby, it didn't seem right to trap a man into marriage, especially one she loved as much as Johnny.

Fortunately, the busy part had been easy. She'd gotten six new clients after the hanging, land cases all, but that didn't matter. She discovered she rather liked civil practice, and even turned down a request to defend an accused killer, referring the case to Patrick Reddy. The distinguished lawyer relished the sport of practicing law as a life-or-death matter. As for Claire, she liked helping people and liked the law when she could practice it more gently.

She was glad for the business for another reason as well. As she counted the days past her monthly, she began to wonder—how would she care for the baby? She could practice law and earn enough money, but who would tend to the infant? And what would her newfound clients think when they discovered their lawyer was pregnant? She thought up a story about an itinerant gambler who'd seduced her, then left her.

She doubted the locals would believe her tale, but as long as she stuck to it, she supposed the mining camp would accept her. After all, in a town with five times more faro tables than churches, how much of a scandal could one pregnant lawyer create? Still, by the end of the month she was worried. She'd missed her second monthly and resented the fact that she had not heard from Johnny. She did not have a plan, and could not make one, until she'd reached an understanding with her child's father.

So, when the Supreme Court papers arrived, Claire fitted herself into her loosest dress, covered that with a dark blue cape, launched out of her office, and marched down Main Street with the vague idea of confronting Johnny. She did not have a plan. She knew she should have one, but her brain had turned to mush on the subject of Johnny. She didn't know which seemed less fair, to punish a babe for the sins of its parents or to trap its father into marriage.

She hurried down Main Street, the late-autumn wind whipping around her, a fat envelope shoved in her pocket, and the scent of snow in the air. She didn't know what she wanted, except to see Johnny and let him know the legal system had finally freed him.

Claire slowed down as she turned onto the street where Johnny lived. She could see his cabin perched in the distance, a neat red house poised on a bluff. She wanted to cry as she approached it, remembering the first time she'd seen it; the day she'd met Fang and Flowers, the kitten. Unaccountably she missed the white dog, and she looked for the beast as she huffed up the street. But she didn't see him and supposed him still missing, the one true victim of Louisa's false accusation.

She touched the papers hidden in her pocket. Some aspects of Johnny's cabin had not changed, however. A half dozen cats draped themselves on the railings. Claire wondered where Johnny had gotten them, and what he would do with this half-wild population when winter arrived and bitter snows kept them indoors. Flowers, the kitten, lazed in the improvised treehouse Johnny had built as protection from coyotes. Claire picked her way through the lounging kitties, mounted the steps, and rapped on the door. Johnny answered, wearing his new red fireman's shirt, a double row of black buttons defining the line of his powerful chest muscles.

"Here." Claire pulled the envelope out and shoved it into his washboard-flat stomach. "You're free. The Supreme Court's reversed your conviction."

"Yeah?" He accepted the fat document from her, looking far more handsome than she remembered. His shirt had a softly rolled collar. It made him look bolder, more grown-up. He smacked a kiss on her mouth. "Thanks."

Stunned, she remained on the porch, the sun warming her back, the kiss warming her heart. "Is that all you're going to say?"

He grinned, the lopsided smile. "You did a great job. I can never repay you, but Mother has left you some money."

Claire stifled the impulse to slap him. She felt foolish now that she'd come here. Why should he care if she was pregnant? She was only his lawyer. That seemed clear enough. The rest had been merely the natural reaction to all the travails they'd been through together. So why did she still want to kiss him? To hold him? To lay her head on his chest and tell him she loved him? Had he simply been lying when he'd said he loved her? And why had she never admitted until this moment that she couldn't envision living without him?

She turned, thinking perhaps she'd walk into the mountains and keep on walking forever. She couldn't go fishing; this late in the season the fish would be sleeping. Still, she felt so stupid she had to do something. A long, long hike sounded appealing. But a warm hand on her forearm restrained her, and a frisson of delight shivered through her.

"Are you all right, Claire?"

"Sure." She toyed with her top button, wondering

if she already looked fat and whether she'd look repulsive pregnant.

"Come get your money. You've earned it."

"Maybe later." She tried to pull away from his grasp, but he kept a firm grip on her elbow.

"Come on." He slid his hand to her back and turned her around. "You've not seen my house."

She tried to resist, but found she couldn't. With twice her bulk and three times her strength, Johnny had scarcely to push in order to move her. He opened the door to his house. Two gold cats padded past them, followed by Flowers. Claire trooped in last. Just inside the doorway, she paused.

His parlor didn't surprise her, though she supposed it should have. It looked like the lair of a tinsmith gone crazy, all agleam with silver and varnish, the wall studded with memorabilia, badges and medals and trophies lined up like toy soldiers on all the flat spaces. A cast-off barber's chair dominated one corner, a reclining behemoth of brass and red leather. A wizened old lady rocked in the other, the only object in the room even remotely domestic. Claire blinked, though the woman did not surprise her. Claire didn't know what had happened to Johnny's mother, but it was just like the softhearted firefighter to end up living with a little old lady, and a total stranger to boot.

Claire lifted her cape and walked to the rocker. "Hello." She took a strong, warm hand into hers. "I'm Claire Butler."

"Amy—" Johnny tapped the brown envelope on his palm. "I'm free, and this is the woman who did it."

The woman flashed Claire a wide, toothless smile, then rose in a swish of soft cotton. "Oh, you're the lawyer who fixed up the deed to our house. Such a dear boy, your Johnny. He's nice to live with, but I'll be glad when he finds a place of his own."

She patted Claire's cheek familiarly. Claire tried to remember where she might have met her.

"Would you like some tea, dearie?" She looked like a dried-up toy doll, with a round face and a thin, toothless mouth.

Claire nodded, still wondering. " 'Our house'?" she asked Johnny, as the slightly stooped lady disappeared into the kitchen.

Johnny grinned. "Amy and I are tenants-in-common. Her son left her here while he's off prospecting. Remember? You filled out the papers."

Claire frowned. She didn't remember the case. Since she'd done only a few since she'd come to Bodie, it horrified her to think she'd forgotten. She wondered if pregnancy had affected her brain and if she should quit the law quickly before her memory lapses became too apparent. She gave Johnny a look of frustration. "Does she think you're moving?"

"That's what I told her." He took Claire by the elbow and led her to the bentwood rocker. "She's the woman whose son I traded the mine to. Remember? You wrote up the quit claim."

"Oh." Claire resisted the pressure to sit in the chair. "Yes." She glanced at the door to the kitchen, then looked down at the papers in her hand. "But I gave you a springing interest." She bit her lip. This had not gone at all as she'd planned. "You regained your right to the house when the Supreme Court freed you.''

''Don't lecture, Claire.'' Johnny plopped her down firmly. ''I remember the terms of the grant deed.'' Grinning, he pantomimed destroying the papers.

''All right.'' Claire clutched the orders more tightly. She knew what he'd say if she persisted. He'd compare her with Chauncey and say she'd been married too long to the banker. ''You're the lord of the manor. Give your house away if you want to.''

''That's right.'' He loped to the door of the kitchen, peeked in quickly, then returned to the rocker. ''I'm not kicking an old lady out.''

Claire folded her hands in her lap, feeling wary. She didn't know where he might be going. She thought again about his Tahiti plan. ''Where—?''

''Your house, I hope.''

Amy's voice drifted out of the kitchen, along with the scent of warm apple pie. ''You've got a dear husband. I surely hope you patch up your quarrel.''

'' 'Husband'?'' Claire said in a low voice.

''Remember?'' Johnny bent down and spoke softly, his breath on her ear. ''We told her son we were eloping.''

''You didn't say we got married?''

''Why not? We did, in a manner of speaking.'' He kissed her wrist, the pulse point of her forehead, then breathed a warm kiss into the curve of her neck. ''Besides, I kept hoping . . .''

''Hoping what?''

''You'd reconsider my proposal of marriage.''

She almost melted. She'd forgotten how lovely his touch was. "You did?"

"Of course." He unbuttoned the top of her cape.

She stilled his hand. "Well, why didn't you come and ask me again?"

He crouched beside her, his thigh muscles flexing, resting evenly on the balls of his feet. He ran his lips over her fingers. "Because I was waiting."

A primitive shiver spiraled all the way through her. She ached for him to the core of her being. She had to steel herself to her purpose. "For what?"

"For you to calm down. You looked pretty upset the day of the hanging."

"Yes. Well. I'm calmer now. I've had some time to collect my thoughts."

"All right." He went down on one knee, his expression good-humored, that lopsided smile splitting his face, but something dead serious beneath the surface. "Would you like to be married?" He placed one broad hand on his wide chest. "I know I've been a bit of a wastrel, but I've gotten a job, at least after a fashion. Mother set up a fund for the fire department. I'm going to be Bodie's first paid fire captain. You don't have to give up being a lawyer—"

"No."

"What?"

"No." She cleared her throat and locked her fingers over her stomach. "I don't accept." She stifled the catch in her voice and pushed herself to act coolly. "Because of the baby."

"What baby?" He sounded surprised, but that didn't fool her. She could read him quite well, and had thought he might try this. His false rape hadn't misled her. His false astonishment wouldn't either.

"You know what baby."

He stalked to the barber's chair in the corner, vaulted into its bulk, crooked a finger at Flowers, then stared at her from beneath lowered lashes. "No, I don't."

"My baby. You know—" She patted the flat spot on her front, wishing she looked a bit more pooched out, but it was too early in her pregnancy for her outside to show what her inside felt like. "This one."

Flowers hopped on Johnny's lap, curled into a circle, and started to purr. Johnny stroked the cat slowly, an odd effect, for it made Johnny's bulk look even more massive. "You've gotten pregnant?"

"Of course."

"By whom?" he asked, his expression serious.

Claire jumped. She wanted to smack him, but a small scuff caught her attention. Amy was returning from the kitchen, her black cotton dress whispering softly.

"Here's your tea, dearie."

"Thank you." She kept her voice even, though she stared daggers at Johnny. She didn't see Amy's expression, but she knew she'd been rude. The old lady was making small hopping movements.

"I think I'd like to go for a walk," Amy suddenly said in a voice thick with false cheer.

Claire continued to glare at Johnny, too livid to care about the old woman's feelings. "Thank you," she repeated in a voice of dismissal.

Johnny rose, not looking at Claire. He took a black

wool coat from the stand by the door, helped Amy into the covering, and led her out onto the porch.

"Is it too cold for you?" Claire heard him ask.

"No. No." The old woman patted his hand. "You just make up with your lady. I'm taking a walk. I'll be back in a minute."

Johnny closed the door softly behind him. "Why didn't you tell me?"

Claire curled her fingers around the warm teacup. His voice sounded lethal. Claire hadn't expected his anger and didn't know what to make of his reaction. "I told your mother."

"That's nice."

She sipped the tea slowly, caught in a trap. She hadn't expected him to be jealous or to question whether he was the father. Nor had she really envisioned Alice Van Kessel keeping her secret. It flashed through her mind that this was a ruse, but dismissed that idea as being too calculated an effort for a man as straightforward as Johnny. He'd know enough to pretend surprise, but he wasn't all that good at acting, nor canny enough to pretend to be jealous. "She really didn't tell you?"

"No. She didn't."

"Be serious."

"I am." He took a creamy white envelope from a shelf by the kitchen. "She left you some money in this, bought me a truck for the fire station, stayed long enough to see me made captain, then took the next train to New York. Here—" He flipped the paper into her lap. "You should probably count it."

She waved the money away with a gesture. "No.

It doesn't matter. I'm doing well in my law practice."

"Count it." He took one menacing step toward her. "She meant this to be in addition to what I would pay you."

Claire placed the teacup on the floor and opened the note with shaking fingers. She wanted to weep at her own folly. She should have known Johnny would be jealous. She'd lived long enough with Chauncey Lyman to realize men's common sense left them when it came to the subject of faithfulness.

She unfolded the stiff cream-colored paper. Three bills slipped out—three thousand-dollar bills, rigid and crisp and deceptively simple, enough to live in Bodie for ages.

Claire read the note with tears in her eyes. *The money is for saving my baby. I haven't told Johnny about the new one. I promised myself, when I let him come West, I'd not interfere with his business. I think it's time to return to that pledge. Married or not, please accept my best wishes. And please send for help if you need it.*

Claire folded the money into the note, then set the whole business down on the saucer. She kept her gaze lowered, afraid she would cry. She swallowed, regained her composure, and looked at the man she'd just rejected. "You didn't know—really?"

Johnny was standing in the kitchen doorway, his ankles crossed, his arms folded over his chest. "I told you."

"So that was a genuine proposal of marriage?"

"Of course. What did you think?"

She stood up, feeling creaky, puffy, disjointed, and

weepy, halfway between relieved and frightened. She bent down to retrieve the envelope. In two strides, Johnny reached her. He steadied her with a hand to the elbow.

"Read it," she said without looking up at him, hoping she wouldn't regret this.

He took his mother's note from her. Claire could scarcely breathe as he perused it. She didn't know what she wanted from marriage, or from a man, or from her occupation. Nor could she see how it all fit together. But right at this moment that didn't matter. She loved Johnny's nearness. His masculine scent and bulging chest muscles. His impulsive nature and chivalrous conscience. She'd long since forgiven him for the death of her father. She didn't know what he'd done with her silver bullet, but she hoped she'd never again have to see it.

In fact, she loved Johnny himself. She'd told him the truth out there in the mountains. He was brave, resourceful, and virile. And if marriage wasn't what she wanted exactly, it was probably just what she needed. A partner in life. Different from her, but with a sense of adventure that allowed him to conquer whatever life sent him, including a divorced lady lawyer who'd just presented him with a baby.

Looking up, she realized he'd finished reading. He brushed a wisp of hair from her forehead. "I'm sorry," he said evenly. "Are you angry I doubted the baby was mine?"

"No." She leaned into his chest, hoping he wouldn't see the tears. "But could you repeat your offer of marriage?"

"Done." He lifted her chin and kissed her lightly. "Marry me, Claire. We'll spend our lives in the bad town of Bodie. I'll be its first paid fire captain. You'll be its first lady lawyer."

The door creaked about an hour later, and Amy peeked in through the narrow opening.

"Come in," Johnny whispered. He sat in the rocker, making rude sketches of baby cradles. He'd discarded three as being too fragile and was perfecting the fourth when the tiny elderly lady returned. "But be a little bit quiet."

Amy glanced at Claire, who had fallen asleep in the big red barber's chair. Johnny had covered her with a blanket, the patchwork quilt they'd used in the mountains. She looked beautiful beneath the dark patterns, her golden hair an ethereal halo. He vowed he'd never throw the blanket away, or get so old that he couldn't take the baby, go camping, and have an adventure. He vaulted out of the creaking rocker, strode to the window, and watched as the sprightly old lady crept over and studied the beautiful, golden-haired woman, his former lawyer and his future wife.

"Well, did it work?" Amy whispered in the softest of voices.

"Yes," he said equally softly.

Amy pulled the covering up to Claire's neck. "I made this quilt, you know."

"It's very lovely."

She walked to the rocker and picked up the teacup, Johnny's appeal, and the cradle drawings. "She seems a nice lady."

"The greatest."

"You're shaking."

"Sometimes she does that to me."

Amy grinned, a toothless but friendly smile. "She's pretty stubborn, your lady lawyer."

"Yeah."

"And clever."

"True."

She strolled to the kitchen, her hands full. "Are you frightened about being a father?"

"No." He walked past Claire. The deep gold of the afternoon sunlight flooded the front room of his little cabin. He loved this house, but he wouldn't mind moving. He could learn to live on the good side of Bodie. "I think it's exciting. I just didn't want to father a bastard."

"I can imagine." Amy laid the papers on the kitchen table, then walked to the sink. "You won't forget your promise to me?"

"No. Of course not. You can help with the baby."

"You don't think she'll mind that?"

"No." He put a hand on the doorframe, thinking about names for the baby. "I'm sure she'll love it. She'll never give up being a lawyer, so I presume she'll need help with the infant."

She set down the cup and took off her coat. "You don't think you'll regret it?" She folded the wool over her arm. "I mean . . . it seems kind of risky. What if she wants to divorce you? She won't even have to hire a lawyer!"

"Naw." Johnny grinned, remembering the days in the mountains. "I don't think I'll regret it." From outside the window, the Standard Mine moaned. The plink of pianos wafted in from Bonanza. Flowers the cat tripped into the kitchen. The scent of pie filled the air. "In fact, it's going to be great." Johnny flexed his arm muscles, thinking about the new fire truck his mother had bought for the station. "I survived eight years as a bad man in Bodie." He bounded forward and picked up Amy, twirling her in a wild spin. She giggled. He dropped her on her feet gently. "But that'll look like nothing—nothing—compared with the adventure of spending my life trying to outwit a lawyer."

Our Town

...where love is always right around the corner!

All Books Available in July 1996

__Take Heart by Lisa Higdon__
                    0-515-11898-2/$5.99
In Wilder, Wyoming...a penniless socialite learns a lesson in frontier life — and love.

__Harbor Lights by Linda Kreisel__
                    0-515-11899-0/$5.99
On Maryland's Silchester Island...the perfect summer holiday sparks a perfect summer fling.

__Humble Pie by Deborah Lawrence__
                    0-515-11900-8/$5.99
In Moose Gulch, Montana...a waitress with a secret meets a stranger with a heart.